When the Fairytale Ends

When the Fairytale Ends

Dwan Abrams

www.urbanchristianonline.com

Urban Books, LLC
78 East Industry Court
Deer Park, NY 11729

ISBN 13: 978-1-60162-898-5
ISBN 10: 1-60162-898-6

First Printing April 2011
Printed in the United States of America

10 9 8 7 6 5 4 3 2 1

Distributed by Kensington Corp.
Submit Wholesale Orders to:
Kensington Publishing Corp.
C/O Penguin Group (USA) Inc.
Attention: Order Processing
405 Murray Hill Parkway
East Rutherford, NJ 07073-2316
Phone: 1-800-526-0275
Fax: 1-800-227-9604

When the Fairytale Ends

Dwan Abrams

In loving memory of Rosalyn Facia Graham

Acknowledgments

Thanks be to God for blessing me to pen my sixth published novel. It's been a journey that I'm thankful and grateful to have been chosen to travel.

Thanks to Alex and Nia for giving me all the love and support that I needed to pursue my passion of writing.

Thanks to my mom, Gwendolyn Fields, and my dad, Gary Abrams, for being in my corner. Thanks to my sister, Ireana, for making me laugh and helping me to stay current.

Much love to my niece, Carrington. Tee-tee loves you!

Thanks to my cousin, Omar Scott, for reading all of my books and keeping it real with me.

A great big thanks to Jessica Barrow-Smith for your tireless dedication and input on this project. You're a godsend, and I look forward to a lasting relationship.

Thanks to my editor, Joylynn Jossel-Ross.

Thanks to my writers group, Faith Based Fiction Writers of Atlanta, for the monthly fellowship.

A special thanks to all of the authors on the Nevaeh Publishing roster. You inspire me, and I'm looking forward to great things for all of us.

Thanks to Sheila Levine for having my back.

And a great big thanks, as always, to my readers.

Peace and Blessings,
Dwan Abrams

Prologue

A bitter, coppery taste filled his mouth, and his tongue felt like one huge swollen blister lolling around. Battering rams seemed to simultaneously slam against both his temples. He wasn't sure if his eyes were open or not, because whether open or closed, he seemed to be swimming in darkness—a darkness that was so utterly black, the fear of being blind constricted his heart. He tried to take in a deep breath, but it felt like slabs of concrete were compressing his chest.

"So, you finally decided to rejoin the land of the living?"

That voice. Female. Familiar. It wasn't a stranger's voice. He tried to place the voice, but the battering rams in his head banged louder. He gritted his teeth against the excruciating migraine and tried to reach for his head, only to realize that his hands were restrained at the wrists. Cold restraints. Metal restraints. He fought against the restraints until it felt like he had broken every piece of cartilage in his wrists. He felt the cold metal around his ankles too. A rough, coarse rope kept his knees firmly glued together, and the coarseness of the rope dug into the tender skin at the underside of his knees. Though he gave a good struggle, the most he managed to do was to scrape all the skin from around his ankles—but the rope didn't give an inch.

"You should stop straining like that, Greg. You're going to hurt yourself."

There was that voice again. Close to his right ear. Vaguely familiar. And she knew his name.

He tried to place the voice again, but every time he started concentrating, the battering rams became deafening and pain reverberated back and forth from one temple to the next. Opening his eyes as wide as he could, he strained to see through the darkness, and finally made out a pair of white eyeballs staring back at him. He licked lips that were Sahara dry and tried to wet his mouth so he could speak. Only squeaks came out.

"Water?" she asked.

He nodded, then instantly regretted it. The battering rams exchanged themselves for band cymbals, pots and pans, fork tines against metal.

Greg felt something cold against his lips, and he touched his chin to his chest, trying to sit up as much as he could to sip on the cool water. Each swallow felt like a ball of fire inching its way down his throat, and his tongue felt ten sizes too big for his mouth. He scanned his mind, trying to figure out where he was, why was he restrained, and who was this woman with the voice and glass of water? And how did she know his name?

When he spoke, it sounded like his vocal chords had been grated with sandpaper, and his swollen tongue made him sound funny. "Who are you?"

He heard the smile in her voice. "I could be your fantasy, or your worst nightmare. Which would you prefer?"

Her words chilled his soul and raised goose bumps across his skin. He wet his lips again. "Where am I?"

"Ocho Rios. How could you forget so soon that we're in Jamaica?"

As soon as she said the words, everything started coming back to him. The money from the will. The trip. His wife. His wife. His wife.

"Where's Shania? Where's my wife? Is she okay? What have you done to her?"

"Shut up and settle down," the woman said, and Greg felt her fingernails start at the inside of his ankle and graze up his leg to his crotch area. She had stripped him of all his clothes. "That little mutt of yours is in good hands. She hasn't been hurt, and she won't be as long as you cooperate with us."

"Cooperate with who? Who are you? What do you want from me?" Greg wasn't sure which beat louder, his head or his heart. But he knew this much; if they so much as harmed a hair on Shania's head, even though the Bible said thou shall not kill, God was going to have to forgive him on this one.

"You know exactly what we want, Greg. We want what you stole from us."

Who was "us"? And what in the world had he "stolen"? He wasn't a thief; the only thing he could ever remember stealing was grapes from the local grocery store, and that was only because he nibbled on them throughout the store, so that when he paid for them, they wouldn't weigh as much. But other than that, what had he stolen? He wasn't a taker; he was a giver. They must have him confused with somebody else; that's what it had to be. They—whoever *they* were must have the wrong person.

"You got the wrong person," he squeaked out. "I swear. It's not me. I've never stolen a thing before in my life."

Again, her demonic laughter filled the room. "You sure about that, Greg?"

How in the world did she know his name?

"Think long and hard about that." He listened to her footsteps as she walked around the bed—that's what he figured he must've been tied down to—and placed her lips merely centimeters away from his left ear. "You stole something from us. And you can either give it to us the easy way . . ."—her claws shot out and grabbed his testicles, and she twisted until a scream ripped from his throat—"or the hard way. Whichever you prefer." She let go of his precious jewels, and as bad as he wanted to hold himself, massage himself, shield himself, the restraints wouldn't allow his hands to move.

Despite the throbbing in his head, he racked his brain, trying to recall his last memories before waking up in this place of torment. He remembered arriving at the island; he remembered Shania and her horrible attitude; he remembered going to the bar, having a drink with two of the Jamaican guys he had met at the shore to relieve some stress. That was the last thing he remembered—sitting at the tiki bar with those two men, sipping a virgin piña colada. Maybe those men had put something in his drink. Although this woman's voice sounded vaguely familiar, and he was sure if she turned on a light, he could identify her instantly, those two Jamaicans at the bar were complete strangers. He had never seen them a day before in his life. So why would they drug him? And that's what *had* to have happened. That was the only explanation for his swollen tongue, the sour taste in his mouth, and this cataclysmic migraine.

But why would they do such a thing? They didn't know him. Even though he was wealthy, he didn't exude wealth. He had worn a pair of sandals, khaki shorts, and a plain white T-shirt. No flashy jewelry or anything of that sort. And he and Shania had stayed in a lavish hotel. The hotel was breathtakingly beautiful, without a doubt, but it didn't scream: *The people who room here are rich!* So why had they singled him out?

"I'll give you time to think it over, Greg, but when I come back, you better be ready to talk business. You better be ready to agree to everything I ask for. Or else I will bring your wife's pretty little fingers to you one by one."

"You touch her and I will kill you!" he screamed and ignored the pain in his throat.

"How? You're going to spit on me to death? It's not like you can move."

Rage forced him to try his best to break through the shackles. He only succeeded in making his headache worse, scratching more skin off his ankles and wrists, and pulling a muscle in his left thigh. He screamed out in fury and frustration, frightened for himself, but even more frightened for his wife. What if they were lying? What if they had killed her already? And where were those two men? If they weren't in here with him, that meant that they were in there with her. What had they done to her? What were they *doing* to her? His vivid imagination alone nearly sent him spiraling over the edge.

"Help!" he screamed at the top of his lungs. "Help! Somebody help! Help me! Somebody help!"

Something long, hard, and cold muffled his screams. Even in the pitch black darkness, it didn't take a rocket scientist to know that she had jammed the barrel of a gun into his mouth. But was it loaded or unloaded? That was the question. He wasn't sure if he really wanted to find out.

"Pull another trick like that," she growled, "and you'll live to regret it. That's *if* I let you live." She shoved the gun deeper in his mouth, until the tip slid down the upper portion of his esophagus. He gagged, and his stomach heaved. She snatched the gun out his mouth, and he turned his head in just enough time to throw up.

"I'll be back in an hour or two," she said. He heard her footsteps retreat. Next, he heard a door squeak open before slamming shut. Then he counted at least three dead bolts click into place.

He lay in the dark silence, quiet, listening, making sure he was completely alone while he strained futilely to make out his surroundings. Once he was sure he was in the room by himself, he fought against the restraints with every ounce of his strength, even attempting to twist his arm out of the socket just to get loose. Finally, he gave up and yelled out from the pits of his soul. He held his breath for fear that the door would come open and she would jam the gun in his mouth and, this time, pull the trigger. He held his breath in fear that the door would fling open and she'd be standing there, holding up one of Shania's fingers to show him that her threats were by no means idle. But when seconds ticked by and became minutes, and minutes dragged by for what seemed like lifetimes, he figured he was "safe" for now and prayed that Shania was okay as well.

As he lay there, his arms shackled to either side of the bed, his legs tied at the knees and shackled at the ankles, he felt like a reincarnation of Jesus, just without the nails. Hot tears slipped from his eyes and puddled in his ears as he stared up at the ceiling feeling utterly hopeless, and whispered, "Yea, though I walk through the valley of the shadow of death, I will fear no evil, for thou art with me . . ."

One

"Let me pay you something, just to show my appreciation, Gregory."

The entire time while she spoke, Greg cleaned his hands on his pants and stubbornly shook his head. "I refuse to take a penny of your money," he said, and waved the proffered twenty dollar bill away. "Anytime you need something done over here, just call me. I'm one phone call away."

Greg took his time as he stepped down from the ladder, and once he was safely on the ground again, he closed the ladder and returned it to her shed. "And I can guarantee you this. Next time we get a storm shower like that one we got yesterday, you won't have to worry about setting out pots and pans to catch leaks." He pointed up at the top of her house. "That's a good, strong, sturdy roof. Slate roofing. Mother Nature can try, but she can't harm that right there."

Mother Washington looked at him, smiling her toothless smile. "God's gonna bless you, you know that, right? He rewards good works."

Greg nodded his head and unhooked his tool belt from around his waist. "God has already blessed me, Mother. He allowed me to live to see another year."

"Another year?" She frowned at him. "It's only May, suga. What you mean by that?"

His smile broadened. "Today's my birthday, remember?"

Mother Washington held up her cane like she was about to hit him with it. Greg held up a hand to shield the blow and laughed while he jumped out of her way. "That's how you repay me?" he said, chuckling. "I fix your roof, then you beat me black and blue with your cane?"

"If you would've told me today was yo' birthday, chile, I would've never let you get out that bed and come over here first thing in the morning just to lay me down a new roof."

"And that, Mother Washington, is why I didn't tell you." He gave her one of his winning smiles, and watched as her anger melted like butter left setting out on the counter. "But if you don't mind, Mother, for my birthday, can you cook me one of your famous peach cobblers?"

"I sure will. I'll make you two, one for you and one for that gorgeous wife of yours. But you let her eat her whole cobbler by herself. She's just as beautiful as she can be, but she ain't nothing but skin and bones. Feed that chile, Gregory. Make her eat something."

"Oh, I'll try." Greg laughed and reached over and gave Mother Washington a tight hug before offering her his cheek. She kissed his cheek, then patted the spot a few times.

"God ain't bless me to have no boys," she said, "but if he would've, I'd have wanted a son just like you."

For some reason, Mother Washington's words brought tears to his eyes, and it surprised him when he had to blink quite a few times to clear his vision. He tried to find the right words to say, but he didn't trust himself to speak. So he simply nodded, kissed her forehead, then told her he'd see her at church on Sunday. He looked over his shoulder and backed his wife's Range Rover out of Mother Washington's driveway.

Since Mother only lived a few streets over from their housing complex, it didn't take him much time to return home. Though the clock on his car radio informed him that it wasn't even quite eight o'clock, he was sure that Shania was already up, in the kitchen or the basement cooking something. She had a huge wedding to cater this weekend.

When he walked through the door, the faint smell of bacon greeted him, and he inhaled deeply and smiled. She must be cooking his birthday breakfast, and he couldn't wait to see what else would fill his plate besides her cooked to perfection, not too crisp, not too chewy bacon. But before ducking into the kitchen, he made a pit stop at the bathroom and relieved himself. He had wanted to use the bathroom at Mother Washington's house, but her plumbing wasn't in the best of shape, and sometimes the toilet flushed, and sometimes it didn't.

Glancing at the ceiling, he made a solemn vow that as soon as he got a chance to take a break from work, he was going back over there to redo the entire plumbing in that old house.

He finished using the restroom, then washed his hands in the sink. While he washed his hands, he glimpsed at his reflection in the mirror. He still looked the same—neatly edged, faded hair, trimmed mutache, thin sideburns. No crow's-feet at the corners of his eyes just yet; no smile lines permanently creasing his face. No bald spot materializing in the center of his head, thank God. But yet and still, knowing that today was his thirty-fifth birthday made him feel a bit...old. He tried to shake the feeling and convince himself that age was a state of mind more so than a number. He dried his hands on the hand towel and glanced at his reflection again. Was that a . . . was that a . . .

He leaned in to take a closer look, hoping it was just the lighting. No such luck. It was exactly what he thought it was. A silver strand of hair stuck right out of the front of his head, teasing him like a little kid saying, "Nahnee-nahnee boo-boo."

Swearing that gray hair hadn't been there the night before, he huffed as he searched for the tweezers to pluck the unruly strand. He found the tweezers in the top pullout drawer and braced himself against the vanity as he pulled the wiry hair. The pain of the pluck pulled tears from his eyes. Rubbing the tender spot in his head, he held the strand up to the light and stared at it.

"Hey, babe," he yelled, twisting the hair in the light, still trying to determine whether the hair was black, off-brown, or truly gray. "Hey, babe!" he called again.

"Coming," Shania called back, and he listened as her footsteps brought her closer to him. His wife, still dressed in lingerie, walked into the bedroom, looking fresh faced and radiant as she kissed him on the lips. Her breath smelled like minty mouthwash. "Good morning, birthday boy." She crossed her arms beneath her breasts and leaned against the door frame of the bathroom. "Where'd you head off to so early this morning? You beat the birds."

"Over to Mother Washington's. Had to fix some of the shingles on her roof. Does this look gray to you?" He held up the tweezers that still held the questionable hair hostage.

Shania dropped her jaw and gave him "the look." "I know you didn't just call me all the way in here to look at a piece of gray hair. Are you serious?"

"So it is gray?" Greg said, and held the tweezers up to the light. He squinted and stared hard at the hair. "You sure it's gray? It doesn't look off-brown to you?"

Shania stared at him and blinked a few times. "This is pitiful, Greg." Against his protests, she took the tweezers from him and dropped them back into the pullout drawer.

"Hey!" he said, retrieving the tweezers and glaring at her. "I wasn't finished."

"Come on, I cooked you breakfast," she said, and though he continued to protest, she hooked her arm through his and dragged him out of the bathroom. "You left in such a hurry, you left your phone on the nightstand. It's been ringing off the hook. Nearly all the calls are from Franklin."

He knew exactly what his co-worker Franklin was calling for, and it wasn't just to say happy birthday. About a month ago, he had seen this beautiful BMW motorcycle on a TV commercial. On a whim, he had told Franklin that he was going to treat himself to it for his birthday. Though he had said it half jokingly, Franklin, a die-hard biker and collector of vintage cars, had taken his vow to heart; and from that day forth, he had continually bombarded Greg with enough magazines, brochures, and biker jargon to drive even the savviest motorcycle mechanic insane. He had to admit, though, had it not been for Franklin's incessant pursuit of the whole bike issue, Greg wouldn't even be considering slipping off to the BMW dealership to take a look at the motorcycles.

Still tugging at his arm and leading him down the steps into the kitchen, Shania said, "I figure since Franklin was calling so much, you two must have plans for today."

"Not big plans," he promised her, being deliberately aloof.

"Well, good, because I want you all to myself today."

Greg frowned. "But don't you have that big wedding coming up next weekend?"

"Yes, I do," she said, "but that big wedding is going on the back burner. I have plans to make your day as special as possible."

"Just being my wife is special enough." He pulled her to a stop in the middle of the kitchen floor and tucked her into his arms, kissing her lips repeatedly. He ran a hand through her relaxed hair and gazed into her large, almond eyes. "You look delicious in that little slip."

She caught his bottom lip between hers and said into his mouth, "Do I?"

His hands slid down to her thighs, and he hooked his thumbs under the hem of her lingerie, lifting it slowly. With his lips close to her ear, he said, "But you'd look even better without it."

"No, no, no," she said, laughing, and whisked out of his arms. "You had me up all night, giving you an early birthday present, and I'm still sore. That, my friend, will have to wait until later."

Still laughing, she opened the oven, and he watched her long, shapely legs, seemingly endless as she bent over much more than was required to remove the domed silver tray. She was teasing him, and it took plenty of willpower to keep from scooping her up and carrying her back to the bedroom, flinging her onto the bed and ravaging her. They'd been at it a lot lately, probably because their wedding was just over three months ago, and technically, they were still in that honeymoon stage.

She pointed at the table. "Have a seat, Mr. Crinkle."

As if on cue, his stomach growled, and he licked his lips, savoring the taste of their kiss as he strolled to the table and pulled out a cushioned chair. She removed the dome with a theatrical twist of her wrist and held her dainty hand in the air, singing, "Voila!"

Eggs Benedict, three slices of bacon, buttery grits, and mixed fruit. Not too heavy, and not too light—just the way he liked it.

"This looks great, babe. I appreciate it." He leaned over and puckered his lips for a kiss, and she gave him a peck.

While Greg ate, Shania left the kitchen, then returned moments later with his iPhone. He thanked her and scrolled through his missed calls. Yeah, she was right. Twenty missed calls and fifteen of them were from Franklin, along with about a dozen text messages that all basically said the same thing:

> Aye man, we still going? Aye man, answer the phone. Aye man, u ignoring me? Man, I knew u was gonna punk out. U worse than a female.

He laughed at the last text message, then decided to keep Franklin in suspense a little while longer while he returned his parents' call as well as calls from his brother and sister. After he thanked them for their wellwishes for his birthday, he finally dialed Franklin's number and held the phone away from his ear as Franklin exploded.

"Oh, so now you wanna call me back?" Franklin roared into the phone. "Man, forget you! I been calling you all morning. I thought we was gonna leave first thing this morning and get that bike. I knew you was gonna punk out. Something told me you was just spitting out hot air. Man up, Greg. You a thirty-five-year-old, rusty-behind, grown-behind man. Why you gotta get permission from your wife to get a bike? You already know she's gonna say no. Now, you got me sitting here, all geared up, thinking I'm about to help my man pick out his first bike, and you straight stand me up. So that's how we do things now, Greg? That's how we do it?"

Once his friend finished blowing steam, Greg put the phone to his ear and said, "You still coming or what? I can be ready in like fifteen, twenty minutes."

"A'ight, cool, dog. I'm on the way."

Greg ended the call and chuckled to himself. That boy was a fool. Even though he had Franklin by two years, he often felt like he had him by twelve. Franklin was irresponsible, wifeless, childless, girlfriendless, only used proper English when he was at work—and even then, slipped in his Southern slang every now and then. And the only things he cared about were his bike and vintage cars. Greg figured that if Franklin could ever find that one good woman, handpicked, packaged, signed, sealed, and delivered to him by God, he would finally grow up and realize that there was so much more to life than toys and laughter.

Greg finished his breakfast and licked his lips. Shania cooked even better than his mother, and that was no easy feat, he surmised. He checked his watch and realized that Franklin would be arriving soon. After taking a quick shower, he tied a towel around his waist, and though he tried his hardest to ignore the mirror, he glimpsed at himself once more. He scratched his scalp and picked up a handheld mirror to check the rest of his head. As far as he could tell, his freshly faded hair was still black. Maybe that hair wasn't gray, after all; maybe it was off-brown. He considered shaving his head again, but he didn't have time to deal with that now.

Sighing, he put the mirror down, realizing that aging was inevitable. The only exception was death, and he wasn't ready to die yet.

He went into the bedroom and changed into a ribbed crew neck shirt, jeans, and motorcycle shoes. The smell of chocolate cake wafted up through the vents, which could only mean one thing. Shania was downstairs in the basement, finishing another batch of those chocolate fudge cupcakes to complete the top tier of her cupcake pyramid. *What happened to today being all about me and no work?* he thought to himself, chuckling. But that was okay with him. As long as she was occupied, she wouldn't bombard him with a thousand questions about what Franklin and he were up to.

Two horn toots from outside signified Franklin's arrival, and Greg peeked his head in the basement, told Shania he was gone, and hurried outside to jump in Franklin's truck. He prayed that he didn't punk out.

Two

His butt had barely settled in the seat good before Franklin started in on him with the technicalities of the situation.

"Now I'm just gonna be real with you," Franklin said, pulling onto the highway. "That bike you saw on TV was the real deal, ain't no denying that. But that bike had to be at least 1000 cc. You try to drive something like that and you'll find yourself wrapped around a tree somewhere."

"Thanks for the encouragement," Greg said dryly.

"No problem, buddy," Franklin replied and gave Greg a heavy-handed pat on his back. "Get you something with that same design but shoot for 249 cc, maybe 449 at the most. And we're gonna look at the V-twins only, no I4s. Boy, those I4s are like driving a horse! All that power in the head—it ain't for beginners, you feel me?"

"I'm not a beginner," Greg reminded him. "I do have my license, and I've been riding bikes for years. I just never owned one."

Greg usually rented a bike every couple of months. He stuck to highway riding or familiar biker trails. He hadn't rented any bikes since getting married, because Shania didn't know he had a motorcycle license.

"Yeah, yeah, whatever." Franklin increased the volume on the radio, nodding and singing off-key to a throwback song from the Commodores. Then he lowered the volume and said, "I can't believe Shania's actually cool with you getting a bike."

"Who said she was cool with it?"

Franklin lifted his eyebrows, then jabbed Greg's side with his fist. "Let me find out my boy has a little heart! But when you bring that bike home, let's see how long you keep it before she makes you bring it back."

"Who said I was bringing a bike home? I said I would *look* at it. I didn't say I was going to buy anything."

"Oh, you'll buy," Franklin said, nodding. "You wait until you find that right bike, the one that you can see your reflection in. And you wait until you sit on that seat and put your hands on those bars, and feel as though that very bike was created for no one else on this earth but you. And I guarantee you'll buy."

"Okay," Greg said and popped his lips. "We'll see."

"Oh, we will see."

Though he tried to conceal it, Franklin's words sent a flood of excitement flowing through Greg's veins. It was bad enough that he was even considering window-shopping for a bike, but at the thought of feeling that bike beneath him, fitting his body so perfectly, and owning it forever, he began to create drafts of a budget within his mind. As long as it wasn't more than twelve thousand, he'd at least *consider* buying it.

His fascination for bikes began a long time ago, on one drafty summer day when he had stumbled upon something covered in tarp near the back of his father's barn. Curious, he had lifted the tarp, and when he saw his father's old polished motorcycle gleaming like a forgotten gem, his seven-year-old imagination had run away with him. He had hopped atop that bike and pretended as though he was zooming through a motorcycle marathon; he'd won first place at that marathon and then switched into his imaginative leather gear and taken a cross-country tour. He was halfway across the United States when the barn door flew open, and his mother's frame appeared at the door, her face twisted in an almost comical expression of horror. She had given him the butt-whooping of his life, and he never got on his father's old bike again.

After his mother told his father about the bike incident, Greg just knew that his father would give him another whooping on top of what he'd already received from his mother. But instead of beating him too, Mr. Crinkle brought him a load of biker publications and looked through them with him, giving him insight on the different bikes and answering any question that his son posed.

Unbeknownst to his mother, Mr. Crinkle would gather him and his brother, and they would go visit the local bike shops. He never understood why his dad wouldn't indulge himself and get a newer bike; and for the life of him, he couldn't understand why his father wouldn't take the bike he had out of the barn, fix whatever was wrong with it, and go riding down the interstate.

It wasn't until Greg was a senior in high school and begging for a bike as a graduation gift that his dad confessed to him that he had actually owned a bike for many years before getting married. However, when he married Greg's mom, at her urging, he gave up his biker lifestyle in exchange for a wife and kids. To keep peace in his relationship, he hadn't ridden a bike since.

"You ain't listening to a word I'm saying, are you?" Franklin said, snapping his fingers near Greg's face.

"Yeah, yeah, I was listening," he said, and he wasn't completely lying. Even while lost in thought, he could still hear his friend's ceaseless, never-ending, go-on-for-days—even if not a soul was listening—chatter.

"All I'm saying is this," he said and put on his turn signal as he waited for traffic to pass so he could turn into the dealership. "Money talks. If you pay cash, you can talk them down on the price, at least ten percent."

"Okay, Frank, I'll keep it in mind."

They pulled into the dealership and went inside with Franklin's mouth still running a mile a minute. The salesman that approached them didn't get a chance to speak a word to Greg before Franklin took over. But to Greg's relief, his friend at least switched to proper grammar, for sake of propriety.

"Listen, sir, uh . . ." Franklin moved the man's collar out the way so he could see his name tag. "Kyle. My man here is looking for a bike. Now, he's a new rider, not real experienced, but not a total newbie either. What do you have that's not too torquey, not too much top-end horsepower? But look, though, if you show us the V-twins, don't show us something that's going to vibrate like crazy when he pushes seventy."

"Okay, okay." Kyle nodded at Franklin, then said to Greg, "I have a few things you might be interested in. Just let me know the type of bike you're looking for, throw me a price range, and we'll make magic happen."

They followed Kyle into his office, where Greg filled out some paperwork; then Kyle grabbed a set of keys and told them to follow him outside. A look of wanderlust appeared on Greg's face as they walked behind Kyle, watching and listening as he pointed at the bikes and gave them a brief, but succinct explanation of each. The moment his eyes landed on the sparkly black BMW motorcycle with shiny chrome, he knew it was the bike for him.

"Excuse me," Greg said, getting Kyle's attention. "I don't mean to cut you off, but tell me about this bike right here."

"Yes," Kyle said, nodding, "she's a beauty, isn't she? She catches a lot of eyes."

While Franklin bombarded the man with the specifics, Greg walked circles around the bike, admiring its sleek design and the detail that was put into its manufacturing.

"Can I?" Greg asked Kyle and motioned at the bike seat.

"Sure, not a problem."

Greg steadied himself on the handlebars and flung one leg over the bike. When he slid back onto the seat and let one foot slide atop the pedal, he felt like he had meshed with a half of him that he never knew was missing. A smile tugged at his lips as he thought about Franklin's earlier words. He was right. There was no way that he could walk away from this dealership without this one.

"That's the one," Franklin said, smiling at Greg's face and nodding. "It's all over your face, boy. That's your baby." He turned to Kyle and said, "How big of a dent are we looking at here?"

"Well . . ." Kyle shoved his hands into his pockets and straightened his back. "That one's sixteen."

"Thousand?" Franklin and Greg asked at the same time.

Instead of answering their question, Kyle nodded his head and said, "But I guarantee you, it's worth every penny."

Franklin put a hand on Kyle's shoulder and leaned in close. "Listen to me, bro," he said, giving Kyle's shoulder a little shake. "You can tell my man really likes this bike, right? So what if he gives you big faces right now, twelve fresh ones straight from the bank? You think you can shave some off that asking price?"

"Uhh . . ." Kyle's face didn't seem optimistic. "I don't know if I can do that . . ."

"Yeah, you can do it," Franklin assured him. "If Greg drives out of this parking lot with a bike that *you* sold him, that's commission, baby. Your money doesn't come from a paycheck. It comes from making sales. Don't you want to make a sale? I'll tell you this much. Twelve in the hand is better than sixteen in a bush."

"Well . . ." Kyle's face seemed a smidgen more optimistic. "Let me go talk to my boss. Then I'll tell you what we can do."

"And while you're in there," Franklin called after him, "bring the keys to this baby so he can take her for a test ride."

Once Kyle was out of listening distance, Greg slapped hands with Franklin, then gave him their brotherly handshake that they'd been doing for years. "Man, you are good!"

Franklin grinned and popped his collar. "Yeah, yeah, I'm a'ight."

"See," Greg continued, "that's why you don't ever have to worry about Mutual Living letting you go. Boy, you sell people insurance like you're selling them chocolate cake."

"Oh, you heard the rumor about the possible downsizing too?"

Greg sat back on the bike and crossed his arms. "Who couldn't have heard the rumor? That's all everybody's been talking about at the job."

"Are you worried?"

"Nope."

"You sure look worried."

Greg sighed and uncrossed his arms. He leaned forward and held on to the handlebars, pretending to rev up the motorcycle. "Maybe a tiny bit. But you know what?" He didn't wait for Franklin to respond. "As much as I like the stability of having a nine-to-five, I wouldn't be opposed to starting my own business."

Franklin stood there in thought; then he put his hands in his back pockets and leaned against the glass siding of the dealership building. "We're children of God, right?"

Surprised at his words, Greg looked over at his friend and frowned, then nodded. "Yeah, we are."

"Then we ain't got nothing to worry about." He pointed up at the sky, at a black bird that was coasting just below the clouds. "If He takes care of the birds . . ." Franklin held his hands out and shrugged.

Greg knew his friend was right, and though he tried his best not to think about the possible downsizing, the question always seemed to linger somewhere in the nether regions of his mind. But before he could ponder the situation longer, Kyle appeared with the motor-cycle key, and his smile was blinding.

"Here's the key, and I think we can go down on the price some," Kyle informed his potential customer.

"Twelve is good," Franklin said.

Kyle pinched his lips and said, "Twelve thousand, five hundred."

"Okay," Greg added in. "I can do that—"

"No, you can't. Either twelve thousand, or no deal. We'll look at something else."

Greg looked at his friend, ready to ram him through a window. Twelve thousand five hundred for a bike that was originally sixteen? He couldn't beat that.

Kyle turned red from his neck up; then finally he shrugged his shoulders and passed Greg the key. "Okay. Twelve thousand it is."

Greg felt light-headed at the sound of Kyle's words, and he looked over at Franklin, who wore a very confi-dent smile. With his eyes, Franklin said. "Told you, I'm bad." Greg had to give it to him. His man knew what he was doing.

They left to go to the bank, and Greg took the money out of his account. But when they returned, Kyle was working with another customer. So Greg and Franklin went back to Greg's choice bike and stood around it talking, waiting for Kyle to finish.

Franklin's cell phone started ringing, and Franklin held up one finger and stepped to the side. Once he ended the call, he said to Greg, "Hey, birthday boy, I'ma have to catch you later."

Greg frowned. "Why?"

Franklin's smile filled his face. "Remember the lady I met at church last Sunday, Sister Catherine, the one with the really big—" He motioned at his chest, and his eyes expanded.

Greg sighed and rolled his eyes. "You mean the one with three kids and five different babies' daddies?" he joked.

Franklin threw up his hand. "Oh, Greg, come on. We've all sinned and fallen short of His glory. And besides, I know Shania and you have plans for today."

"Yeah, well"—Greg gestured at the dealership—"how am I supposed to get home?"

Franklin grinned. "Ride your bike." Still grinning, he started to walk off.

"Frank, get back over here."

He kept walking.

"Frank! Franklin!"

Frank kept walking; then he started to skip, looking like the crazy nut that he was. Not once did he look back.

Kyle rejoined Greg and apologized for the wait. They both stared after Franklin, and Kyle stood there looking confused. He shifted from foot to foot. "So . . . uh . . ."

This time, Greg's iPhone vibrated in his pocket, and he answered. It was Shania wanting to know how much

longer he and Franklin would be out. He promised her
that he'd be there shortly, and almost told her that he'd
be arriving on a bike, but decided to withhold that information because he knew without a doubt that she'd
try to talk him out of it. But what in the world would he
say once he pulled up at the house on a motorcycle? He
knew what he'd say; he would tell her that he was the
head of the household and that if he wanted a bike, he
could darn well have one. He smoothed his hand over
his goatee and shook his head. That wouldn't work
with her. Their relationship had been built on trust,
mutual respect, and communication. There was no way
he could get away with such a dismissive attitude.

"Everything's okay?" Kyle asked, wearing a look of
apprehension.

Greg figured that the salesman was probably scared
that he would renege on the deal since his spokesper-
son had left the scene. But he wasn't going to renege.
He liked this bike, and he liked how it made him feel.
Even if Shania was pissed at him and gave him the
silent treatment for a while, he could only hope that
eventually she would understand that this was something he felt he needed to do for himself.

"This is a new bike, right?" Greg questioned.

"Yes, sir," Kyle said and nodded his head so much
that he almost looked like one of those bobblehead
toys.

"Never been driven?"

"No, sir."

"Okay." Greg sat back on his haunches and pulled at
his chin hair. He knew if Franklin was here and heard
what he was about to say, he'd probably go into cardiac
arrest. But Franklin wasn't here. He was too busy playing knight in shining armor to Sister Catherine. "Well,
let's skip the test drive. I mean, it's not like I'm buying

it as is, so if something goes wrong with it, you guys'll have to fix it."

Kyle's green eyes might as well have been dollar signs. Greg half expected the young guy to jump in the air and clap his feet together. But within seconds, Kyle regained his professional composure and tried his best to repress his glee as he complimented him on his choice. He took Greg to his office, and they finalized the paperwork. They shook hands, and Greg felt excited that his dream had come true. The anticipation of riding his brand-new bike made him feel as eager as he had the day he got his driver's license when he was a teenager.

He clutched the keys in his hand like he had been given a precious gem and allowed his excitement to overshadow any apprehensive thoughts.

The salesman continued, "Thank you for doing business with us, Mr. Greg Crinkle, and your ride is ready and waiting for you."

The corners of Greg's mouth curled upward as he shook the salesman's hand with his free hand, securing the deal.

In need of a helmet, he went to a different section of the store and browsed the various helmets. A woman with big brown and blond curly hair, and brown doe eyes that seemed too big for her face, browsed the helmets as well. He wondered if she rode a bike; she wasn't wearing biker gear. There was no possible way that she could ride a bike in pants that tight. And, boy, were those pants tight. It looked like she had put them on with a paintbrush. She glanced over at him, caught him staring, and he quickly averted his eyes. A glossy black helmet with a red design caught his eye, so he picked it up.

"I like that one too," she said and stepped close enough to him that he could smell the fragrance of her perfume. A floral sweetness, not too strong, but not too subtle, either.

As she stared at his face, her glazed lips formed a perfect O. "Minister Crinkle?"

Hearing her call him "minister" took him by surprise, especially since he was the youth pastor, not the pastor of the church. He stared at her long and hard, trying to place her face, but he knew for a fact that if he had seen a face like hers in the sanctuary, he would've remembered.

"Yes, that's me." He nodded. "And you are?"

She held out her hand. "Kristen."

He shook her offered hand, and her palm felt soft and warm. When he tried to let go of her hand, she kept holding on to his.

"I haven't lived here in years, just in Georgia visiting family. My mother goes to Saved and Sanctified Baptist Church, and she insists that anybody staying under her roof, whether living there or otherwise, goes to church. I went on Sunday, and I saw you there. You're over the youth, right?"

Wearing a look of pride, Greg nodded. "Yeah, I am. If you're still in town on the fifth Sunday of this month, you should come. Fifth Sundays are youth Sundays, and the youth preside over the entire Sunday morning service."

"Sounds interesting," she said, not sounding the least bit interested. Again, Greg attempted to retrieve his hand out of hers, but she tightened her grip. She wore a seductive expression as she spoke. "I didn't know ministers were into motorcycles." She emphasized the word *ministers*. Her voice sounded melodic.

The way the young lady ran her tongue over her white teeth made Greg have an inappropriate thought. Inside, he admonished the thought and forced himself to stop staring at her perfect mouth. Using as much force as was required, he pulled his hand out of her grip and fought the urge to wipe his hand on his pants. Somehow, her touch made him feel like he'd been tainted.

Averting his eyes to the helmet, he said, "I've always had a thing for bikes." He placed the helmet on his head to see if it was a snug fit.

"And I've always had a thing for a man on a bike," she teased, then stepped in even closer to him. "Here, let me help you." She stepped against his body and flattened her breasts against his chest as she stood on tiptoe to reach the clasp beneath his chin.

To bystanders, this may have seemed like an innocent move. But discretion, and the increased amount of blood that was rushing from his head to between his legs, told him otherwise. He tried to back away from her, but the shelf of helmets behind him hindered his escape.

"Is it a good fit?" she asked, and he wasn't sure if she was talking about the helmet or her body against his.

"I'm married," he said and cursed his body for betraying him.

She shrugged one shoulder. "I see the ring." She pressed her body against him even more, and he was sure that she could feel his hardness through his pants. Her lips stopped inches away from his ear. "But are you happy?"

"Very much so. Extremely very much so."

Chuckling, she stepped away from him and every fiber of his being screamed for him to run. So he did. He whipped off the helmet and headed to the front counter, removed his wallet from his back pocket, and slapped down more than enough for the helmet, then hurried outside to his bike. To his dismay, she followed him.

"Minister! Minister!" she called out.

Against his better judgment, he stopped and turned to face her. He had to bite his tongue to keep from yelling, "What do you want?" and instead, politely said, "Yes?"

She had the decency to look somewhat remorseful as she reached through her curls and scratched the back of her head. "I apologize for back there. I was out of line."

"Yes, you were."

She held her hands behind her back and shifted her weight from one leg to the other. Then she gestured at his motorcycle. "Is this you?"

Trying to remain polite, Greg replied, "Yeah, I just bought it."

"So how long have you been riding bikes, Minister?"

He didn't like how she said the word *minister*. It almost sounded like she was taunting him, challenging him. Again, he cleared his throat. "Actually, this is my first bike. I've always wanted one, but I . . ." He forced his eyes to look away from her hips and focused on his bike seat. "I finally decided to treat myself, since today *is* my birthday."

"Well, happy birthday!" she exclaimed and put a hand on his chest. He looked down at her hand, then stared at her with eyes that assured her that the little game she was trying to play was not going to work with him.

She removed her hand and swallowed. "I have a sister," she said. "She's really into bikes and cars and stuff. That's why I'm here. She has a birthday coming up pretty soon, and I thought I could find her a pretty pink helmet for a gift."

Greg's iPhone vibrated against his leg again. He slipped the phone out of his pocket and glanced at the screen. It was a text message from his wife that only said two words—*hurry up.*

"Look, that's great," he said, and pulled the helmet over his head, clasping it beneath his chin, "but I really need to get going. Good luck. I hope you find the helmet you're looking for, and have a nice day. Be blessed."

Not too fond of her abrupt dismissal, her face turned sour, and she stepped away from him. "That was pretty disrespectful for a so-called minister."

Her words stopped him in his tracks. Disrespectful? If anyone was disrespectful, it was her and her unwanted advances. And who did she think she was, calling him a "so-called" minister? He wasn't one of those types of church folk who only wore their titles while they were in the sanctuary. Christianity wasn't religion to him; it was a way of life. Rather than take a jab back at her, Greg looked up at the cloud-filled sky and mentally put the situation in God's hands.

"Is that invitation to church still open?" she asked.

He had half the mind to tell her no but instead nodded his head and said, "The invitation to God's house is always open. Bring your sister too, if you can."

To his relief, she smacked her lips and turned and walked away with her back straight and her head held high. He figured she wasn't used to getting rejected, and he understood why. She was a very attractive lady with an hourglass figure that women envied and men dreamed about. Greg noticed more than a handful of men at the dealership entranced by her spell, and though she added an extra twist to her curvaceous hips, he didn't allow her cat walk to distract him any further.

Pushing the disturbing encounter aside, he allowed himself to drink in the warm summer breezes and relished in the warmth of the bright sun beaming on his face, causing a moist layer to form on his forehead. He stared at his reflection in his bike—*his* bike—and noted the twinkles of delight that starred both eyes. It would be nice to see that same twinkling in his wife's eyes when he showed Shania his bike.

If nothing else, Shania had to admit that this bike was beautiful, absolutely gorgeous; and if the bike was human, she'd probably look about as attractive as Halle Berry. He snapped his fingers. That's what he'd call her—Halle Berry, in honor of his beloved actress.

Remembering Shania's text, Greg decided not to postpone his departure a second longer. He threw one leg over the motorcycle as he shifted his weight onto the seat. He pulled his face guard in place and checked again to make sure his helmet was secured. A few more moments passed as he acquainted himself with the feel and the weight of the bike. Then he took a deep breath and slipped the key in the ignition. The low rumble and purr of the motorcycle sounded like a chorus of heavenly angels. The feel of this much power between his legs gave him a rush and made him feel like he was taming a beast. Once again, he was that seven-year-old boy in his pajamas, sitting atop his dad's old bike, feeling like he was one step away from being on top of the world. He said a prayer for God to keep and cover him, then revved the engine and drove out of the dealership on his brand new-bike.

As he darted into traffic, his heart thudded in his ears. A rush of adrenaline flooded his veins each time he shifted gears. With the wind whipping his body and bugs splattering on his windshield and face guard, he sped past the numerous vehicles traveling the interstate. His vision became acute as he noticed every passing car and truck. Greg felt alive. He had secretly rented bikes numerous times in the past, but nothing compared to owning one. Hopefully his wife and mother would respect his decision. Any repercussions would have to be dealt with later, but at that moment, nothing, or no one, could rob him of the joy he felt.

Three

Rounding the corner into his Alpharetta subdivision, a suburb of Atlanta, Greg slowed his pace. He passed by numerous brick houses with well-maintained lawns before pulling into his circular driveway and parking his bike in front of his three-story brick house. He paused for a moment, still getting used to the idea of living in such a massive house. The 6,000-square-foot home once belonged to his wife's parents, who died in an automobile accident ten years ago. They willed the house to Shania and her younger sister, Cheyenne. However, to show her gratitude for all that Shania had done for her, Cheyenne chose to let Shania have the house.

The son of an Air Force pilot, Greg grew up on military bases. Most of his childhood homes were a third the size of the estate standing before him. Then there was the three-bedroom house he owned in Stone Mountain, another Atlanta suburb. He chose to rent it out, as opposed to selling it after the wedding. That house wasn't anywhere near as luxurious as Shania's seven-bathroom, six-bedroom home. He found himself feeling as though he lived on an episode of the TV show *MTV Cribs*. And now he had the perfect bike to go along with the perfect home.

He removed his helmet and got off the bike, glancing at the windows of the house to see if Shania was staring out at him. If she was, he could imagine the look of horror on her face. She'd probably think that her eyes were deceiving her. She'd be furious that he bought a bike without discussing it with her. Then she'd probably be scared for his safety. She tended to be a worrywart.

He kicked down the stand and the metal sparked as it scraped the concrete. As he tugged on his pant leg, he admired his new toy and grinned. He felt the urge to kiss her, but to avoid looking like a fool in case he did have unseen onlookers, he settled on patting her instead. Hopefully, Shania would understand—after all, it *was* his birthday.

He inhaled, and the smell of freshly cut grass caught his attention. Noticing the big brown bags sitting at the curb, he figured that the lawn guy must've come by that morning. The hedges were trimmed with designer mulch lining the bushes. Fully bloomed bright purple hyacinths, yellow daffodils, pink zinnias, and white and red roses decorated the flower bed by the door. His home felt so inviting to him that he looked forward to coming there every day.

Sighing, he inserted his key in the door and entered. He placed his helmet beneath the foyer table and pushed it way back, then called out to Shania. The gentle click-clack of her sandals brought her down the hallway into the foyer. The way her face lit up when she saw him filled him with a pleasant warmth that reverberated throughout his body. She had a way of making him feel loved and appreciated. That alone endeared her to him. Maybe telling her about the motorcycle wouldn't be as difficult as he thought. Maybe she'd be just excited as he—perhaps a little disappointed that he hadn't touched bases with her first, but nevertheless enthused.

He cleared his throat and grabbed her hand. "Babe, don't be mad, okay?"

Her smile flipped upside down and she sighed. "Greg, you know I hate when you say that. Oh, my God, what did you do? Don't make me throw up. My stomach's been bothering me all day."

"I can show you better than I can tell you." He paused. "Close your eyes." Perhaps if she could feel his excitement about the bike, maybe she could muster up some enthusiasm of her own.

She gave him an incredulous look before closing her eyes and following his lead. He told her not to peek as he guided her out the door. When they reached the bike, he touched her lower back and told her to open her eyes.

Shania opened her eyes and her jaw dropped as she clutched her stomach. For a second there, he thought she might actually throw up after all.

"What's this?" When she spoke, her eyes blinked rapidly, her neck snapped from side to side, and she looked less than thrilled. She might as well have been looking at a blow-up doll rather than a bike.

His heart sank. "I just bought it," he explained. "It's a BMW motorcycle."

"I can see that." She folded her arms across her chest, expressing her disapproval. "Why did you feel the need to get a motorcycle? Are you going through an early midlife crisis or something? My God, if you do this at turning thirty-five, what in the world are you going to do when you turn forty?"

Her words stung, and he found himself questioning his motives for wanting that bike at this stage of his life. How did she know that a part of him felt like he was getting old and turning into his dad? Nothing against his pops; he had the utmost respect for him as a man and a father. As far as Greg was concerned, he couldn't have asked for a better role model to teach him how to be a man. Greg's point of contention was that he never knew the biker side of his dad. He only knew the disciplinarian and provider side. And now, here was his father, well over sixty, and no matter how much the family moved around and changed residences, that beloved bike remained covered up and parked.

He refused to fall into that same trap. Before he and Shania started having children, Greg wanted to cross off a few more items from his bucket list, like owning a bike. What was the point of only existing in life when a person had the opportunity to actually live it?

"I—I," he stammered, unable to get his words out. He couldn't believe that she had tripped him up like that. He felt like punching himself in the face for acting like such a coward. Franklin was right. *Man up*, he demanded.

"And furthermore," Shania continued, still working her neck, "how dare you make such a major, and *dangerous*, decision without consulting me?" She rolled her eyes. "But I can't solely put the blame on you, because I know that Franklin put you up to this foolishness."

Greg felt the need to defend his friend. "Franklin might've rooted me on, but I'm the one who made the final decision."

"Oh really? So what should I do, applaud you?"

Greg sighed and dropped his shoulders. He pinched the bridge of his nose and stared up at the sky. "Babe, I don't want to argue with you."

"Then you shouldn't have purchased this bike." She dug her hands into her hips. "How selfish and inconsiderate can you be?"

"Well, it *is* my birthday, sweetheart. Can I buy me something that makes me happy? Why are you making such a big deal out of it?"

"Excuse me?" She took a step away from him, and her face had lost its color.

He clenched his jaw. He and Shania didn't usually argue, and he didn't like hearing her speak to him in such a harsh tone. And the look on her face wasn't helping, either. He stared down at his feet and pretended to become entranced by a tiny weed that had sprung up from a thin crack in the pavement. A million thoughts raced through his mind as he tried to figure out a way to restore the peace in their relationship while keeping his bike.

"Shania, I've been wanting a bike for a while now, and I know you might not—"

She halted her hand inches from his face. "The last thing I want to do is stand in the way of your happiness, but I wish you would've talked to me about this first." Her sable eyes stared into his light brown ones. She tossed her hands up and sighed. "You had to know that I wouldn't be okay with this. For Christ's sake, my parents have already been taken from me. I couldn't deal with another phone call telling me that someone I love so dearly has been taken from me. I can't, Greg . . ." Her voice trailed off, and she looked down at the ground.

"Babe, don't cry. Come here. Shania, come here."

When she didn't budge, he went to her and pulled her into his arms. He knew that Shania had taken her parents' death hard, and even though ten years had helped heal the wound, she still struggled with their death at times. He could only imagine what she had gone through; a twenty-two-year-old woman, in her senior year in college, looking forward to walking across that stage, and suddenly being slapped with the news that a drunk driver had slammed into her parents' vehicle, killing them instantly. As if that wasn't bad enough, to have to take a leave from college to go home and raise her ten-year-old sister. Although she didn't get to walk across the stage, she took her finals the following semester and received her degree in the mail a few weeks later.

Greg felt a tinge of sadness as he mulled over the demise of his in-laws. He wished that he could've met them just one time so that he could thank them for the exceptional job they'd done raising Shania. He appreciated the spiritual foundation Shania's parents had given her. She had proven to be a woman of strong character, integrity, and faith by the way she stepped up to the plate and took on a stage of motherhood that she hadn't asked for or expected. He didn't know of many young women who would've taken on that responsibility. That made him respect her even more.

"Baby, listen," he said and kissed her forehead, then used the hem of his shirt to wipe her tears. "I should've talked with you first, I know, and I apologize for not doing so. It's just that owning a motorcycle has been a lifelong dream of mine, and I didn't want you to try to talk me out of it. You *know* you would've done everything in your power to talk me out of it."

Shania softened her tone and smiled. "You're right," she said and nodded. "You should've talked to me first, and I would've talked you out of it." She unfolded her arms and placed them at her sides. "After you told me that your brother had gotten a motorcycle, I sensed in my spirit that something was going on with you. So I'm not completely surprised, but . . ."

He took her hands in his. "But?"

She sighed deeply. "Marriages work because couples learn how to compromise. And . . . even though I want to demand you to go take that bike right back where you got it from . . ."

Greg lifted his eyebrows in optimistic anticipation as he waited for her to finish.

"I guess it's okay."

Greg felt like doing a backflip, and if his spine hadn't already seen thirty-five years, he probably would've. "So I can keep it?"

She gave him a begrudging smile. "But if you have an accident and hurt yourself really bad, I will kill you."

Greg laughed at her concern. "Nothing will happen to me, baby." He stepped to the side so that he could look her in the face. Though she wore a hint of a smile, her eyes were filled with sadness. He held her chin and placed a soft kiss on her lips. "I appreciate your worry. I understand your worry—but you do too much of it. God'll take care of me. And I promise you, I'll be careful."

She bit her bottom lip and lowered her head.

Just the thought of causing Shania pain hurt his heart. He slipped his hands around her waist and pulled her close. With her head resting on his chest, he stroked her straight, shoulder-length hair.

Trying to lighten the mood, Greg said, "Wanna go for a ride?"

She gasped. "I said compromise. I didn't say I was crazy."

He nuzzled her neck, then sucked on her earlobe. "Wanna go for a different kind of ride?"

Her naughty smile matched his, and he pumped his hands in the air as she hooked a finger through his belt loop and pulled him into the house. Nothing like a good serving of birthday sex to make everything all right.

While she stood beneath the shower's spigot and washed away the traces of their lovemaking, Shania promised herself that she wouldn't think about the vehicle that was sitting outside in her driveway. But who was she kidding? That was the *only* thing she could think about. She tried hard not to be mad with Greg, yet she found it impossible not to be. Her cheeks felt hot every time she thought about that motorcycle. What in the world was he thinking? She concluded that his actions seemed reckless and irresponsible—unlike the Greg she knew and loved. She hoped that he wasn't starting to change and take her for granted. For crying out loud, they had only been married a little over three months. Wasn't it too soon for the fairytale to be over?

She stepped out of the shower and gritted her teeth in frustration while she dried off. As she lathered her body with creamy body butter, she let out a sigh. She didn't want anything, including her foul mood, to interfere with the plans she had for Greg's birthday.

Birthdays had always been special to Shania. Growing up, her parents used to throw lavish parties for both her and her sister. She liked the way those celebrations made her feel . . . special, like a princess. She liked making her loved ones feel special too. She knew that the only way she was going to release her anger was to pray.

With Greg in his home office, using the computer, she closed the bedroom door and kneeled down beside her bed. She shut her eyes and prayed that God would give her peace about the situation and keep Greg safe.

When she finished praying, she pulled out her wedding album and perused the professional photos, reminding herself how much she loved her husband. She then closed the album and touched up her makeup and brushed her dark hair. She was already dressed in fitted jeans and a sexy shirt, so she slid on a pair of open-toed, wedge-heeled sandals that showed off her hot pink pedicure and went down the hall to get Greg.

Standing in the doorway of Greg's office, Shania saw Greg reading the birthday card she had left for him on top of his keyboard, smiling. She knew that he liked more meaningful cards, so she had read several before selecting the one that best conveyed her feelings about her man.

He looked up at her and closed the card. "Thank you, baby."

"Glad you liked it." She shifted on her foot as she read his expression. "Everything's okay, right?"

He placed the card on his desk and nodded as he exited out of his e-mail. "Yeah, everything's fine."

But from the tone of his voice and the expression on his face, she knew everything was not fine. She invited herself to sit in his lap, and she held his cheeks while she stared into his face. "What's wrong?"

His hand went to his chin and he tugged on the little patch of hair that was there. "I just checked my e-mail, and, uh . . ."

"And?"

He scratched the back of his head with both hands, then let his arms flop down to his sides. "You know the five new insurance policies that I signed last month?"

A sour feeling settled in the pit of her belly. "Yes."

"Well . . ." He scratched the back of his head again. "I just checked my e-mail and four of the policyholders canceled their policies."

"They can't cancel," Shania said, racking her brain as she recalled the policy guidelines. "I thought that if they didn't cancel in thirty days, they're locked in by contract for at least six months."

"True, but . . ."— Greg looked at the ceiling and blew air from his lips—"it hasn't been a full thirty days yet."

Bummer. At a loss for words, Shania turned in his lap and faced the computer. Then she looked over her shoulder at him and said, "Don't be so stressed about it, honey. So what if they canceled their policies? The same way you got them to sign on, you can find others to sign on."

"It's not that easy, baby."

"Please tell me what in life *is* easy?" She shrugged her shoulders. "I mean, if it's about money, don't worry. I still have plenty of savings left in my account, and we have more than enough in our joint account. Plus, I have this huge wedding to do this upcoming weekend, and I actually got a letter today from the governor's secretary. She wants me to concoct a sample menu for the governor's induction ceremony."

"And that's all good news," Greg said, nodding his head, "but, babe, I told you about the rumor going around the job. My policies keep getting canceled. My clients keep pulling out. This is not a good look. If Mutual Living does decide to downsize, I'll be the first one out the door."

"Can you stop with all this negativity?" Shania stood to her feet and stared at her husband, shaking her head. "You are a minister. You of all people should know that you have to look at things with eyes of faith, and right now, you are not speaking life. You are speaking death. And furthermore, if you are praying about the situation, which I hope you are, then you need to let it go, because worry cancels out prayer."

"You're right. You are right," Greg said, nodding. "Thanks, babe, for reminding me who I am, and whose I am. I needed that." She watched him shut down the computer and stand to his feet. "Instead of that thriller movie, let's go see a comedy. I feel like we both need a good laugh."

When Greg came near her, he brushed past her, leaving the faint scent of his Euphoria cologne behind, reminding Shania of how good he smelled. The fragrance affected her like an aphrodisiac. She felt like ripping his clothes off. She grabbed ahold of his muscular arm, and he tilted his head in her direction.

"You get me started again," he said, "and you can cancel going to the movies."

The thought did sound appealing, but she decided to hold off on it. She and Greg had been going at it like rabbits lately, and though she tried her best to take her birth control pills at the same time every single day, some days slipped her mind. She knew they were playing with fire, and though kids were definitely on the menu, she wanted to enjoy her full-course meal first.

Once she settled into the passenger seat of Greg's Mercedes, Greg pressed the button to open the garage, and he backed out of the yard. As he passed by his motorcycle, he touched her hand and said, "Baby, I was wrong for not talking to you first, okay? In the future, I'll consult with you on all major issues. I promise." His smile conveyed his level of sincerity.

Any anger that Shania may have been feeling melted like an ice cube sitting on top of a hot stove. Although she wasn't thrilled about Greg having a motorcycle, she realized that she had no control over another adult. She couldn't tell him what to do any more than she could stop him from doing something he really wanted to do. The ultimate decision remained his. She patted his chest, and he flexed a toned pec. They both seemed amused.

"You don't regret getting married, do you?" Shania asked, believing she already knew the answer. She just wanted to hear him say it.

"Of course not, baby." He shook his head. "You're my rib. Don't ever doubt my love for you. *He who finds a wife finds a good thing*. That's biblical, baby. Can't argue with God."

Greg's words made her weak in the knees. Every time she thought of herself as his wife, her insides quivered. Holding his arm a little tighter, Shania teased, "And don't you ever forget it."

They left for the movie theater and enjoyed the two hour action-comedy film, filling up on buttered popcorn and soda.

Shania preferred romantic comedies. Since it was Greg's birthday, she let him pick the movie and sucked it up. She found herself enjoying the movie more than she cared to admit and jumped at the explosions. She dared not tell Greg, because she didn't want him dragging her to those types of movies on a regular basis.

After the movie, they went back home and changed clothes. They were ready for a game of tennis. They ran around the community court, sweating and panting. After serving the match point, Greg rejoiced in his victory while Shania pretended to pout.

"You know I let you win, right?" Shania joked as she guzzled some bottled water. "Since it's your birthday, I didn't want to beat you too bad."

With his racket, Greg gave Shania a playful smack on the rear end and burst out laughing. "Beat that." He took off running.

"Oh no, you didn't," she yelled as she sprinted behind him all the way home.

As soon as they walked through the door, the cool air hit them in their faces like a towel and dried their sweat. The air-conditioned house was a welcomed contrast to the seventy-eight humid degrees they had just escaped.

They made their way to the upstairs bathroom, took off their clothes, and showered together. Shania then filled up the Jacuzzi and turned on the bubble jets. Feeling romantic, Shania put in an old-school, baby-making CD and lit sugar cookie scented candles, her preferred candle scent. She submerged her body into the bubbling tub, where Greg was already waiting for her, and closed her eyes as she leaned her head back.

"This feels so good." She relaxed every muscle in her body as Greg massaged her foot. He gave the most incredible foot rubs. They tended to put her to sleep. His hands felt magical. "Are you enjoying your birthday so far?"

He sucked her big toe, sending chills up and down her spine, and she giggled. Her eyes sprung open, and she gave Greg a "come hither" look. She couldn't believe how much Greg turned her on. He released her foot, and she sat up, exposing her bare skin to the elements. She straddled Greg and enjoyed the intimacy that soon followed.

Two hours had passed and they had taken their act to the bedroom and fallen into a deep slumber. Awakened by the telephone ringing, Shania noticed that the time read 4:00 P.M. She reached across her husband and answered the phone.

Her sister said in her high nasal tone, "It's four o'clock in the afternoon. I know you're not sleep."

Shania yawned. "Yeah, I dozed off. What do you want?"

"I just wanted to let you know that Jonathan and I will meet you at the restaurant for Greg's birthday dinner."

Shania slapped her forehead with her open palm. "God, I'm so glad you called. Greg wore me out. I almost forgot about dinner." She got out of bed, careful not to cause any noticeable movement, and put on a robe. She glanced at her husband who looked so peaceful with his long lashes resting against his smooth, creamy peanut-butter-colored skin; then she tiptoed out of the room.

Shania confirmed that they had six o'clock reservations at the Sun Dial, Atlanta's only tri-level dining
complex featuring a revolving upscale restaurant. She
had selected the Sun Dial because that was where she
and Greg went on their first date, and the restaurant
offered a breathtaking 360-degree panoramic view of
the city's skyline.

Cheyenne told her that she and her husband, Jonathan, were already two and a half hours into their
three-and-a-half-ride from Valdosta and assured Shania that they'd be on time.

Two hours later, Shania and Greg met Cheyenne and
Jonathan at the Westin Peachtree Plaza. They greeted
each other with hugs and kisses on the cheek and
boarded the scenic glass elevator to climb the hotel's
seventy-three stories to the restaurant. Once inside,
Shania looked around and noticed that the restaurant
had a nice-sized crowd. Live jazz music filled the air.
She felt Greg's arm reach around her waist and pull her
close, making her feel even more safe and secure.

They didn't have to wait long before being seated at
their table and placing their drink and food orders. Shania glanced out the window and admired the lit build-
ings. She couldn't believe how much had changed in a
few short months. Who would've thought that the four
of them would be on a double date without Shania wanting to strangle Jonathan? She remembered how she felt
when Cheyenne first started dating him. They were ju-
niors in high school, and Shania didn't think he was good
enough for her little sister. Not long afterward he became
a high school dropout and occasional street pharmacist.
In her eyes, he lacked ambition and his very essence
meant trouble. But in Cheyenne's eyes, he was her gift
from God.

It wasn't until Jonathan had been shot in the abdomen after an altercation and hospitalized that Shania felt compassion for him. Although she felt devastated when she found out that Cheyenne had run off and eloped with Jonathan, she decided to give him a chance.

"We have a surprise for you, sister." Cheyenne's eyes glowed, and she sounded excited.

A surprise for her? Why were they giving her surprises on Greg's birthday? Shania stopped looking outside and looked at Cheyenne. She held her breath, hoping that Cheyenne wasn't about to announce that she was pregnant. If her sister's lips so much as formed a p-word, she was going to flip. When it came to Cheyenne and Jonathan's relationship, Shania needed to take baby steps, not quantum leaps.

Squeezing Jonathan's hand on top of the table, Cheyenne announced, "Jonathan got his GED. He's even going to attend the fall semester at Valdosta State along with me."

Cheyene was a sophomore at Valdosta State and Shania felt proud of her younger sister for going to college, because it was no easy feat getting her there. In high school, Cheyenne was notorious for skipping classes. It was a favor from God that allowed her to graduate. Shania had never seen someone miss as much school as Cheyenne and still graduate with honors.

Shania exhaled, and a smile spread across her face. She could tell that her sister was proud of him, and even though she was reluctant to admit it, she was proud of him too.

"I'm so glad to hear that. Congratulations," Shania said.

Greg chimed in, "That's terrific. Very smart decision."

Jonathan eyed Greg and Shania. "I owe y'all a lot." He raised a brow. "When I was coming up, my mom abandoned me and my brothers and sisters. For a while, I lived on the streets. I was homeless." He tilted his head to the side. "I sold drugs to survive—am I proud of that?" He paused. "No. I was just doing what I had to do." He placed his hands on his lap and exchanged glances with Cheyenne. "Then I met my boo, and everything changed."

Cheyenne leaned over and kissed Jonathan on the lips; then she leaned back in her seat. For the first time, Shania could see how her sister might be attracted to Jonathan. Beneath his thuggish veneer lay a decent guy trying to find his way.

Jonathan took a sip of water and swished a cube of ice around in his mouth. "Man"—he shook his head— "I coulda been dead. When I got capped, all that stuff people say about your life flashing before your eyes is true, the bad and the good. While I was in that coma, it was like a presence was all around me, keeping me. You know what I'm sayin'?"

All eyes were on Jonathan until Greg broke the silence.

"It wasn't your time," Greg said. "God has a plan for your life."

"I know that now," Jonathan relented. He looked at Shania. "I had always heard people talk about the Lord, but I wasn't a believer. I just thought black people had too much religion. Like it was an excuse for not trying hard. I used to hate when my grandmamma would say, 'I'ma pray for you.' I used to be like, 'Pray for yourself.' She was poor and seemed to be happy. I couldn't understand that." His mouth formed a circle as he wiped the corners of his mouth with his hand. "Now I know better. That's because of you, Ms. Shania." He pointed his index finger at her.

Shania's eyes misted as she remembered how hard she and Cheyenne had prayed for Jonathan's recovery while he lay helpless in that hospital bed.

He continued, "I used to hear people talk about the Lord, but they were doing just as much dirt as me. I wasn't feelin' that. But then I met you. You were the first person I ever met who talked the talk and walked the walk. And then when you came to the hospital and prayed for me even though I knew you couldn't stand me . . ." He snickered. "I knew there was something different about you."

Shania let out a slight chuckle.

He composed himself and said, "Then you took the time to talk to me about my salvation afterward. That changed my life. Maybe if the guys I used to hang with had somebody like you all in their lives, they'd be all right too. You guys are the only family I've got."

Shania dabbed the corners of her eyes with her napkin. She had no idea that she had made such an impact on Jonathan's life. The fact that he considered her to be family came as a surprise to her as well, especially since she hadn't gone out of her way to embrace him as a member of her family. Until now she had considered him to be the bane of her existence. In her mind, he was merely a test that she needed to overcome. Now she realized that she had been way off. The Lord had used her to bring Jonathan to Christ.

"Sister, are you crying?" Cheyenne teased.

Shania's nostrils flared. "Shut up. I'm not crying. Just trying to make sure my eyeliner's not smeared."

Cheyenne smirked. "Sure you are."

The waiter arrived with their food. Shania welcomed the distraction. Although she appreciated the bonding moment that she and Jonathan had shared, she thought he had gone too deep. She wanted to lighten the mood and make the evening more festive. After all, they were celebrating Greg's birthday. So, she cracked a few jokes, and everyone laughed.

They finished eating dinner and ordered coffee to go with the birthday cake they planned to eat for dessert. Shania had picked up a caramel cake, Greg's choice, from her friend who owned a bakery and brought it with them to the restaurant.

Before slicing the cake, they sang "Happy Birthday," and Greg opened his gifts. Cheyenne and Jonathan got him a silk tie and expensive cuff links. Shania could tell by the look on his face and the way he kept thanking them that he loved his gift. Then he opened the jewelry box containing the onyx ring Shania had gotten for him. He showed his appreciation by giving her a kiss.

They enjoyed the buttery caramel cake while making small talk and sipping coffee. When they finished, they all stood and followed each other outside. Although Cheyenne and Jonathan would be spending the night at the house with Shania and Greg, Shania hugged her little sister like she never wanted to let her go. It was still hard for her to accept the fact that as Cheyenne's husband, Jonathan came before her. After so many years of providing for and protecting her little sister, it was difficult for her to accept that now provisions and security rested solely in Jonathan's hands. Despite the fact that he now had a GED and had changed his lifestyle, she still felt that God had greater plans for Cheyenne . . . than him.

On the drive back home, Greg thanked her for making his special day exquisite, and though he wouldn't admit it, she could see the exhaustion from the day resting in his eyes.

"I need to make a quick stop. Is that okay?" Greg asked, covering a yawn with his hand.

Curious as to where he was going, she nodded and called Cheyenne's cell phone to tell her they had to make a stop. Cheyenne told her that they'd just meet them at the house rather than following them. Shania ended the call and sat quietly for the rest of the ride. She wasn't surprised when about forty minutes later he pulled into Mother Washington's driveway. He left the car running as he jogged up the steps and used his personal key to open Mother Washington's door. She watched as her husband ducked into the house and closed the door behind him. Greg was a total sweetheart, and it touched her heart that he looked after Mother Washington, always checking up on her and helping her with the upkeep of her house.

Mother Washington had bounced around from church to church, but when she had visited Saved and Sanctified Baptist three years ago, she had instantly considered the place her home and had taken Greg in as her "adopted" child. Rumor had it that Mother Washington had two daughters, but if she did, she never talked about them. Shania wondered why.

Greg came out the house a few minutes later, looking bothered.

"Something wrong?" Shania asked as he clicked his seat belt in place.

"She has a really bad headache. Said it's been bothering her all day."

"You want to stop and get her something?"

Greg shook his head and drove off. "She said the only thing she wants is darkness, silence, and sleep."

"I know that's right." Shania settled in her seat and stared at the headlights of the cars as they passed by. She nodded to the music and before she realized it she had drifted off to sleep. She didn't awake again until she felt Greg's arm slip beneath her knees and the other arm behind her back as he hefted her out of the passenger seat and against his chest. Still sleepy, she rubbed one eye.

She held on to his neck while he balanced her against one knee and used his free hand to unlock the front door. While he carried her to the bedroom, she could hear the sound of the TV coming from Cheyenne's closed bedroom door. She snuggled her head into the curve of his shoulder and inhaled the cologne that faintly clung to his shirt, as well as the masculine musky scent that belonged to only him.

Once inside their bedroom, he closed the door behind him, undressed her until she wore not a stitch of clothing; then she held her hands high in the air as he pulled her favorite raspberry red night slip over her head. Then, to top it off, he picked her up and tucked her in bed.

Shania cooed in contentment. "You are too sweet to me. I love you so much."

"I love you too, babes. Now, shhh."

She smiled as he placed a finger against her lips.

"We had a long day today, and you're going to need your rest for tomorrow," he explained.

She kissed the finger against her lips, moved it out of the way, then grabbed the back of his head and pulled his lips down to hers. She thanked God for blessing her with a husband who was so caring and considerate. Even if he had made a selfish move by purchasing that dreadful bike without her input, considering the totality of the circumstances, she could let that one mishap slide and continue loving him for being the excellent husband that he was. Flaws and all.

Four

Greg lay in the bed looking at Shania as she slept. His chest stuck out just thinking about the care his wife had taken to make sure that his day was special. What a birthday. He scratched his head and stared over at his wife, whose body was only half covered by the satiny sheets. One of his hands dragged along the inside of her uncovered thigh, and she moaned his name in her sleep and turned toward him. For half a second, he considered waking her up for an energy boost to start his day off right, but he decided against it. Yesterday had been long, and he was sure that she would spend all day in the kitchen, rushing to make up for lost time.

The wedding was only six days away, so she had her work cut out for her. As much as he enjoyed morning sex, he allowed his sleeping beauty to get a few more minutes of rest before she got up and started to get ready for Sunday morning service.

He leaned against the headboard, not ready just yet to shed the blanket of tranquility that the bed offered. Mentally, he did a quick run-through of the notes that he'd speak on during today's youth service—depression. It always surprised him how much his students went through during each week. Sometimes it was a breakup with a boyfriend or girlfriend, or grades plummeting in school, failed exams, dealing with bullying or peer pressure, and dealing with broken homes and absent, distant, or inadequate parents. Adults oftentimes failed to realize that even though the youth didn't have to deal with major bills, job stress, or marital problems, they still had a wealth of issues to trudge through. Greg could only hope that the words of encouragement that he filled them up with every Sunday morning was enough to carry them and guide them throughout the week, and throughout their lives.

A glance at the clock told him he needed to get out of bed and put some pep in his step. He was never late to work, so he didn't need to be late to God's house either. He hurried up and showered and shaved. When he finished getting dressed, he wrote a note to Shania telling her that it was his turn to be in charge of the youth services and that he'd see her at the 11:30 A.M. service.

After placing the note on his pillow, he kissed her cheek, and she didn't even stir. So he left the room without making a sound and went into the garage, where his convertible Mercedes and motorcycle were parked. He eyed Halle, itching to ride her, but he dismissed the urge and unlocked his Mercedes instead. He didn't feel like answering a bunch of questions about his new purchase, or having the kids harass him about giving them a ride when they knew full well that wasn't going to happen. The elders and mothers of the church would probably disbar his membership if he pulled up on church ground wearing a Sunday suit on the back of a motorcycle.

As soon as he walked through the doors of Saved and Sanctified Baptist Church, the few young people that were in the main sanctuary ran up to him and greeted him with hugs, daps, and high fives.

"What are you all doing in here?" he asked them after greeting each one in turn. "Shouldn't you be in the youth department?"

"We're headed that way," the oldest of the crew, a freckle-faced kid, said. "We just wanted to say hey to Pastor Ray first."

"Okay then. Just make sure you're in your seats by 9:30 A.M."

"Yes, sir, Minister Crinkle," they said in unison.

Greg smiled at them and tousled a few heads and patted a few shoulders as the youth left out the main doors in the direction of the youth department. Greg scouted the sanctuary for Franklin, but he wasn't there yet, which was expected. On a good day for him, he usually didn't show up at church until the praise team had reached their second or third song. On a bad day, he got there seconds before the pastor had asked everyone to stand so he could give the benediction.

Greg saw his pastor speaking with one of the deacons, and he waited patiently until they finished before he walked over to his pastor and gave him a manly hug. Pastor Ray asked him how he was doing and inquired about Shania, to which Greg admitted that she was a bit tired, but she'd be there for Sunday morning service.

As he headed toward the back, he bumped into Mother Washington as she was leaving the restroom.

"Good mornin', suga," Mother Washington said.

Dressed in a purple suit with a matching hat that had a feather sticking out the side, Greg thought Mother Washington looked real good this morning, considering how bad her head was bothering her the night before. But he expected her to be dressed sharp because that was her motto: you could half step it throughout the week, if you so desired, but on the Lord's day, you gave Him your Sunday best.

"Good morning, Mother Washington," Greg said as he bent over and gave her a big hug. The smell of Bengay® assaulted his nostrils. "How're you feeling today?"

She sighed and massaged her temple. "You know, suga, my head ain't bothering me as bad as it was last night, so I consider myself blessed. These old bones have seen better days, but I won't complain." She gave her signature smile, one that lacked about three teeth on the top row and five or six on the bottom. "I made two cobblers this morning. Got 'em sitting on the stove cooling. You make sure you come by and get 'em, okay?"

Greg nodded, licking his lips in anticipation. "Yes, ma'am. I'll come by after church and get them. Thank you, Mother."

"Where's that beautiful wife of yours?" She looked around as if she were expecting Shania to show up at any moment.

Whenever he heard other people refer to Shania in such an endearing way, his chest filled with pride. It reminded him that he had made a good decision in making Shania his wife. He believed she deserved all of the accolades people gave her, and more.

"She's a little tired. We had a long day yesterday, but she'll be at the 11:30 A.M. services," he explained.

Mother Washington snickered and elbowed his side. "I guess you put it on her, huh?"

Greg felt his cheeks grow hot, and he looked around to see if anyone else was standing nearby. One thing about Mother Washington was that she didn't bite her tongue for anybody. If she felt it, she said it.

"Don't be blushing," she said, and pinched his cheek. "Y'all is married folk now. It's all right in God's eyes. And I know y'all have only been married a few months, but don't do like a lot of these modern couples." She wagged a finger.

Greg furrowed a brow, wondering what she was talking about.

As if she had read his mind or his expression, Mother Washington didn't miss a beat when she said, "I'm talkin' 'bout babies, suga. Don't get so caught up with stuff that don't matter that you forget about your family. Life is short." She looked him in the eyes. "People get married and think they got forever to sort everything out. Marriage is forever, but we got a limit on life. Give that woman a baby and don't wait too long. Ain't nothing more important than your family, suga." When she said these words, she held her crumpled handkerchief against her lips, and her milky eyes glazed over with tears. She said into the handkerchief once again, "Ain't nothing more important than your family." She looked back up at Greg and added, "And blood ain't always thicker than water. Sometimes water thicker than blood."

Greg appreciated her words of wisdom, even though he didn't understand it all. He definitely wanted to have children with Shania one day. Right now, though, he enjoyed their time alone together, and he especially loved the spontaneity of their relationship. He liked the freedom they had. They could make love anywhere in their house, no matter what time of day or night. When they wanted to get up and go, they could. Besides their honeymoon on the island of St. Croix, most of their trips weren't planned in advance. They'd simply pack a bag, gas up the car, and decide where they wanted to go. The two of them had taken mini vacations, as they liked to call them. The trips ranged from weekend getaways to five-day excursions. So far they had gone to Destin Beach and Disney World in Florida, Charleston and Myrtle Beach, South Carolina, Chattanooga, Tennessee, and Savannah, Georgia. There was never a dull moment. With Shania, he had fun—not to say that having children would dampen that fun, but it would definitely make things different. And right now, he liked things as they were.

"Thanks for the advice, Mother," he said with sincerity, and touched her elbow as he glanced at her trembling chin and misty eyes. "Are you okay?"

She clamped her lips together and nodded. He knew she wasn't okay, but he didn't press the issue. Once Mother Washington pressed her lips together, that was a done deal. He couldn't squeeze a word out of her anymore than he could squeeze the very last drop out of a tube of toothpaste.

Greg walked her to her self-assigned seat at the front of the church, leaned forward and kissed her rogue cheek, then told her he'd see her in a little bit.

Still wondering what had made Mother's mood change so quickly, Greg tried to momentarily push those thoughts away as he hurried downstairs. As soon as he opened the doors to the youth department, he could hear music blaring through the halls. One of the associate youth pastors had already started getting the kids hyped up. Greg felt like dancing and found himself bobbing his head when he heard Kirk Franklin say, "Put ya hands up."

As soon as Greg entered the room filled with teenagers, he was met with laughter. He could tell that the kids were having a good time by the way they were singing along and dancing. He looked around and wished that he could freeze that moment in time. The boys had on jeans that fit, not sagging down to their ankles and showing their underwear, and the girls looked like little girls. They weren't wearing makeup and many had childlike hairstyles. Such a refreshing change from what he normally saw on the street.

Greg walked to the front of the room and high-fived the other youth pastor. The guy turned down the music, and Greg welcomed the kids.

"How's everybody doing today?" he asked, and the room filled with chatter as the kids began to shout their responses at him. "Okay, okay," he said, waving his hands for them to simmer down. "Who remembers what I said the topic for today would be?"

The freckle-faced kid raised his hand and Greg pointed at him. "Depression?"

"That's right," Greg told the class. "Depression." He took a seat at the edge of his desk. "By a show of hands," he clarified, "can someone tell me who they think was the most depressed person in the Bible?"

"Jesus," one of the younger kids in the classroom yelled out, and the class started laughing. The little boy shrugged down into his seat with a look of embarrassment.

"Don't laugh at him," Greg said, hitting a ruler against his desk to quiet the class. "I understand why he would think Jesus. Look at what all Jesus went through, all he had to suffer for our sake. For the average man, that could be a bit depressing, and even for Jesus, I'm sure it got difficult at times. But not once did he ever sin, and since we want to become more Christ-like, we need to learn how to go through our hard, depressing times sin-free. Easier said than done, this I know. But you have to start somewhere."

Greg held his ruler high and circled it in the air. "Somebody give me another name from the Bible who you think suffered from depression."

One of the older young ladies in the group held her hand up and Greg pointed at her. "Job," she said softly.

"Job," Greg repeated loudly. "That's the first one that came to my mind. Who knows the story of Job?"

They spent the next twenty minutes or so reading passages from Job and discussing the obstacles he had to face in life. Greg made all the kids stand to their feet, and with the associate youth pastor's help, he assigned them different roles: one person was to be Satan, the others God, Job, Job's wife, Job's three friends, the messengers, and Job's children and cattle. They reenacted the scene from the Bible to make the story more realistic for them.

Afterward, he asked the kids to retake their seats, then said, "Does anyone know why Job's story is relevant to you guys?"

For once, the class was silent, and no one raised their hand.

Greg cleared his throat and walked around the tables as he talked. "Job's wife continually told him to curse God and die. Basically, she told him to kill himself. After all he had been through, after all he had to suffer through, the average man would've probably done just that—killed himself. That's why I chose Job's story." He looked around and stared at each pair of eyes, making sure the kids were listening to him. "Sometimes, life can get so depressing that you might desire to take your very own life. Youth suicide is on a rise, and this is nothing but the enemy doing his job. Stealing, killing, and destroying young lives. I don't want anybody to raise your hands, but I can guarantee you that somebody in this room has seriously considered or at least thought about ending it all at some point in time in their life."

For the next hour, Greg talked to them about teenage suicide, and why that was never a good idea. He explained that life was only temporary, and that circumstances were temporary too. The children openly discussed their thoughts of suicide and battles with depression. Hearing about some of their home lives saddened Greg. It broke his heart to hear their various stories. Some of them had one or both parents addicted to drugs or alcohol. Others had parents in jail. Many were being raised in single-parent homes. Some had headed or were on the verge of heading in the same direction that Jonathan had taken. Their plights seemed never ending. Even still, Greg tried to be a beacon of light and told them that no matter what they were going through, God knew about it, loved them, and cared about what happened to them. He finished up with a group prayer, but offered individual prayers as well.

After services were over, Greg laughed and joked with some of the students. Interacting with the youth made him feel energized and alive. He felt his iPhone vibrate in his pocket and saw that it was Shania. She must've been looking for him. He answered as he made his way down the hall and up the stairs to meet his wife. He told her that he was en route and ended the call.

When he walked into the church vestibule, he had to stop and greet one member after the other. It wasn't until a woman with a familiar face caught his eye that he thought about the woman from the bike dealership, the one with the body carved out of a fantasy. He stared at the brown-eyed, black-haired woman for the longest time and could almost swear that it was the woman from the dealership. But something about her looked... different. This woman didn't have that look of danger in her eyes. And plus, the woman at the dealership had curly brown hair with blond highlights. This woman's hair was jet-black. And even in the modest white dress she was wearing, he could tell that she had a nice shape, but it was nothing like the hourglass figure that had turned every head at the dealership.

To his surprise, he watched as the woman headed over to Mother Washington, and he watched as Mother Washington hugged her tight, rocking her from side to side, as though she had known this woman for a very long time. With unanswered questions eating at him, Greg continued staring at the woman until her eyes just happened to catch his. In her eyes, he saw no recognition. There was no way this could be that same woman from the dealership. She had recognized him from the church instantly, even in his casual weekend gear. So he knew she would recognize him in the congregation.

Perturbed, Greg decided to drop the issue and scanned the congregation for his wife and Franklin. Franklin was still nowhere in sight, but Sister Catherine and her three kids were already sitting on the fourth row from the front. He saw his wife standing in the hallway, accompanied by Jonathan and Cheyenne. He greeted a few more members, making sure to give the women innocent church hugs, then made his way over to his wife. All the while he couldn't stop thinking about that woman. He wondered who the woman was that looked so much like the woman from the dealership. Or was it the same woman? If it was her, what kind of game was she playing with him?

Five

"Greg's on his way," Shania explained to Cheyenne and Jonathan.

They stood in the hallway outside of the sanctuary next to the water fountain. Shania observed people as they entered the church. Some of the older women were dressed in colorful suits and hats of varying sizes. Most of the men wore dress shirts with slacks; a few had on suits and ties. She saw a cute little boy wriggling his hand, trying to free himself from his mother's grip. She smiled as she imagined herself in a similar predicament one day with the son she hoped to have.

Turning away, she spotted Greg walking toward her with a troublesome expression on his face. She hoped that the kids at youth church hadn't been too hard on him. Dealing with the youth could be unpredictable. Those kids tended to be more moody than a woman going through menopause.

"There's Greg," Shania announced.

Cheyenne and Jonathan looked in his direction.

"I hope you guys weren't waiting too long," Greg said as he approached. He then kissed Shania on the cheek.

"Not that long," Shania assured him. "You all right?"

He took a sip from the water fountain and dabbed his mouth on his shirt sleeve. "Yeah, I'm okay." He exhaled. "We talked about some heavy stuff today in youth church."

Shania gave him a half smile, but something in his expression still worried her. "It's tough being a kid these days. They're forced to grow up so fast."

Greg nodded his head. He touched her lower back, sending a shiver up her spine, and ushered her into the sanctuary with Cheyenne and Jonathan following behind. Something in his demeanor still struck her as disturbed and distant, but she decided to let it go. At least for now.

They took their seats in the front row, greeting the people sitting around them. Services started with praise and worship, followed by the congregational scripture reading. When they finished, it was time for altar prayer. After a couple of songs performed by the choir, the congregation acknowledged visitors and gave their tithes and offering. Then the pastor came out and delivered a powerful sermon titled "The Kind of Friends That Are Dangerous." The pastor preached from the book of Job and gave a breakdown of Job's friends. He then told the congregation to walk in integrity wherever they were, because God saw what they were doing. He encouraged the people to hold on and trust God. If people waited on God, He would go after their adversaries.

Shania stood to her feet and shouted, "Preach, Pastor!" She knew that he was speaking the truth.

After services ended, they hugged some of the members and wished them well before heading out. Greg walked with Shania, Cheyenne, and Jonathan to Shania's Range Rover, and he held the door open for her. He leaned in and pecked her cheek, then said, "I'll meet you at the house later."

She frowned at him. "Where're you going?"

Greg reached across her and buckled her in. "Franklin didn't come to church today, so I'm going to swing by there and check up on him."

"Really?"

He frowned at her. "Are you mad?"

She wiggled her hands in the air. "No, I'm not mad, per se. I'm just not feeling this aura, this vibe you're putting out in the air. What's wrong with you? You've been acting strange all morning."

"And what's wrong with you?" he tossed back. "You've been having a real funky attitude lately."

Shania glared at him and ignored the gasps and whispers that reached her ears from the front and backseat passengers. "Move out of my way so I can close my door, please."

"Babe," he said and reached out for her hand. He held her hand and gave it a squeeze before placing a kiss across her knuckles. "I'm sorry, okay? I just . . . I have a lot on my mind."

She tilted her head to the side. "You want to talk?"

"Maybe later." He thumped the roof of the car, then stepped out the way so he could close the door. "I'll meet you at the house later."

She knew that whatever was on Greg's mind would eat at her until they finally talked about it and put it out in the open. For now, she would let the situation rest.

During the drive home, Shania struck up a conversation with Cheyenne. Although they talked on the phone daily, having Cheyenne at home meant the world to Shania, even if it was only for the weekend. She missed having her sister around since she had gone off to college. As much as she knew she needed to let her go, it was difficult to do. The twelve-year age gap between the sisters seemed to lessen as they got older. The more mature Cheyenne became, the better their relationship got. To Shania, they were beginning to feel more like sisters instead of the mother-daughter role they had been thrust into.

The thought of Cheyenne being a sophomore in college spoke volumes about God's favor. Shania was even more surprised that Cheyenne decided to major in engineering. She had always pictured Cheyenne majoring in journalism or English, because she loved writing poetry. She had to admit, though, it pleased her that Cheyenne went for a male-dominated profession; she wished that more women would challenge themselves and not be intimidated by professions that required heavy math or science concentrations.

"So," Shania began, and glanced at the passenger seat to make sure Cheyenne was listening to her, "how's school coming along?"

Cheyenne whistled and let her hand glide through the air. "It's a breeze. I'm making As in all my classes and passing all my exams. Thanks to my hubby"—she glanced over her shoulder at Jonathan and they shared a smile—"who stays on me all the time and makes sure I start on my papers well ahead of time."

"Oh, how sweet," Shania wanted to say, but refrained from doing so because she knew it would come out sounding very sarcastic. So instead, she plastered a strained smile on her face and said, "How are you liking your new apartment?"

At first Cheyenne lived in the dorms. After getting married, Shania had helped her sister move into a cute one-bedroom apartment in a gated community near the campus. Shania even went to Valdosta to help her decorate and make sure she was settled in.

"We're loving it," Cheyenne said with an even bigger smile, and Jonathan and she shared googly eyes again.

At the sound of "we're," Shania visibly cringed, and at the sight of their googly eyes, she felt like throwing up. For the life of her, she couldn't understand where this bitterness and attitude were coming from. This was not like her; it must've been getting pretty close to that time of the month.

Trying to be nice, Shania looked at Jonathan in the rearview mirror and asked, "Have you thought about what you want to major in?"

He grinned, revealing a chipped tooth in the front of his mouth. "I wanna major in finance." She was impressed until he said, "Somebody's gotta help Cheyenne manage all of that money she's gonna get when she graduates from school."

Shania's eyes bucked, and she almost ran off the road. She wouldn't be surprised if smoke tendrils were escaping her nose. Her fingers dug into the steering wheel as she navigated the car to the side of the road and slammed on the brakes, causing everyone inside to jerk forward. She placed the car in park. Whipping her neck around like a scene from the horror movie classic *The Exorcist,* she looked Jonathan straight in the eyes.

Without blinking, flinching, or smiling, she said, "I know that you and Cheyenne are married. I get that. But there's one thing I want to make perfectly clear." She held up her index finger to express her point even though she really felt like sticking up the middle one. "I'm the executor of my parents' estate. That means Cheyenne doesn't get a dime without my approval. I don't know what Cheyenne told you, but she will not receive all of the money in her trust until she's thirty-five years old. So, if your whole purpose for eloping was to get her money and run, you can forget that."

Cheyenne gasped. "Why would you even say something like that, sister?"

"Because you know it's true!" Shania hit the steering wheel and rolled her eyes. "When he saw you, he saw dollar signs, and you know it."

She knew that her statement about Cheyenne not receiving all of the money in her trust until she turned thirty-five wasn't completely true. She really said it for shock value. The truth of the matter was that their parents had left them $2 million; each parent had a million-dollar life insurance policy. Her parents had planned their estates so well that they even had a mortgage pay-off in the event of their death, so Shania and Cheyenne didn't have any mortgage payments. Their house had been paid for.

Because Shania was the oldest, she had control of the money. In her parents' will, they left instructions for the money to be divided equally between the sisters. Since they didn't want to risk the girls losing the money, they put stipulations on the distribution. Shania received $400,000 right away, because she had met the age requirements. She received $200,000 more when she turned twenty-five, and another $200,000 payment on her thirtieth birthday. Her final payment would be received in three years, on her thirty-fifth birthday.

Shania used some of her money to start a catering company, Eat Your Heart Out. She remodeled her base-ment and turned it into a commercial kitchen. In the seven years that her company had been in existence, she had become quite successful. She catered everything from private parties to weddings to corporate events. With her company consistently turning a profit, she hadn't needed to spend any more of her inheritance money. Instead, she invested in land, real estate, bonds, and CDs to diversify her portfolio.

As for Cheyenne's portion of the money, Cheyenne received a $200,000 distribution check when she turned eighteen. A portion of her money went toward her college tuition, books, and a Honda Accord. Most recently, they used some of her money for the deposit on her apartment and furniture. The rest of the money went into their family trust, from which Cheyenne received a monthly stipend to help with living expenses. Because of that, she didn't have to work. All she had to do was focus on her studies. She'd receive the rest of her money in equal installments at ages twenty-two, twenty-five, thirty, and thirty-five.

Feeling relieved to have gotten that off her chest, Shania faced forward and blinked. When she glanced into the rearview mirror, she saw Jonathan's cheeks puffed out like a blowfish, and then he blew out the air and started working his jaw. Just when she thought she'd explode if he didn't say what was on his mind, he finally opened his mouth and spoke.

"You think you know me, but you don't know me," Jonathan said to the back of her head.

She put one hand on the steering wheel and used the other to put the car in drive. She waited until she had enough space between cars before easing her way back into traffic.

"If that was the case," he continued, "I wouldn't have been with her this long."

Shania cut her eyes at her sister and then looked straight ahead. Cheyenne didn't utter a word. The tips of her ears were red, and she continued to stare forward as she gnawed her nails down to their nail bed.

"I know that you can't stand the ground I walk on," Jonathan continued, "and I'm sure it would make your day if I would just disappear out your sister's life forever."

Before she could stop herself, her head nodded on its own volition.

"But you know what?" he added. "Whether you like me or not, you should have enough respect for your sister to respect her decision. You think you got me all figured out, but you don't. You think you know me, but you don't know the half. What I do know is that I love your sister, and as long as God allows me to be on this earth, I'm going to do everything I can to keep her happy. And if that's not enough for you, then, hey, it is what it is. But as long as that's enough for Cheyenne, then that's all that matters."

"Okay." Shania smirked. "Let's drop it."

"Yes, let's," Cheyenne added in a soft voice, still nibbling on her nails and staring out the passenger window.

No one spoke for the rest of the ride, which suited Shania just fine. She appreciated the quiet, and used the silence to force herself to calm down.

Once at the house, Greg joined them outside and he seemed a little less disturbed than he had been at church. Jonathan nearly tripped out of the car when his eyes landed on Greg's bike.

"Man, is that a BMW motorcycle?" he exclaimed with his hands on his hips as he gave the bike a good looking over. "I ain't even know BMW *made* motorcycles."

Cheyenne looked at her sister with her mouth hanging open. "You actually let him get a bike?"

Shania rolled her eyes. "I didn't let him do anything, but that's a whole other can of worms that I don't feel like opening right now." She opened the door and hopped down from the Rover. "Come on, Cheyenne. We'll leave the boys out here, and you can help me put something on the stove."

Greg was more than a little ready to show off his new motorcycle and explain all the gadgets to Jonathan. He and Jonathan spent a few moments in the garage doing some male bonding while Shania and Cheyenne went into the kitchen.

Shania looked into the sink and removed the bowl of thawed shrimp and the bag of thawed lobster. Cheyenne went straight to the bar stools and straddled one. She looked up at the small flat-screen television hanging on the wall above the bread box and said, "Where's the remote?"

Shania gave her sister an exasperated stare. "I thought I said come help me put something on the stove."

Cheyenne rolled her eyes and searched the countertops, then began pulling out cabinet drawers. She searched through their contents for the remote. "Shania, you know I can't cook. Found it!" She grinned as she held up the remote, then settled atop the stool again.

As Cheyenne flipped through the channels on the small plasma-screen TV hanging on the kitchen wall, Shania heated a skillet on the front eye and said, "You're married now. Don't you think you should learn how to cook?"

She shook her head. "No. Jonathan looks through cookbooks almost every day. He's always coming up with meals to cook for us, and when he doesn't cook, we go out to eat or order pizza."

Shania shook her head while she lifted the pot top and used the tongs to lower the lobster into the steamer.

As a child, she used to sit in the kitchen and watch while her mom prepared meals for the family. Since Cheyenne hadn't had that same opportunity, Shania didn't want to pressure her, so she continued preparing dinner alone.

The men came in about an hour later, and even though Cheyenne hadn't lifted a finger to help with the meal, she at least had the decency to set the table. They sat at the table; Greg said grace; then they dug into the food. Not many words were said, just a lot of chewing, swallowing, and fork tines scraping against the ceramic dishes. Whenever they did speak, they seemed to tiptoe around the elephants in the room—the huge explosion that happened in the car, the rekindled tension between Shania and Jonathan, and the white elephant sitting on Greg's chest.

After they finished eating, Jonathan and Cheyenne went home, and Greg hung out in his office. Thankful for the peace and quiet, Shania disappeared into her basement kitchen and began making another batch of cupcakes to finish off the wedding's showcase cupcake pyramid. She wondered if she'd ever be able to accept Jonathan into her family.

Six

Greg woke up Monday morning a bit earlier than usual. He wanted to get an early start in the office since he had paperwork to complete and meetings with a few clients scheduled. Today, his plan was to make up for lost ground. For the four policies that were canceled over the weekend, he challenged himself to sign at least five new policies today. That would definitely be no easy feat, but he planned to give it his best shot.

Having beaten the usual morning traffic, when he arrived at the office, he turned on the lights and brewed a pot of coffee. Since he was the first person there, he figured he could get a lot of work done before the crowd.

The coffee finished percolating. There was nothing like the smell of fresh coffee to awaken the senses, he thought. He poured himself a cup and made his way to his cubicle. Once at his desk, he took a few sips of his hot drink, then went through his file cabinet in search of clients who had canceled their insurance policies within the last year or so, and who might be interested in reinstating their policies at a lower monthly price and with a contractual agreement that locked them into a three-month agreement, rather than six.

First, he pulled up a new spreadsheet and created a field for names, numbers, and insurance policy type. After he inserted all the data from the pulled files, he picked up his phone and began making the calls.

Half the clients didn't answer or numbers were no longer in service. Those who did answer either rudely rejected his offer or politely told him they weren't interested and curtly ended the call. Out of the thirty numbers he called, he got one yes and one "Maybe, but call me back next month when my funds are looking a little better." Dispirited, he dialed the last number on his list and sighed aloud when he got the no-longer-in-service message.

"Why such a long face?" Franklin said, inviting himself into Greg's cubicle with his own cup of straight black coffee. He took a seat in the empty chair with his legs spread wide apart and the cuffs of his dress pants rose high, showing off the lower portion of his ashy, hairy legs. "You look like your puppy died."

"I don't have a puppy."

"Well, if you had one, you'd look like he died."

"Shut up, Franklin," Greg said, and clicked his pen closed before tossing it on the desk. "I'm not in the mood for jokes."

Franklin sipped on his coffee, then sat it on Greg's desk. He crossed his hands behind his head and leaned back in his chair. "A'ight, man. Spill it. You still thinking about that girl?"

Greg lifted an eyebrow. "What girl?"

"The girl you told me about that was at church Sunday."

Greg pulled at his chin hair and shook his head. "No, I'm over that. She just looked real familiar, but she wasn't who I thought she was," he said.

"Well, if it's not her, then what's got you so stressed? I ain't seen you look this tense in a while."

Greg smacked his lips and tapped a tuneless beat atop his desk. "You remember those five new policies I opened?"

Franklin nodded emphatically. "That's good news, Greg. Five policies in one week? That's great news, especially for you. You only get about one or two policies per month—okay, okay, I'm overexaggerating—but for you, at least one or two policies per day is good news. You doing good, my brother, so what's the problem?"

"The problem," Greg said, staring at the discouraging data on his computer screen, "is that all the policyholders canceled over the weekend, except for one."

Franklin's face flip-flopped. "You joking, right?"

Greg groaned and held his head, which was beginning a slow, dull ache at the spot directly between his eyes. "Man, I wish I was but—" His office phone let out a shrill ring, and he held up a finger at Franklin while he answered it. "Mutual Living, Greg Crinkle speaking, how can I assist you? Yes, sir, Mr. McDowell, how are you today? Glad to hear it." Greg listened to the man speak, and then his heart dropped. "Yes, sir, today would be the last day that you could do it, but—yes, sir, we do offer a full refund, but—well, before you do that, Mr. McDowell, at least consider opening a different policy. We have a special going that you can open a new policy with no money down, your first month insurance would only be seventy-five dollars, and plus, you'd only have to agree to a three-month contract rather than six." He crossed his fingers and glanced over at Franklin. "Is that something you think you might be interested in, Mr. McDowell?"

His face dropped as he listened to the man shoot down his offer. He thanked him for doing business with them, then ended the call. Greg held the phone in his hand for a few extra seconds after the call ended, then finally dropped the phone on the receiver.

Franklin wasn't smiling anymore. "Let me guess. Another cancellation?"

"Yep." Greg smiled a humorless smile. "All five policy-holders. Now what do I do? If that rumor about down-sizing is really true, I can kiss this job good-bye."

"G, don't say that."

"Don't say what? The truth?" Greg held his hands out to either side of him. "Let's just be realistic here. They want to cut back on employees because of the struggling economy. We have too many seasoned reps in here close to retirement, and I'm not one of them."

"True," Franklin said, "but look at your track record. You have your faithful policyholders that have been with you for years. And you even talked them into opening new insurance policies."

"Yeah, but the boss is not interested in long-standing clients. He's only worried about how many new names we can add to the roster. And that's not something I'm good at. But you, Frank"—Greg pointed at his friend— "you don't understand where I'm coming from because you're so good at what you do. You sign about ten, fif-teen new policyholders every day. The boss isn't going to let you go. You're like gold to him. But me . . ." Greg splayed his fingers over his chest. "I'm dispensable."

Franklin finished off his coffee and crushed his Styro-foam cup in his hands, then leaned forward and dropped it in Greg's wastebasket. "You are what you speak."

Swallowing the lump forming in his throat, Greg re-flected on the thirteen years he had invested in the com-pany. He wondered if his job could be in jeopardy. He then rationalized all the reasons why he shouldn't worry. Franklin was right; all workers had their strengths and weaknesses, and even though acquiring new clients wasn't a strength for him, keeping good, long-standing policyholders was definitely a plus for him. And even though he didn't have a roster full of names, he was still a top performer. His name had consistently appeared in the President's Circle. Not only did he have good relationships with his clients, but they trusted him, and that's what mattered the most.

Snapping out of his reflective state, Greg said, "You're right. I'm over here speaking death when I need to speak life. I just have to trust and believe that God is in control and that He has it all worked out. To be honest, I think we'll both be fine. We don't have anything to worry about." He tried to sound confident as he convinced himself that he was telling the truth.

"Mind if I switch the subject for a minute?" Franklin asked, and Greg nodded before he could finish asking the question.

Greg was ready for a change of topic; no matter how confident he tried to seem, if he reflected on the issue too long, he knew it was just a matter of time before he found his spirits in the dump again.

"You remember when you came by yesterday and I told you I didn't come to church 'cause I was under the weather?"

Greg nodded, then added, "You lied, huh?"

Franklin lifted his eyebrows. "How you know?"

"'Cause it was written all over your face. How long have I known you, Frank? Thirteen, fourteen years? When you're lying, I know it. You slept with her, didn't you?"

Again, Frank's eyebrows shot skyward and he lowered his voice, as though God himself was sitting on the other side of the cubicle. "What?" he whispered. "Did she tell you?"

"No, she didn't tell me nothing," Greg said, and held up a finger while he took a transferred call. He filled out a claims form and faxed it over to the claims department, then returned his attention to Franklin. "So what was supposed to be a little 'date' turned into you going all the way." He posed the question as a statement.

Franklin put his face in his hands and shook his head from side to side. "Man, it's like she knew that's all she wanted from the jump. I got over there, Greg, Sister Catherine wasn't wearing nothing but a robe."

"Nothing but a robe?" Greg's eyes grew wide.

Franklin leaned forward and added, "And nothing underneath. Not even a pair of socks."

"Lord have mercy," Greg whispered, shaking his head. "And then what happened?"

"Man . . . man, what you think?"

"How many times?"

Franklin's eyes were full of remorse, and his Adam's apple bobbed as he tried to swallow. Then he gnawed on his fist and finally admitted, "I lost count after the twelfth time."

"The twelfth time?" Greg pushed back away from his desk and stared at Franklin in surprise. "Dang, bro, you weren't playing no games, were you?"

"No games," Franklin promised him. "I went in there just to spend time with her, but when she dropped that robe and those big ole breasts went flopping everywhere . . ." Franklin closed his eyes and shook his head as though he were savoring the memory. "After six whole months of uninterrupted celibacy, I sinned, Greg. I fell short. But here's the whammy. You ready for it?"

Greg nodded. "Go ahead."

"Usually, after I lay down the pipe," he said, "I feel a little bad because I know it's fornication. But after I finished at Sister Catherine's house, I felt like I'd been playing in dirt, you feel me? I felt so . . . unclean. And so . . . ashamed of myself. You listening to me?"

Greg cupped his ear to show Franklin he was listening to every word.

"And I have never in my life felt that way after sex."

"It's called conviction, Frank. The Holy Ghost makes you feel guilty when you sin. That's actually a good thing. The only time you should get worried is when you do wrong, you know it's wrong, and you no longer feel bad when you do it." Greg thudded his friend on the back. "But don't beat yourself up about it. You sinned, you were wrong. Now repent, and go on with your life."

"Yeah, you're right," Franklin said, and tilted his chair on two legs while he stared at the ceiling. "But, man, while I was doing it, while I was putting in work—"

"Please, spare me the details."

"I ain't gonna tell you the details," Franklin promised him. "All I'm saying is this. While I was doing her, Greg, I felt like crying." He dropped his chair to all fours and looked at Greg with a very serious expression. "I felt like crying, because I want to lay the pipe to a woman who loves me just as much as I love her. I'm tired of the physical thing, you feel me? I want something on a deeper level. And when I do lay the pipe, I want God to look down at me and be like, 'That's right, Frank! Give it to her! Put in work!'"

If his friend wasn't looking so serious, Greg would've bust out laughing in his face. Even when he was serious, that boy was a fool. Trying his best to keep a sober expression, Greg said, "Basically, while you were having sex with Sister Catherine, you realized that you're ready to be married, and you'd much rather be having sex with your wife."

Franklin pointed a finger at Greg, then snapped his fingers. "I knew you'd get it. Exactly. That's what I want, Greg. So now what do I do?"

"For starters," Greg said, then held up one finger to take another call. When he finished the call, he returned his attention to Franklin. "For starters," he began again, "you need to leave Sister Catherine alone, because I don't believe that she's the one God has for you. And then you need to get on your knees and pray for God to send you a wife. While you're waiting on her arrival, pray for Him to prepare you to be a husband."

"That's deep," Franklin said, and nodded. "I like that. I'm gonna do that."

"I hope you will."

"A'ight, man," Franklin said, standing to his feet and smoothing the creases out of his shirt. "Let me get back over to my cubicle before they realize I got missing. I'll catch you at lunch."

Greg snapped and pointed two fingers at his friend. But as soon as Franklin, which was his distraction, left his cubicle, all of Greg's previous worries resurfaced, leaving him feeling deflated. Mentally, he was all over the place. He sat in his chair and considered what he'd do if by slight chance he did lose his job. The possibility didn't sit well with him. In fact, the mere thought vexed his spirit. He had become so good at his job that he couldn't imagine learning a new trade. Even if he elected to stay in the same industry, finding a suitable company to match his current compensation plan could prove difficult.

Then he stopped to consider his age. He wasn't getting any younger. He'd be competing with guys fresh out of college, and here he was just a half decade away from forty. Although he viewed his level of expertise as a plus, he knew that his age would be a minus. Most employers wanted younger employees to train and mold, because they weren't set in their ways.

He massaged his temple, trying not to let himself get stressed out over a situation that hadn't occurred yet. He realized that he was letting fear get the best of him. Fear of being without a job. Fear of not being able to provide for himself and his wife. And most of all . . . fear of failure.

He reminded himself that God had not given him the spirit of fear and composed himself when he heard the office coming to life. People were chatting and settling into their workstations. He focused his attention on his work until 9:00 A.M., when he joined the rest of the team for their weekly staff meeting. They sat around the conference room table, listening to their manager talk about the state of affairs. Greg took copious notes and on occasion looked out the large window, catching a view of the clear sky.

He stopped writing when he heard his boss say, "I'm sure many of you have started hearing rumblings about a possible downsizing." His tone sounded serious as he adjusted his burgundy tie. He sighed. "I'm disappointed to inform you all that it's true."

Outbursts exploded throughout the room. Greg felt like walking out of the meeting. He struggled to stay in his seat.

"Wait," he continued, holding up his hands to shush the crowd. "Let me finish." The chatter turned into a low roar, a dribble, then finally ceased. "Corporate hasn't given us any names of affected personnel. We don't know what they're basing the cuts on, or how many people will be impacted." He leaned on the long table. "I can assure you that I'll fight to keep each and every one of you. I wish I had more to tell you."

His words offered little comfort to Greg. He zoned out for the rest of the meeting, thinking about what he needed to do next. He thought about how his résumé needed to be updated. Even if he wasn't on the chopping block, he didn't like feeling vulnerable. He disliked leaving his fate in the hands of his employer. Maybe he had become too complacent and needed to explore other options, anyway.

He then thought about Shania and how she had turned her passion for cooking into a successful career and thriving business. He wondered if he had an entrepreneurial spirit lying dormant within.

When the meeting ended, Greg couldn't get out of there fast enough. He gathered his belongings, went back to his desk, and logged off his computer. He then grabbed his briefcase and headed to his first appointment of the day.

A few hours later, Greg had met with all of his appointments and secured two new policies. That helped brighten his spirit, but he still didn't feel like going back into the office; he had too much on his mind. He apologized to Franklin for reneging on lunch and decided to take the rest of the day off.

When he got home, he didn't see Shania's car in the garage. A part of him felt disappointed that she wasn't there for him to talk to. Maybe that was for the best; since despite Franklin's prompting, he felt that anything that came out of his mouth at this moment would be all death and no life.

He decided to wait until he found out whether he was getting cut or not before involving her. No point in making Shania worry if she didn't have to. She already had enough on her plate.

He needed to clear his mind, so he changed out of his business attire and into riding clothes. He put on his helmet and took a ten-mile ride on a motorcycle trail that meandered through the deciduous woods along a creek.

As he traveled the concrete road, pushing against the wind, his previous fears resurfaced in his mind. He knew that he didn't have control over what was happening at work, but he knew one thing for certain—God had his back. That belief helped him to silently pray and ask God to handle the situation and do what was best for him.

When he returned home and parked his bike in the garage, he showered and changed into a T-shirt and lounge pants. He poured himself an ice-cold glass of pomegranate juice and enjoyed the refreshing taste.

While leaning against the island in the kitchen, he heard keys fumbling at the garage entranceway. He put his drink down and opened the door for Shania. She was carrying a bag, so he took it out of her hand. She thanked him.

"How was your day?" she asked as she kicked off her heels.

He set the bag on the counter and rubbed the back of his neck. With a slight sigh he said, "It was okay."

Shania walked over to him and stared him in the eyes. "I don't like the way you sounded when you said that. What's the matter?" She raised a brow.

Unwilling to lie to her, Greg told her about the meeting at work and the pending layoffs. She reached out and hugged him. Her soft body felt good to him. They shared a kiss.

With her arms wrapped around his waist, Shania stopped kissing Greg and said, "Honey, you're smart, educated, and professional. If the company you work for is fool enough to let you go, that's their loss. I don't believe you'll have any trouble getting a new job."

He stepped back from her and rested his body against the counter. "It's not as easy to get a job as it used to be. Atlanta is so saturated and competitive."

His pessimistic attitude didn't surprise him, but his words still left a bitter taste in his mouth.

She held up her index finger and gently pressed it against his full lips. "Stop with all the negative talk. You already know who you are and whose you are. You know the source of your supply, and it's not your job."

Greg moved her hand from his lips and placed it over his heart. He allowed her words to marinate in his mind. He knew she was right.

"Besides," she continued, "if push came to shove, you could always work with me. You know as soon as I finish one wedding, I get an invitation to cater another. We'll always have work." Her smile showed her sincerity. She began removing groceries from her bag.

Although he heard Shania say that he could work with her, he processed that as meaning working *for* her instead. He didn't like the idea of not having an outside source of income and having to rely on his wife for financial support. Something about that just didn't sit right with him. He liked being able to pay their household bills, go out to eat at nice restaurants, take his wife on vacation, and buy her gifts. Not being able to provide for her would make him feel like less than a man.

"Hopefully it won't come down to that," Greg said seriously.

A fleeting thought about owning his own company crossed his mind. He did a quick mental rundown of what he liked to do and was good at doing. He realized that he knew how to break cars down and rebuild them. His father had taught him all about cars and motorcycles. He then thought about businesses in his area and couldn't remember seeing any businesses that specialized in restoring classic cars.

With his knack for working underneath the hood, and Franklin's love for vintage vehicles, the idea of owning his own company suddenly became more appealing to him. Did he have what it took to be the head brotha in charge?

Seven

While Greg arose for work, Shania went back to bed to get a couple more hours of sleep. She had tossed and turned all night, and the moments when she finally found a spot comfortable enough to warrant rest, Greg started his own bouts of tossing and turning. Exhausted from her sleepless night, Shania rolled into the middle of the bed, allowing her skin to soak up the warmth Greg's body had left, and within seconds, she had fallen into a deep sleep.

When Shania woke up, she lay in bed for a few extra minutes in a meditative state. She needed clarity of thought and hoped that meditation would give her some insight.

She felt bad for Greg, yet she didn't think he had a need to worry. With his job performance, she was convinced he'd be one of the last people to go. Even if he did get downsized, Shania had a difficult time understanding why Greg was acting like that would be the worst thing that could happen to him. She could understand Greg's anxiety better if he didn't have any marketable skills, but he did. She also thought it would be a good time for him to pray and ask God to reveal his life's purpose. Rather than wallowing in self-pity, she wanted Greg to walk in faith and live his destiny.

Maybe if they had a baby, Greg wouldn't be so worried about his job situation, because he'd have someone else to focus on and give his energy to. She marveled at the thought of having a little one around the house. She wouldn't mind having Greg as a stay-at-home dad. Lots of men were doing that these days, especially with corporate downsizing. Just the thought of Greg changing diapers and getting up in the middle of the night for feedings made her chuckle. To Shania, having her husband as the primary caregiver would be better than leaving her baby with a nanny or day-care provider, especially since she had no interest in giving up her career.

She pulled the sheets up to her neck and stared at the cathedral ceiling. Knowing she could've stayed in bed an extra thirty minutes, she forced herself to get up, get dressed, and finally dial the governor's secretary.

She greeted the secretary in a professional manner on the first ring.

"Hi," Shania began. "This is Shania Crinkle, owner of Eat Your Heart Out Cakes and Catering. I got your letter in the mail a few days ago, but I've been a bit busy, so I apologize for my tardy response."

"Oh, it's no problem at all." The secretary went on to explain the induction ceremony and how they would have a head count of two hundred people. She informed Shania that she was one of the five candidates who the governor had decided to include in their catering pool. Whoever had the most appetizing menu and the most appealing—rich in quality samples—would be the chosen one to cater the event. The governor gave no specifics, except for the fact that he wanted finger foods—hearty finger foods that exhibited fine Southern cooking at its best. "Do you think you could have a sample menu and samples ready for taste testing by this Saturday?"

The wedding was this Saturday, and though she hated to add this extra stress to her already hectic schedule, there was no way she could pass up this opportunity. If she was selected—no, *when* she was selected—only God knew what doors this induction ceremony could open for her business.

Jittery with excitement, Shania promised the woman that she would have something ready by Saturday. She hung up and called her assistant to tell her that she'd need her to set up for the wedding while Shania met with the governor. She then went into the basement and scanned her shelves of cookbooks, pulling out every book that dealt with Southern cooking. She spent the next few hours marking potential recipes in her cookbooks and restructuring certain recipes to turn the final product into something that would constitute a finger food.

After she had a handful of recipes in tow, she began looking through the cabinets, the pantry, the deep freezer and refrigerator for the ingredients. After she gathered everything she'd need to complete the first two recipes, she tied her apron around her waist and washed her hands.

While working, she thought about Greg and his possible predicament. For her, she couldn't imagine working for someone else; she never had the desire to work in corporate America. She liked being an entrepreneur. Her father had always told her that if she pursued her passion, the money would follow. Her love for creating gourmet meals felt as natural to Shania as breathing. Cooking was the one thing in life she'd do even if she didn't make one red cent.

She tore a piece of wax paper and spread it across the counter. She kneaded some dough and sprinkled flour, hoping that she hadn't contributed to Greg's anxiety in any way. A feeling in her gut, call it female intuition, told her she had. She knew that men had fragile egos, and it didn't take much to shatter them. She thought Greg's willingness to provide for her was sweet but unnecessary. She didn't need anyone to support her financially; her parents had made sure of that. What she needed from Greg was his unconditional love and emotional support, which he willingly provided.

In spite of her independence, she worked hard to make Greg feel needed and valued in their relationship. She refused to belittle him or make him feel as though he couldn't do anything for her. She respected him and loved him too much for that. Besides, Greg did plenty for her. She loved Greg's traditional values. Out of all the time she had known Greg, he hadn't so much as asked her for five dollars. He took her to nice places, like her favorite restaurants, movies, plays, and concerts. Above all else, she enjoyed spending time alone with him. They didn't have to be doing anything: just being with him was enough.

In addition to insisting on paying the household expenses, Greg wasn't afraid to help out in other ways. He had no problem taking out the trash without being asked, and he maintained her car by keeping it full of gas, taking it in for scheduled service appointments, and detailing it. Not only did he give her his money, he gave Shania all of him—mind, body, and soul. She appreciated all of it and didn't take him or his love for granted.

Her mother had been a good role model, Shania felt. She admired her mom for the way she had balanced her career and family. Both her parents had worked as dentists and shared a thriving practice, yet Shania's mom still submitted to her husband. Her mom had once told her that just because a woman makes just as much or more money than her man, that doesn't give her the right to tear down his manhood. She had further explained that what kept a man's heart devoted to his woman wasn't her beauty, body, intellect, or wealth, but the way she treated him and made him feel.

Shania wiped her flour-covered hands on a cloth towel and threw it on the countertop. She looked around her modern kitchen and realized how fortunate she was. Being able to get up every day and do what she loved was a blessing she didn't take lightly or for granted. She wondered if Greg felt the same way about his job. He had told her that he liked what he did, but she questioned whether that was the same as living one's purpose.

She grabbed a baking pan and sprayed it with non-stick cooking spray before placing pieces of dough on top. She then turned on the oven and slid the pan inside. Standing in the middle of the kitchen, she evaluated what she had to do next and exhaled. She finished preparing the main course, placed the food in the preheated oven, and set the timer.

While the food cooked, she went upstairs and fixed herself a smoothie. She then called Greg. After several rings, she got his voice mail. An uneasy feeling crept into her spirit. Even though at church Sunday Greg had said she'd been acting weird lately, deep down inside, she felt like he was the one who had been acting pretty weird. Ever since that moment in church when he'd walked toward her with the weight of something pressing against his shoulders, he hadn't been the same. Now, the big question of whether or not he would keep his job hung over his head, and he seemed more distraught than ever.

She tried calling him twice more, but she still got the voice mail. One look at the clock told her that it was a quarter past five, so he was not at work. And if he wasn't at work, then why couldn't he pick up his phone? Instead of leaving a message after the beep, as his voice mail so courteously requested, she hung up the phone and tightened her apron around her waist. Whatever phase he was going through, she hoped he came out of this thing fast. She was not too fond of the new change that was taking place in her husband. Was he going to snap back, or was she going to have to snap him back?

Eight

Greg stared at his iPhone as he contemplated calling Shania back, but then decided that he didn't want to lose focus on the task at hand. He continued working on Mother Washington's pipes until he could flush the toilet repeatedly without the water rising to the top of the bowl, threatening to spill over.

"Mother Washington!" he called, and she hurried into the bathroom as fast as her fragile legs and cane would take her.

When she stepped into the bathroom, her eyes were scrunched in pain, and she was holding the side of her head. "Not so loud, suga," she said, massaging her forehead. "That headache keeps sneaking up on me."

Greg apologized and lowered his voice to just above a whisper. "Watch this," he said and flushed the toilet about ten times. Not once did the water rise.

"You are a doll," she said and hooked one arm through his and gave it a strong tug. "I don't know what I would do without you." She patted his hand softly. "This old house is just falling apart." She cleared phlegm out her throat and spit into the handkerchief that she kept balled in her hand. "Henry wanted me to move outta here before he passed, but I said naw. I been in this house this long. Why leave right 'fore the Lord take me home?"

Greg wasn't sure what to say. This was the first time Mother Washington had ever talked about her late husband with him. He had heard stories floating around church, talking about how her husband's health had been failing for years before he finally passed away three years ago. He'd had a bad everything—a bad heart, bad kidneys, bad liver, bad lungs. Basically, years of unhealthy eating, cigarettes, alcohol, and obesity had finally caught up with him.

He had also heard rumors about her husband being accused, but never convicted, of inappropriately touching young girls in the church. Church folks criticized her for being married to a pervert.

"When Henry got real bad off sick," she said, shuffling her feet as she walked into her cluttered living room with Greg trailing behind her, "that old church I was going to didn't do a thing to help me. They knew I had to take care of Henry and myself, and they knew I didn't have no type of help. They thought taking up an offering was good enough, but it wasn't, Greg." She collapsed into her rocking chair, which was covered by a red, blue, and green crocheted throw. "I ain't need they money, suga. I's got plenty of money. I needed they help."

Greg grabbed her blanket off the couch and covered her legs with it, because even though it was May, Mother Washington always felt cold and liked to have a little heat going. While she talked, Greg went over to her fireplace and lit a starter log and waited until the flames leaped high before he dropped a log of wood atop it.

"Thank you, suga," Mother Washington said and hummed while she picked up a white and blue crocheted blanket she was working on.

Greg sat down at the foot of her rocking chair and watched the dancing flames while she talked.

"And when Henry passed," she continued, "you think anybody came over to help me out? No, siree, not a soul. That old church just took up another offering pan for me, like money is the answer to every problem."

"And that's what eventually brought you to Saved and Sanctified Baptist?"

"Sure is, chile," she said, pursing her lips and nodding her head. "Soon as I walked through them doors, I felt the love in that place. Ain't no denying the love or the anointing in that church."

Greg nodded. He knew exactly what she was talking about, because he had only been going to that church five years longer than her. Franklin was actually the one who'd invited him to church with him. He went one Sunday and had been going ever since.

Mother Washington hummed some more, then said, "Thems little children at that church treat me like I'm they's grandma, and it makes me feel good. And everybody there calls me Mother, and they treat me like a mother too. You know how good it makes me feel to be treated like a mother?" She laughed to herself like she had just said the funniest thing; then she stopped laughing and held her head, wincing in pain.

"Mother, you might want to go get that checked," Greg said, looking over his shoulder at her. "If it's been bothering you for this long, you might need to take migraine medication."

"No, I don't need the doctor's medication. I got the best doctor in town, and He's gonna take sho'nuff good care of me." She kept rocking, then hummed some more. "Did you see my daughter at church Sunday?"

As soon as the words came out of her mouth, Greg immediately knew who she was talking about. She was talking about the girl with the big brown eyes, the jet-black hair, and the white dress. However, he had to wonder whether Mother Washington meant that literally or figuratively, because if that was her biological daughter, they didn't bear any resemblance.

"The woman in the white dress?" Greg asked.

"Yes, chile. Ain't she beautiful? Ain't my baby beautiful?"

"Yes," Greg whispered, nodding. "She was gorgeous."

"See, if you wouldn't have met that pretty little lady you married, I would've wanted you to marry my Kaiya, 'cause then at least you could've been my son-in-law."

"That's her name? Kaiya?"

"Yeah, but she goes by Kai. Just as pretty as she can be. Real sweet-spirited." Mother Washington sighed. "Too sweet-spirited. I wish she had more of a backbone. Wish she was more of a fighter."

"She must look just like her daddy."

"Well, I can't call that one, suga, 'cause I don't know who her daddy is."

"Mother Washington?" Greg looked over his shoulder again, this time with a look of incredulity. Even though she was a "Mother" now, he was sure she hadn't been saved and sanctified always. But yet and still, he found it shocking that she would so boldly admit her promiscuity.

She started laughing again, then stopped to cough up more phlegm in her handkerchief. "No, chile, I ain't mean it like that. Kaiya is my sister's baby. She had two little girls less than a year apart, but my sister passed away when they was real young. So I took 'em in and raised them like they was my own. I ain't never have no kids, 'cause though I got pregnant seven times, I could never carry the baby long enough for it to live."

The thought of such a kindhearted woman having to suffer through seven miscarriages pained Greg and he reached over, slipped off her shoes, and pulled her feet in his lap.

"No, no," she said, trying to pull her feet out his hands. "You don't wanna massage them things, all those bunions, calluses, and corns."

Despite her protests, Greg held her cold feet in his lap and warmed them and massaged them with his hands.

"What about the other daughter?" Greg asked.

"Oh, she's a hateful old somebody," Mother Washington said, making a sour face and shaking her head. "See, I found out later that men touched her when she was a young girl. They touched her down there a lot. And I guess she turned bitter because of it. And even though I took her in and raised her, she give me 'bout as much respect as someone would give a rabid dog. She like a vulture, Greg. Just sitting around, waiting for me to die. She blames me for not protecting her."

Greg's cell phone rang again, and this time, he answered it. "Shania, baby, I'm coming, okay?"

"Where are you?"

If he didn't know any better, he could've sworn that she'd been crying.

"Babe, are you okay?"

"Gregory Crinkle, where are you?"

"I'm at Mother Washington's house."

"Do you know what time it is?"

He glanced at the cuckoo clock that hung above the fireplace. It was a quarter to eight. How had time gotten away from him so quickly? "Babe, I didn't realize that—"

"Would a courtesy call have been too much to ask?"

Yeah, those were tears in her voice.

"Babe, I'm sorry, okay? I'm on my way right now, okay, Shania?"

Her answer to his question was the dial tone. Greg pulled the phone away from his ear and stared at it, struggling to believe that his wife had just hung up on him. He looked over at Mother Washington, who was wearing a smile on her face.

"I—I don't know what's going on," Greg said, pocketing his phone and standing to his feet. "She hasn't been herself lately. I don't know what's gotten into her."

"I know what's gotten into her."

Greg stared at Mother Washington, even more confused, but she simply gave him her toothless smile. "Go'n home to your wife, Gregory. She needs you. And don't you stress no more about that job. God's gonna work everything out for your good. Just know that whatever happens, it's for your good. You hear me?"

"Yes, ma'am," he said and disappeared into the back room, only to come forward with a pair of thick, furry socks. He slid the socks onto her feet, tucked the cover close around her, and kissed her forehead. "Take it easy, Mother."

"You take it easy, son. And be careful on that bike."

"I will." Greg smiled. He liked when she called him son.

He hurried outside to his bike, jumped on, and heeded Mother's warning as he drove only five miles above the speed limit to his house. When he got there, Shania was curled into a fetal position on the couch, wrapped up in a blanket, with a half-empty box of Kleenex and a pile of balled tissues lying on the couch beside her.

Guilt stricken, he realized that when he hadn't called her, she probably thought something bad had happened to him.

"Oh, baby," he said and scooped her against his chest as though she was a small child. She must've been too tired to remember she was mad at him, because she threw her arms around his neck and held on tight.

He carried her to the bed, and as much as he wanted to make love to her, he simply held her and stared at her beautiful face until his own eyes became too heavy to hold open and he drifted off to sleep.

The next day, he woke up early in hopes that he could get to the office and see if he could add some more clients to his roster. He slipped out of bed, careful not to wake Shania, and prepared himself for work.

Within the confines of his cubicle, he worked hard and diligently, pulling more old files and calling even more numbers. Even when Franklin came over with a cup of coffee and every intention of chatting, Greg shooed him on his way and told him he'd talk to him some other time.

He reaped a few benefits from his hard work; he got a definite yes from four of the callers, and a possible yes from one. That boosted his ego until his boss's head peeked around the side of his cubicle as he tapped on the vinyl siding.

"Mr. Crinkle, you got a moment?"

Greg straightened his tie and sat a little straighter in his chair. "Follow me," his boss said as he led Greg into his office.

If his heart beat any louder, there was no way that he could hear a word that his boss spoke. Mentally, he tried to remain optimistic. He thought about the President's Circle, his long-standing clients, the four, possibly five, deals he had just secured within a two-hour frame. But as soon as his boss took a seat in the vacant chair and said, "You are an excellent worker, Greg. You really are. Without you, this company would not be where it's at now. However . . ."

As soon as he reached the "however" mark, Greg blanked out. He had worked there long enough to know what kind of speech his boss was giving him. This was the you-just-got-cut speech.

Though the man's mouth continued to move, Greg's mind was a mile away from the current conversation. He looked over the desk into the round red face of his boss, who was in the process of firing him. As he stared at the man's moving lips, he knew his boss was in the middle of telling him the canned spiel from human resources about his severance package and eligibility for unemployment benefits.

Greg sat there in numb amazement as he wrote down his system passwords on a piece of paper. Turning over the passwords felt like the final nail in his professional coffin. He had always been told to safeguard his passwords and not to write them down or share them with anyone. He unclamped his ID badge and placed it on the desk. Staring at his smiling photo, he remembered how happy he had been when he first started working for the company. He couldn't believe that he, along with fifty percent of the people in his office, had been let go. His boss had apologized and seemed to have genuine concern, but that was of little consolation for Greg.

While half listening to his boss, the desire to cuss him out clouded Greg's brain. He felt like telling his boss where he could go and how to get there. To keep from going off, Greg clutched his iPhone so tight that he expected it to shatter in his hand at any moment. To say he felt angry would be an understatement. He felt like straight punching someone. His nostrils flared as he mentally reminded himself to breathe and not lose his cool. He didn't want to lose his religion and be seen as unprofessional, especially since he might need a reference.

Standing up from his seat, Greg's boss extended his hand to Greg and said, "I'm gonna miss working with you, buddy."

Greg clenched his jaw. He stared at the stiff hand before him and contemplated smacking it. He thought the better of it and shook his hand anyway. Then he walked out and found a box from a storage closet so that he could clear out his cubicle.

As he made his way to his soon-to-be former work-station, he noticed that some people were teary-eyed, others were crying, and some gathered around expressing their shock and disbelief. Greg tried not to get caught up in the emotion and cleared out his desk without talking to anyone. While removing the items from his desk, he felt an overwhelming sadness. He wondered how thirteen years, worth of stuff could fit in one box as he picked up his stress reliever ball and shook his head.

"Lot of good you did," he said to himself, giving the ball a squeeze, then tossing it in the box.

He knew it was just a matter of minutes before Franklin appeared in his cubicle.

"Man, this better be a rumor about you getting cut."

Greg swooped a hand around his bare cubicle, which no longer held a trace of his presence. "Does it look like a rumor to you, Mr. You Are What You Speak?"

"Don't try to throw my words back in my face. I ain't the one who fired you."

"No, you're not. And also, you're not the one who got fired. So you can go back to your cubicle and leave me the heck alone."

Franklin sincerely looked hurt.

Too angry to apologize, Greg ignored his friend and pretended not to see the pain in his eyes. He pulled tape across his two boxes, stacked them on top of each other, and left his cubicle. He carried his boxes stuffed with office supplies, personal photographs of him and Shania, notebooks, and assorted papers to his convertible Mercedes and popped the trunk. He placed the boxes inside and considered going back to apologize to Franklin but changed his mind. He didn't want to go back in that place and see the looks of pity from individuals who would undoubtedly keep their jobs. Besides, he didn't feel like being bothered. He wanted to be alone with his thoughts. Since he wasn't one for emotional outbursts, he just got in his car, dropped the top, and headed home.

As he drove along the interstate, panic kicked in. For the first time in his adult life, Greg didn't have a job. So much of his identity had been tied into his professional accomplishments. What was he going to do? he wondered. Making a mental checklist, he figured that he could live off his severance package while he looked for a new job. Maybe he'd solicit the services of a headhunter. Perhaps he'd do some market research for a start-up company.

Feeling a slight throbbing in his temple, Greg grabbed the bottle of pain medication that he kept stashed in his center console and took two pills, which he washed down with a half bottle of Sprite that had been sitting in the car for only God knows how long; it tasted like lemony spit water. He grimaced as he forced himself to swallow it down.

Out of the corner of his eye, he could see a median separating him from the oncoming traffic. The thought that the median was the only thing keeping him from colliding head-on with another car nagged at him like a hangnail. So much in his life was so wrong; his wife and he weren't getting along for the first time since saying "I do" on Valentine's Day; he had just intentionally thrown a jab at his one and only best friend; and for crying out loud, he had just been fired. The image of him turning his steering wheel all the way to the left, crashing into the block of cement, and smashing his car like an aluminum can flashed across the screen of his mind. For a fleeting moment, suicide seemed to be the solution to his problems.

Greg gripped the steering wheel tighter and shook his head. Through clenched teeth he mumbled the words, "The devil is a liar."

An image so vivid of a crying and inconsolable Shania popped into his brain. It seemed so real that he wanted to reach out and touch her. He had never seen so much pain etched in Shania's pretty face. Then he saw Franklin, tears streaming from his eyes, no laughter in his face as he stood over his friend's casket and said his final farewells.

Oh, Lord, and what about his parents? He could see his dad, trying to stay strong; his mother, lost in despair. Just the thought caused him to shudder. He realized that taking his own life would be the most selfish and faithless thing he could ever do. Too many people loved him for him to cause them such pain.

The sad realization that by even contemplating killing himself demonstrated Greg's lack of faith in God and what He could do made Greg call on his Savior's name. He began repenting and apologizing for thinking that his circumstances were greater than the one he served. Greg wondered when he had developed such a lack of faith. He spent the rest of the drive having an intimate conversation with his Father.

By the time Greg rolled up to his house, he felt mentally drained. He wished he could say that he felt at peace about the situation, but peace eluded him. Feelings of embarrassment and failure weighed him down.

When he came into his home, he could feel a calming presence there. The smell of aromatherapy filled the air. Flickering candles greeted him throughout. Struggling to put on a brave face, he paused for a moment to collect his thoughts.

"I thought I heard you come in," Shania sang out. "You're here pretty early."

She went to hug him, and he retracted.

Frowning, she said, "If this is about last night, you're already forgiven. I just . . . my emotions just got out of control, and I didn't know how to handle the situation. I'm sorry for being a nag. I'm sorry for hanging up on you, and I'm sorry for giving you so much attitude all the time. You forgive me?"

He kissed her offered lips. "Yes, I forgive you. And do you forgive me for not at least shooting you a courtesy call about my whereabouts?"

"Yes, I forgive you," she said and held the back of his head while she gave him an even deeper kiss. She cut the kiss short, then retracted her neck a bit. "What's the matter with you? Why are you still acting so strange? Everything's cool now, right?"

Greg fell silent for a moment, then shook his head. "No, babe. No, everything's not cool." He glanced away from her before choking out, "I got fired."

Shania parted her lips on a gasp. "Honey, I'm sorry. Tell me what happened."

He grabbed her hand and led her into the media room, where they sat on the couch. Unable to look her in the eyes, Greg reclined on the couch and closed his eyes. For a split second he escaped into thoughts, hoping and praying that this day had been just a bad dream. When he opened his eyes and saw that Shania had fixed her gaze on him, he knew his world had changed. He went on to explain that under the directives of corporate, half of his office had been downsized.

"There was no rhyme or reason." He sounded frustrated. "There were top performers and average performers. Some people had lots of seniority, and others didn't. I guess I got the short end of the stick."

"What about Franklin? Did he get cut too?"

"Puh-lease." Greg rolled his eyes and shook his head. "Franklin is their gold mine. They'd have to be a fools to let him go. But me . . . I guess I was just mediocre."

"You were not mediocre," she promised him, rubbing small circles in his back. "They just didn't realize your full potential. But it's okay, babe. If God closes one door, He'll open another." Shania continued to comfort him with her touch and her encouraging words.

He knew that she meant well and wanted to help, but he wasn't in the mood for any pep talks. Since Shania had never worked for anyone other than herself, he figured that she had no clue how he felt. She couldn't possibly relate.

He wanted to clear his mind, so he left Shania sitting on the couch while he went to change into his riding gear. While he was changing, his cell phone received a text message from Franklin. It read: Wanna go 4 a ride?

The timing couldn't have been any more perfect. Greg texted him back an affirmative, and told him to meet him at the stoplight by the park. He then told Shania that he'd be back and jumped on his bike to go meet Franklin. When they met, they exchanged no words, simply nodded at each other, and took off riding, with Franklin leading the way.

As they drove in peaceful silence, Greg allowed himself to become at one with nature. He focused on the charcoal gray rock and cement and broken white lines that seemed to go on forever. He wondered where the road would lead him, if he just stayed the course.

Biting his lower lip and swallowing the lump forming in his throat, he compared the road to life's journey: mysterious, filled with unknowns, unpredictability, yet in a strange sort of way, exciting. Although he would've preferred to change his plight in life, he understood that if he stayed on track, he'd be okay; God was in charge, and He knew what lay ahead.

After riding on the open road for thirty minutes, Franklin signaled that he needed to stop for gas, and Greg nodded because he needed to stop too. As they pumped the gas, pollen swirled in the air, tickling Greg's eyes without relief. Franklin offered to pay for the gas, but Greg declined the offer. He capped off his tank and secured the cap before going inside the store and buying a soda. He paid for the soda; then he popped the top of the soda and tilted his head back to quench his thirst. While he drained the can, he glanced outside and saw a throwback car roll in front of the convenience store, and the car would've been in mint condition had it not been for the blubbery piece of rubber that represented the back passenger tire. Greg emptied the can, belched, and tossed the aluminum into the trash; then he stepped outside.

By the time he made it outside, Franklin had gone over to the vintage car, probably more so to talk about the make and model rather than help with changing the tire. When the driver stepped out of the car, Greg's jaw dropped, and so did Franklin's. Even with her hair swept up into a bun, Greg immediately recognized her as the brown-eyed girl from church. Franklin had hearts in his eyes, and he might as well have had "in love" stamped across his forehead.

"You, uh, need help changing your tire?" Franklin asked, making it very obvious that he was impressed by both the car and the woman who drove the car.

"No," she said in her soft voice. "I know how to change it."

"I'd hate to see you get your hands dirty. You're too beautiful for that. Please, ma'am, I insist."

She smiled at Franklin with her lips and her eyes. "Well, since you insist," she said and gave him a little bow as she stepped out the way.

Franklin turned and looked at Greg, biting down on his index finger hard and saying with his eyes, "Greg, this chick right here is *hot*." Greg smiled at his friend and went and sat on his bike while Franklin helped the young lady. He thought about offering to help but then decided not to because he didn't want Franklin to think that he was game-blocking. What should've taken no more than ten, fifteen minutes at the most took a whole half hour, mainly because the two were chatting about the different makes, models, and years of vintage cars that they owned.

Greg tried to wait patiently, but after a while, he gave Franklin a birdcall and motioned with his head that he was leaving. Franklin gave him two thumbs-up, a wink, and yelled that he'd catch him later.

Sincerely wishing his friend the best of luck in his pursuit, Greg put his sunglasses and helmet back on and headed home. When he arrived, he sat in his drive-way and counted the bricks on the house . . . anything to take his mind off of being unemployed. For as far back as he could remember, he'd always had a job. As a tween he had a paper route. Then he mowed lawns in the summer and shoveled driveways in the winter to earn extra cash. His parents used to praise him for being an "enterprising young man," as they often called him.

He let out a loud sigh as he prepared himself to go into the house. Knowing Shania like he did, he figured that she'd do whatever it took to cheer him up. Although he appreciated her care and concern, he wanted to work through this in his own time, in his own way. He didn't want to be reminded of things he already knew. Nor did he want to be made to feel guilty for feeling the way he felt. He just wanted to be . . . left alone.

Nine

Shania didn't know what to think when Greg came home and breezed past her without saying a word. She tried not to show it, but her feelings were hurt. She understood that Greg had a lot on his mind, and she wanted to be sensitive to his emotional needs, yet she could feel him shutting down. She hoped that he wasn't slipping into depression. She wondered if she should try and talk to him. "No," she said to herself. One thing she had learned from being in a relationship with Greg was that men tended to mull things over in their minds and tried to figure out solutions to their problems themselves, unlike women, who liked to talk about their problems.

As difficult as it was for Shania not to be all up in Greg's face, trying to get him to communicate with her, she sat alone at the dinner table and ate the bow tie pasta with shrimp and salad that she had prepared for two.

When she finished eating, she put away the leftovers, poured herself half a glass of blackberry wine, and relaxed on the couch in the media room. She thought about what she could do to make Greg feel better. She tried hard to put herself in his shoes and imagined how she would feel if she had been let go from a company to which she had given years of faithful service. She determined that she would feel humiliated, confused, and, of course, sad.

After she took a sip of wine, the sweet flavor lingered on her taste buds. Shania decided to call her first cousin and best friend, Rayna. She needed Rayna's input on the situation at hand.

Thankful that Rayna answered after the second ring, Shania skipped the small talk and went straight to the heart of the matter. She told her cousin all about Greg losing his job and how he seemed to be sulking. Then she asked for some advice on how to handle the situation.

"Cuz, I'm sorry that Greg lost his job." Rayna's tone sounded sympathetic. "This doesn't have to be a huge setback in your relationship. You know you and Greg have that whole fairy-tale-type relationship going on." She chuckled.

"What do you mean?"

"I'm just saying. You prayed about that brotha and waited until you got married before you gave him some. You did it right and waited for your prince," she said and then paused. "Did you read Steve Harvey's book *Act Like a Lady, Think Like a Man?*"

"Yes, I did," Shania admitted.

"Then you should remember the part where he talks about men being simple. He said that men are driven by who they are, what they do, and how much they make."

Shania remembered reading that and wanted to laugh at her cousin for sounding like she had quoted Bible verses.

"I mean, come on, think about it, Shania. Up until this point, Greg had fulfilled his destiny as a man. He had a steady job and made a good living. Then he went to work one day, and the whole bottom fell out." A pregnant pause followed her words. "You shouldn't be surprised by his reaction. As a man, he feels the need to provide for his family. And how's he supposed to provide without a nine-to-five?"

"Actually, it was an eight-to-five."

Rayna smacked her lips. "You know what I'm trying to say, Shania."

Shania nodded her head, and when she realized that her cousin couldn't see her nodding through the phone, she added, "I get that, Rayna. I really do." She took another sip from her wineglass and let the bittersweet flavor play on her tongue before swallowing. "I respect my husband. Although I want my man to work, I don't want him to feel pressured to provide for me."

"This isn't about you, cuz. You remember when you first met him? The thing that attracted you to him the most was the fact that he wasn't impressed by your bank account. He wasn't concerned about what all you had to offer him. He wanted to show you what he could bring to the table."

Again, Shania nodded. Her cousin was right.

Rayna continued, "It would be different if Greg was some playboy looking for a woman to take care of him, but he's not that guy. He's decent all the way around. He's not going to be happy living off your money."

Shania traced the rim of her glass with her finger. "He doesn't have to live off me. He could help me run the business or start his own. It's not like we don't have the money for it."

Rayna chuckled. "I hear you. But is that what Greg wants?"

Sighing into the receiver, Shania said, "I can't really say. He's never talked to me about wanting to start a business. As far as I know, he likes getting up and going out to work every day."

"Exactly." Rayna sounded like she had just announced a victory. "Some people aren't meant to be entrepreneurs. They like the security of getting a steady paycheck every couple of weeks."

"My company has a steady cash flow, and I earn regular paychecks too," Shania defended.

"You're the exception, not the norm."

That was why Shania loved talking to her cousin. No matter what, Rayna always brought clarity to the situation. "So . . . should I help him find another job, or should I—"

"You should," Rayna said loudly, clearing her throat, "shut up, sit back, and let that man be a man. If he needs your help, he'll ask for it."

"True." Shania finished off her drink, rubbed her finger along her chin, then added, "Well, what if we took a vacation to get his mind off his problems?"

"Shania! What happened to shutting up, sitting back, and waiting on him?"

"What?" she exclaimed, smiling. "It was just an idea."

"Okay," Rayna said, laughing. "That wouldn't have been my first thought. However, that could actually work. Must be nice," Rayna teased. Then Rayna questioned her about the wedding Saturday and asked her if she had everything ready.

As Shania settled in front of the computer, she hurried her cousin off the phone so she could surf the Internet and scout out a few possible vacation locations. She spent an hour researching different islands and finally settled on Jamaica. She had never been and wanted to go. Excitement bubbled over inside her as she clicked on photo after photo of white sandy beaches and water so clear, she could see the tropical fish shimmying beneath the surface and starfish clinging to the ocean floor. Then she imagined herself splashing in that same water in an all-white two-piece, her skin bronzing beneath the glow of the sun. She calculated the package price for flight tickets, transportation, and a one-week hotel stay, and the calculation placed a smile on her face.

No matter how tight Greg might try to be with money now that he'd lost his job, even he would have to agree that such an economical price for such a breathtaking getaway was unbeatable. She shot her travel agent an e-mail, asking her to see if she could find tickets to Jamaica at a cheaper price than what she'd already found. But she knew that before she could purchase tickets, she'd have to touch base with Greg. In his sour mood it would probably take a whole lot of persuasion to get his consent. What better time to start the persuasion than now?

Shania went upstairs to her bedroom and noticed that Greg was already asleep. She tiptoed into the bathroom and closed the door behind her. Careful not to blast the water, she took a shower, dried herself with a warm towel, and crawled into bed next to her husband. He turned over on his side and faced her. His eyes popped open, and she smiled at him.

Touching the side of her face, Greg said, "I love you."

She leaned in and pecked him on the lips. "Want a massage?"

He grinned as he lifted the covers. "Why are you naked?"

She shrugged, then watched his eyes fall closed and listened to the low timbre of his moans. He let her love him in that special way that she only offered to him on occasion.

"I love you, babe," he breathed into her mouth, and she hungrily swallowed every word. She prayed that for this one moment in time, he would set aside all his worries and anxieties and give her all of him: heart, mind, body, and soul. And he did. They reached their peaks together and collapsed back against the bed, clinging to each other as though their bed was a storm-ravaged sea, and they were each other's only anchor.

Ten

"Man, I'ma marry her."

Greg almost laughed into the phone. "Frank, you just met this girl like what, two days ago? How are you already talking about marriage?"

"All I know is this, man . . . we click. We click on a whole 'nother level. Okay, so you already know she likes vintage cars, right? That car you saw her with at the gas station, that's the only vintage car she owns. So you know I took her to my bat cave and showed her my collection. Man, G, this chick is the only female I've ever showed my collection to, and she was just as excited about it as me! Do you know how that feels?"

"No, I don't," Greg replied truthfully, because though he could appreciate a nice-looking throwback, he didn't have the passion for collecting cars like his dear friend. "It must feel pretty good."

"Greg, listen, man, that ain't even it."

Greg lowered the job search screen on the computer so he could give his full attention to the conversation. "Tell me the rest, Frank."

"You really want the rest?"

"I want the rest, Frank," he assured him.

"I mean, do you *really* want the rest?"

Greg rolled his eyes and let out a sigh. Franklin wouldn't be Franklin if he wasn't over the top, theatrical. "Bro, if you don't shut up and just say it."

"Man, she rides bikes too!"

"Word?" Greg smiled. He always liked to see a woman on a bike. To him, it said something about her character, that she wasn't afraid to step out and do something that was considered risqué or out of the box. "Did y'all go riding together yet?"

"Did we?" Franklin laughed into the phone. "Dude, we went riding that same day that she got that flat. She met me at the park, and we rode all over Alpharetta. Rode our bikes until the sun came up. I'm dead serious."

This time, Greg chuckled and nodded his head. "Let me find out that my man done tripped and fallen into a puddle of love."

"I'm drowning in it, man," Franklin admitted. "And I like how it feels. I'm gonna marry this girl. That's my wife right there. Her name's Kaiya."

"I know her name."

"Huh?" Franklin smacked his lips into the phone and Greg could imagine him rolling his eyes. "Please don't tell me this is one of the chicks you used to bone before God delivered you."

Greg held his side and laughed. "No, Frank, I never 'boned' her." He laughed again. "But look, you two are just getting to know each other, so I don't want to ruin the surprise. Take her out to a nice restaurant and ask her about her past. You might be shocked what you learn."

"Shocked like in a good way, or shocked in a bad way?"

"Bye, Frank. You're interrupting my job hunt."

"How's that coming along for you?"

"Slowly but surely." He considered telling Franklin that he was thinking about starting his own company but decided to wait until he had made a more concrete decision.

"A'ight, my man. I'll holla at you later."

Still smiling, Greg ended the call and pushed the phone aside. No matter the trials and tribulations he was going through in life, he was happy for his friend. If anyone deserved a good woman who he could mesh with in life, Franklin was definitely deserving of one.

Greg took in a deep breath, pulled up his job hunt screen, and flipped to a fresh sheet of paper on his notepad. He spent the rest of the morning online applying to jobs posted on popular job sites. He figured that if he treated his job search like a full-time job, he should be able to land a job in a reasonable amount of time. He then wondered what "reasonable" meant. One week? Two weeks? A month? Six months? What was reasonable?

Feeling frustrated, he got on the phone and called friends, colleagues, and even former clients who he thought could help with his job search. He put out feelers first to see who was in a position to either hire him or refer him to someone who could. He wrote down names, telephone numbers, and e-mail addresses of every referral. By the time he finished making phone calls, his mind felt like it had been on a treadmill.

He then looked down at his notepad and had a nagging feeling that he should seriously check into starting his own company. He wrote down: "Classic car restoration and accessories shop." He searched online for a market research company, placed a phone call to them, and provided them with all the information they needed to begin doing a market analysis for him. They even scheduled a follow-up conference call. Then he called a guy at his church and asked for his help with writing a business plan and applying for a business loan. He knew the guy at church could do it for a reasonable cost. At least that way it would be done right.

He wanted to get a small business loan so that he'd have a line of credit available, even if he didn't use it all. As a business major, he learned in college that most businesses failed during the first five years due to lack of resources and working capital.

He smiled at the fact that he had taken the first steps toward becoming an entrepreneur and decided to take a break. So, he left his home office and went to check on Shania. He found her in the basement, sliding a pan in the oven.

When she saw him, she wiped her hands on her apron. "I didn't think I'd see you at all today with the way you've been cooped up in your office."

He wrinkled his forehead. "Been looking for a job."

She gave him a hug and kissed his cheek. "How'd it go?"

"Got some leads that I plan to follow up on."

She held his hands and looked him in the eyes. "I spoke with my travel agent today, and she found a good deal on a trip to Jamaica."

He stepped back; his brows knitted together. He wondered if he had heard her correctly. He tried to wrap his brain around why Shania would want to take a trip when the rug had been pulled from under him. Did she really think he'd be in the mood to sit on the beach, sipping piña coladas, when he didn't have a job and didn't know how long his savings would last? Was she in la-la land?

A part of him felt like Shania didn't have a clue sometimes. Instead of harping in on her like he initially wanted to, he kept a cool demeanor. His wife and he both had been a little testy since they bumped heads at church, and he didn't like it. He knew that he was partly to blame for being consumed with the brown-eyed woman at church and Mother Washington. He couldn't even explain his behavior other than the fact that his gut kept telling him that something was wrong.

He was ready to squash this tension in their relationship and go back to those blissful honeymoon days, where their biggest confrontation was whether they wanted sausage or bacon for breakfast, or whether they wanted to light vanilla-or apple-pie-scented candles.

"Jamaica sounds great, babe. But I don't think this is the right time for a vacation," he said, trying his best to remain calm. "What're you cooking? Smells pretty good."

"Will you let me explain before you shoot it down?" She followed him to the oven. "This would be the perfect time for us to get away, because you don't have any work obligations right now. You could use the time to get clarity about your career options and your future. Sometimes if you remove yourself from the situation, you get a clearer picture, and you realize that your circumstances aren't as bleak as you originally thought." She dropped her hands to her sides.

He allowed her words to sink in, and he had to admit that what she said made sense. A sweet, cinnamon scent captured his attention, and he looked toward the oven again.

Shania sighed and smacked her lips. "They're sweet rolls. Want one? I think they make pretty good finger food."

Shania left him standing there while she removed the sticky rolls from the oven and placed them on the counter to let them cool. His mouth watered as he looked on, watching the glazed walnuts slide down the sides of the rolls.

He walked up behind her, held her hips and placed a kiss behind her ear before reaching around her for a roll. She slapped his hand hard and he pulled away, shaking his stinging hand and frowning at her.

"What was that for? I thought you said I could have one."

"You can . . ." she said, sliding the spatula beneath one of the rolls and holding it near his nose. He inhaled and could literally taste the buttery, gooey treat on his tongue. "If you say yes to Jamaica."

He chuckled and squeezed her waist. "Oh, so you're bribing me? With a sweet roll?"

"They're decadent," she said, sliding the roll back and forth beneath his nose. "Melt in your mouth good."

"Okay," he gave in and took the roll off the spatula. "A getaway just might be what I need." He bit down into the hot roll and moaned while he chewed. Buttery, sweet, just the right amount of cinnamon. It felt so warm and smooth going down his throat. No wonder these people paid so much money for her food. This woman knew exactly what she was doing.

She waited until he finished chewing, then said with a triumphant smile, "So that's a yes?"

She offered him a napkin but Greg shook his head and licked each finger clean. "Girl, you stuck your foot in these rolls." He sucked his thumb clean, then shook his head again. "But I still don't think a vacation right now is a good idea. Who knows how long it will take me to find a job?"

The frown on her face hurt his heart, and he reached out for her, but she moved away from him.

"Shania, babe, don't be like that. You know what I'm saying makes a lot of sense."

"No, it doesn't," she whined, then straightened her back and leaned against the counter. "I want you to know that I have every confidence you'll find another job. But if it doesn't happen right away, please don't stress yourself out about it. It's not the end of the world, Greg. We have enough money to last us—"

"No, *you* have enough money to last—"

"What's mine is yours, Greg." Her voice rose. "It happened the day we said 'I do.'"

Greg glared at her. "Do you really have to yell at me like that?"

"I didn't mean to raise my voice, honey. It's just . . . " Shania threw her spatula on the counter. "I don't get it. I don't get you. You go to church every Sunday and minister to all these young people, teaching them about faith, but when the time comes for you to tap into your own faith, you seem so hopeless."

Greg worked his jaw while he stared at her confused expression. He knew he shouldn't have come down there. He should've just stayed in his office, kept searching for a job, or he should've jumped on his bike and took a relieving ride. One thing he didn't come down there for was another argument. He felt like they had left the door to their relationship cracked open to the devil, and he had come storming in, wreaking havoc every chance he got. Why he thought Shania would actually understand, he had no idea. Yet and still, he decided to give it one more shot.

"Shania, you know I love you, so please don't take this the wrong way." He sighed and stepped closer to her. "You already have enough money to last you a lifetime. Even if your business didn't bring you another red cent, you'd still be okay. You wouldn't have to get an outside job." He made a sweeping motion with his hand. "Your house and car are paid for. And you don't have any real credit card debt."

"*Our* house and car," she corrected him softly. He gave her an exasperated stare, and she sucked in her bottom lip.

"Please, babe. Please. Listen to me."

She nodded her head.

He patted his chest. "Baby, I'm a man. I could never live off you. No matter how much money you have, that's *your* money. I have to feel like I'm contributing and pulling my weight. Without a job, I don't see how I'm doing that."

She removed the lid from the container of icing made from powdered sugar and drizzled the rolls. "I hear you, and I respect that. It's true that the person who earns the most money usually controls the relationship." She glanced at him. "But that's not true for us. First of all, the only reason I have more savings than you is because of an inheritance, not because of my labor. And when it comes to our earnings, after my business expenses, our take-home pay is about the same. Plus, you're a homeowner too. In fact, you have a leg up on me because your property is actually making money."

"I wasn't saying all that to make it seem like we're in some sort of a competition. This isn't tit for tat." He sounded sincere. "I wanted you to understand why it's so important to me to find another job as quickly as possible. I was just pointing out the facts."

"So was I." She used a spatula to lift up a warm roll from the baking pan and picked it up. She walked over to him. "Open."

He opened his mouth and took a bite. The first roll was delicious, but with the icing, the gooey treat practically melted in his mouth. After he finished chewing, he licked the icing off his lips. "What are you trying to do, fatten me up?"

She laughed and wiped icing from the corner of his lip. "No, I'm just trying to shut you up, but in a sweet way."

"Shut me up this way more often, and then everything will be cool."

"I know that's right," she agreed with a smile.

"So these sweet rolls, are they for the wedding too?"

"No, I'm completely finished with the wedding stuff. It's carefully wrapped and stored in airtight containers in the deep freezer to keep it fresh. Now I'm working on the governor's menu in hopes that I'll be chosen to cater the induction ceremony."

She turned to walk away, but he pulled her against him so that her back pressed against his chest. He lifted up her hair, scattering kisses along the nape and sides of her neck. "Tell me what's on your menu."

She purred at his kisses and seemed to struggle to recall the menu. "Rolls. That's my theme. Cinnamon sweet rolls, vegetable spring rolls, Cajun steak rolls with gravy dipping sauce, chicken pinwheels stuffed with spinach and mushrooms, and skewer salads."

"Skewer salads?"

"Everything you want on a salad, but pinned to a skewer—like green leaf, red leaf, and romaine lettuce, red onion, tomato, cucumber, rolled in olive oil, sprinkled with sesame seeds, drizzled with your favorite dressing."

"Oh my God, that sounds so good. But I thought the governor just wanted to sample this stuff. Why'd you make so many sweet rolls?"

"The governor gets a sample." She picked up another sweet roll, but this time ate it herself. "The rest, I baked them just for you."

Her words were like strings that tugged on his heart. Now he knew why he had come down there to bother

her. Because he loved her dearly, and during this dark, cloudy time in his life when he needed a little sunshine, he had her smile to illuminate the darkness.

In one bite, he finished off the roll she'd started on, then turned her in his arms so he could kiss her sweetened lips. He then licked the icing off his fingers and hers, causing her to giggle. He nuzzled her neck and sucked on her skin the same way he had sucked her fingers. What started off as giggles became soft moans, and finally purrs.

Just as he hoisted her up on the counter, he felt a vibration in his pant pocket. He reached to retrieve his iPhone, but Shania grabbed his hand and whispered, "Don't you dare."

For the next twenty minutes or so, the phone was completely forgotten. When they finished with their lovemaking, Shania slid to her feet and said, "Check your phone, sweetie. It might be a job calling you back."

He had completely forgotten that his phone had vibrated. At her suggestion, he pulled his iPhone out of his pocket. He frowned when he noticed it was a missed call from his pastor. Without hesitation, he quickly returned his pastor's call.

"Hey, Pastor Ray," he said and winked at Shania. "When you called, I was a little . . . busy. What's going on?"

"When's the last time you talked to Mother Washington?"

As soon as he mentioned Mother's name, Greg's heart palpitated. "I was just over there last night. Why? What's wrong? Is everything all right?"

"Oh, I don't want you to get all worked up." His pastor attempted to calm him. "She was just on my heart real heavy, and I kept calling over there, but I didn't get an answer. I want to go by there myself to check on her, but I'm out of town, handling some business, and you could probably get over there before I could."

"I'm on it, Pastor."

"As soon as you find out something, give me a call."

"I will."

As soon as Greg ended the call, Shania said, "Honey, what's going on?"

"I don't know," Greg said, already slipping on his clothes. "Pastor just wants me to check on Mother Washington."

"You want me to go with you?" She sounded concerned.

He jogged toward the door. "You can."

"Well, wait up," she said, hurrying up and putting her clothes back on. "I'm coming too."

Minutes later, Greg pulled into Mother Washington's driveway, and he and Shania rushed out the car and ran to the front door. Greg didn't bother to knock; he simply let himself in. When he threw open the door, he half expected to see Mother Washington lying on the floor in a puddle of blood. Instead, what he saw sitting on the couch was almost just as bad. Almost.

"Minister Crinkle?" The woman from the bike dealership looked at him with a wide smile, and the way her eyes glittered reminded him of snake eyes. "How good to see you again! How was your birthday? Pleasant, I hope?"

From behind him, Shania said, "Who is she? Greg, how do you know her?"

Greg stared at the woman as though she was a monster that had managed to crawl out of his worst nightmare. "What are you doing in Mother Washington's house?"

"I'm Kristen, her daughter—technically her niece, but she's always been like a mother to me."

As fragments of the conversation he and Mother Washington had shared the night before wafted up from his memories, Greg looked at Kristen hard, but the adrenaline and fear pumping through his veins distorted his perceptions. He was unable to make the connection that she was one of the two daughters Mother Washington had told him about.

"Where's Mother Washington?" Greg wanted to know.

Kristen rose from the plush chair, and when she stood and he saw what she had on, he had no choice but to look away. She was braless in a white wife-beater that was tied into a knot at the back, showing off her ironing-board-flat belly and her angel belly ring. She wore a pair of shorts so tiny and tight that he was surprised she could actually move in them.

She looked over Greg's shoulder and said to his wife, "We met on his birthday, the same day he bought that beautiful bike of his. I actually helped him pick out his helmet. You know, the red and black one."

He felt Shania's hand give him a light shove. "You didn't tell me about meeting any woman at the dealership."

What he wanted to say was he didn't meet a woman at the dealership, he met a slut, and she was standing right in front of the helmets. Instead, he said, "I didn't think it was important." Which, in essence, was the truth.

"Well, I'm Shania," she said and held out her hand to the woman. "I'm his wife."

"Kristen." Instead of shaking the offered hand, Kristen stared at it like it was a disease until Shania's cheeks reddened, and she retracted her hand.

"So she's your wife?" Kristen asked, looking at Greg curiously. "You never mentioned anything about having a wife. To be honest, I don't even recall you wearing a ring on that day."

"Excuse me?" Shania said, grabbing Greg's shoulder and turning him to face her.

Greg went into a coughing spell as he choked on his spit. He couldn't believe this woman was standing there telling bald-faced lies. When he could breathe again, he said, "You know what? I don't know what games you're trying to play, but I'm not playing it with you. Where's Mother Washington?"

"You sure didn't mind playing my little game at the BMW dealership."

"Greg!" Shania hit his shoulder so hard she made his teeth knock together. "What all exactly happened at the dealership?"

Glaring hard at Kristen, Greg turned soft eyes on his wife and said, "Babe, I promise you nothing happened. I swear it to you, nothing happened. The only thing that happened is what's happening right now. I ran into this . . . this . . ." he couldn't fix his mouth to say the words *woman* or *lady,* so he finally said, "This *female* at the dealership. She made some advances that I didn't appreciate, and that was that."

"If you're gonna tell her the story, you might as well tell her the whole story," Kristen said.

Greg said, "What is the whole—"

"Greg!" Shania shouted.

"I'm not dealing with this!" Greg yelled and threw a hand up at Shania and Kristen. "Save your little games for another day. Now is not the time. For the last time, where is Mother Washington?"

Kristen retook her seat and had the decency to cross her legs like a lady. "She's asleep. She had a migraine, so I gave her a few pills."

Greg sprinted into Mother Washington's bedroom, but her bed was neatly made, and she was nowhere to be found. His heart pounded in his ears as he repeatedly screamed her name. He looked in the closet, then went to the bathroom, and that's where he found her, crumpled on the floor.

"Oh God, Shania, call 911!" he yelled.

Greg dropped to his knees and picked up Mother Washington's frail body. He checked her neck for a pulse and breathed a sigh when he felt one, even though it was faint. Kristen ran into the room with the most inauthentic look of surprise on her face that Greg had ever seen. There was no doubt in his mind that Mother was in her current condition because of something Kristen had done to her.

"What did you do to her?" Greg gritted through his teeth.

"She had a headache, so I gave her some pain relievers, that's all," Kristen explained in a casual tone that bordered on sounding defensive.

"Show me what you gave her."

Kristen went into the bedroom, then returned with a brown prescription bottle. Greg snatched the bottle from her and read the label. The prescription was made out to Henry Washington, and it was 1600 mg Percocet.

Greg's nostrils flared. "How many did you give her?"

Kristen shrugged her shoulders. "Maybe two."

Greg didn't believe a word coming out of her mouth. He yelled at her, "You idiot! It's not her name on the bottle. These were her husband's painkillers. This is way too strong for her."

Kristen shrugged her shoulder. "Well, I didn't know. Sorry."

Never in his life had Greg wanted to slap a female as badly as his palm was itching to connect with Kristen's face. How could she find her so-called mother unresponsive on the bathroom floor and the only thing she could do was shrug her shoulder and apologize? What kind of a monster was she?

Shania rushed into the bathroom, frantic. "I called 911. They're on the way. They should be here any minute now." She dropped to her hands and knees beside Greg and asked him if there was anything she could do to help.

Greg didn't want to move Mother Washington much, but he couldn't leave her lying on the cold tile floor; it just didn't seem right. So he had Shania help him move her to the bed, and then he grabbed hands with his wife and began praying for Mother Washington's health and strength.

Just when he finished his prayer, they heard the paramedics knocking on the door. As Greg went to open the door, he noticed that Kristen had slithered back into whatever snake hole she had crawled out of.

After explaining to the paramedics the few details he knew, Greg went looking throughout the rooms of the house in search of Kristen, but she was nowhere to be found.

The paramedics loaded Mother Washington onto the ambulance, and it crushed Greg seeing her tiny body strapped to the stretcher. A pale green plastic breathing mask was covering the majority of her face.

Greg got in the car, and he and Shania held hands and prayed as they followed the ambulance to the emergency room.

At the hospital, Greg called Franklin. The day that Greg mentioned to Franklin that he should ask Kaiya about her past, he had done just that. Franklin told

Greg that Kaiya had opened up to him about her rela-
tion to Mother Washington. Franklin admitted that he
had a lot of questions, but Kaiya assured him she'd give
him answers—one day.

In the meantime, Greg told him what was going on.
It just so happened that Kaiya was there with him.
When he got off the phone with Franklin, he and Shania waited anxiously in the waiting room for any news
from the doctor. Kristen was still nowehre to be found.

While waiting, Franklin and Kaiya burst into the waiting room and both wore anxious and fearful expressions.
Greg stood to his feet and touched fists with Franklin,
then greeted Kaiya. This time, as he stared into Kaiya's
face, he immediately drew the connection. Kaiya and
Kristen looked nothing like Mother Washington, but
the two sisters shared so much resemblance, they could
almost go for twins. The only difference was that where
Kristen had this dark edge about her, Kaiya's character-
istics and demeanor showed a sweet-spirited, loving individual. No wonder Franklin could fall for the young lady
so fast and so hard.

"Is my mother okay?" Kaiya asked, looking from Greg
to Shania.

Greg nodded his head. "She's still alive, and they're
pumping her stomach now. The doctor seemed pretty
optimistic that she was going to pull through."

Kaiya looked relieved as the stress lines went out
of her face and her shoulders relaxed and dropped.
She folded herself into one of the hard-backed waiting
room chairs and looked off into the distance, shaking
her head. "It's my fault," she whispered.

"No, it's not, baby girl," Franklin assured her, and he
dropped on his knees between her legs and held both of
her hands in his. "Don't blame yourself."

"I have to," she said, still looking off into the distance with blank eyes. "My sister and I haven't been home in four years, since we went off to college on the West Coast. We graduated not that long ago, and it was my idea for us to come home." She sighed. "I knew that there was bad blood between Kristen and Mama. That's why I don't like leaving her alone with Mama. I don't trust her. I should've been over there while she was at the house, but Kristen tricked me." Kaiya looked over at Greg, and her eyes seemed to plead with him to believe her. "She was asking me about my plans for today, and I told her that I was spending the whole day with Frankie. I should've known right then that she was up to something for questioning me about my whereabouts. Kristen is sneaky. You have to watch her."

Greg didn't need someone to tell him that. He'd had plenty of firsthand experience to attest that what Kaiya had just said was no opinion—it was a fact. Greg looked over at Shania and squeezed her arm, making sure that his wife had just heard what Kristen's *own* sister had said about her.

"Well, it's still not your fault, baby girl," Franklin promised her, and tugged at her hand until she looked at him. "You don't have control over other people's actions. You can't blame yourself for something another adult did. Your sister's gotta answer to God for herself."

Before Franklin could finish, the doctor walked into the waiting room, and since he was smiling, Greg took that as a good sign, and rightfully so. The doctor explained to them that they had pumped Mother Washington's stomach, and she was feeling better already—awake, talking, alert, and ready to get out of the cold hospital.

Greg could almost see a comforting blanket of pure relief settle upon everyone in the room.

Then the doctor said, "She says the last thing she remembers is taking a handful of Excedrin to help with a headache, but what we pumped out of her stomach was not Excedrin. Does anyone know how she could manage to take such a high dose of Percocet?"

Kaiya spoke up first and her eyes were large, round circles, edged with what looked like fear. "Mama's eyes aren't good," she explained. "She must've grabbed the wrong bottle."

Greg stared over at the young lady, and it took all his willpower to keep his jaw from dropping. Even now, looking in her eyes, he knew Kaiya didn't buy her own story a bit more than he did. Why was she taking up for her sister? Why was she covering her tracks? Was it because she was scared of her? Was it because she didn't want to see her sister charged with criminal negligence? Or was it something else? Was she in on this thing as well?

He recalled from his memory Mother Washington saying something about one of her daughters being like a vulture, just sitting around and waiting for her to die. What if both of her daughters were vultures? What if both of them were putting on a show? And what if they took up for each other, covering each other's tracks so that no one would figure out what they were doing and exploit them?

"You know what?" Greg said aloud, even though he was talking more so to himself. "When they release Mother Washington, she's coming to stay with us, Shania. There's no way I could leave her there by herself again. Thank God we got there when we did. What if the next time we show up too late?"

No matter what Kaiya, Kristen, or anybody else said, in his heart, Greg felt like this was a failed attempt to send Mother Washington to an early grave. Though this time was a failure, Kristen, and/or Kaiya, would make sure that the next attempt was a success.

The doctor told them that if all went well, they would release Mother Washington first thing in the morning. Kaiya asked the doctor if it was okay for her to have visitors. When he nodded, Kaiya was about to go visit her, but Greg asked if he could go in first. Upon Kaiya's approval, Greg left.

He pressed open her room door slowly and walked into the room, smiling big. It pained him deeply to see her under the covers of a hospital bed, her arm outstretched and hooked to an IV.

"How're you feeling?"

Mother Washington gave him her toothless grin as he pulled up a chair beside her bed. "Well," she said with a smile, "at least my headache is gone."

He knew she had said that to pull a smile out of him, but he didn't feel like laughing. He reached out and held her cold hand. "Mother, when I went in there and found you on that bathroom floor—" He choked up and looked down in his lap, shaking his head. His voice broke when he said, "I was so scared."

"Don't be scared for me," Mother Washington said, and leaned forward just a tad so she could grab his knee and give it a good shake. "When the good Lord is ready to call me home, ain't nothing you or a soul can do to keep me here. And you best believe this. When God's ready for me, I'm ready for Him. I's got peace in my soul."

He nodded his head as he let her words soak in. Then he said, "Mother, when they release you from the hospital, will you please come stay with me and Shania— just for a little while? I want to be able to keep a close eye on you."

Mother Washington pursed her lips tight. "I don't like the thought of Satan running me outta my own house. But God gives us common sense too. So I think you're right, Gregory. It may be best for me to stay with you and your wife for a little while."

Relieved, Greg leaned forward and kissed the back of her wrinkled hand.

"I know my baby Kaiya out there somewhere, ain't she?"

Greg nodded.

"Can you send her in to me, bless her heart? I need to talk to her."

"Yes, ma'am," Greg said and stood to his feet. He kissed her forehead, told her he loved her, then headed out to the waiting area.

He told Kaiya that her mother was asking for her; then he wrapped an arm around Shania's waist, gave Franklin a dap, and left the hospital. Once seated in his car, he called his pastor and gave him a heads-up on the situation.

No sooner than Greg got off the phone, all sorts of thoughts about Kristen and Kaiya infiltrated his brain. He didn't know what was up with those two, but he was determined to find out.

Eleven

The next morning, Greg forced himself out of bed bright and early just so he could lock himself in his office and have a conference call with the representative doing his market research.

When he finished, he called the hospital to see what time they were releasing Mother Washington, only to find out that her release time and date hadn't been determined yet. Concerned, he asked to be transferred to her room, only to find out that she had been moved to another room and was currently undergoing lab work.

"Lab work for what?" Greg questioned.

The nurse on the phone replied politely, "I'm sorry, but I'm not able to disclose that information over the phone. But when a patient goes down to the lab, it's basically for blood work, to run a few tests—things of that nature."

"Okay," Greg said. "Should I try calling back in an hour or two?"

"You can give it a shot."

Greg thanked the nurse and hung up the phone. He glanced at his iPhone and saw that he had a new text message. The message was from Franklin and it read: About to ride to Macon. Wanna join me?

Greg texted back: don't u have a job?

Franklin replied: yeah, but I called off today; need a break from that place. u riding w/me or what?

He had to agree with Franklin; he needed a break too. Furthermore, he looked forward to any opportunity to stop by and see his parents. Since he hadn't seen them in a while, a visit was definitely in order.

He woke Shania by placing a kiss atop her forehead.

She yawned and smiled at him, then said with her eyes still closed, "Where you headed?"

"Out riding with Frank. Is that okay?"

With her eyes still closed, she nodded. "Love you."

"Love you too, babe." He kissed her forehead again and took a few moments to stare at her beauty, which continued to radiate on her face even when she was sleeping. It touched his heart that his wife chose to believe in him rather than the lies that Kristen had tried to feed her yesterday. Her trust meant everything to him, and he would never intentionally do anything to breach the trust she had in him.

He leaned over for one quick peck on the lips, then grabbed his riding gear and headed outside. Greg met up with Franklin at Franklin's garage. Franklin told him that he didn't have any particular reason for going to Macon other than he just felt like going, and he wanted to feel the wind whipping against his face. Greg figured the trip was spontaneous, considering the short notice Franklin had given him.

"How much sleep did you get last night, man?" Franklin asked him.

As guilty as he felt to admit this, Greg said, "Boy, I slept like a baby. I was just so wore out. Me and Shania."

Franklin pulled on his helmet. "I stayed up with Kaiya all night. Yesterday really shook her up, man. We had a real long, deep conversation. I've never had a conversation so deep before with a chick." Franklin threw his leg over his bike, then said, "Serious question, G.

How much you know about Kaiya and her sister? About their past?"

Greg gave his head a good scratching over before donning his helmet. "To be honest, not much, man. I only know that their biological mom died at a young age, and Mother Washington took them in and raised them like they were her own children. That's about it."

"Well, she told me everything last night. Everything."

Greg revved up his engine and Franklin revved his up as well. In order to be heard over the loud purring of the motors, Greg yelled, "Real talk, Frank. You think she had something to do with Mother Washington and her overdose?"

Franklin emphatically shook his head. "No, man. That was all Kristen. Guarantee it."

Greg hoped that his friend was telling the truth. He hated to think that Mother had two vultures circling her. Kristen alone was bad enough. Forcing himself to push thoughts of Mother Washington and her two adopted daughters aside, he followed Franklin and merged onto the highway. They stopped at a red light that held much longer than they expected, and while they waited for the light to change, Franklin said, "So how're you holding up, man? You had any luck with a job yet?"

Greg shook his head. "No, not yet." A few more seconds passed as they watched the long line of cars make their left turn. Greg said, "Frank, I'm doing market research and applied for a start-up business loan to open a classic car restoration and accessories shop."

"For real, man?" He sounded surprised; then Franklin frowned. "If you want to start your own business, why don't you just ask Shania to lend you the money?"

"'Cause I don't want her money. I want to do this thing myself. Plus, if the business goes under, heaven forbid, I couldn't live with myself knowing I had lost her money like that."

Again, Franklin frowned. "G, man, I feel you, and I know where you coming from. But, man, that's your wife. Y'all are a team. Y'all need to be on the same page, working together."

Greg balanced the bike between his legs and put both hands on the handlebars as the turning traffic finally came to a stop. "Look, if I get the loan, would you be willing to help me? I ain't asking you to quit Mutual Living, or anything like that. Just . . . you know, lend me your expertise, help me get some business, just to get the ball rolling."

"You know you my dude, and you know I got you. If you in, then I'm down for whatever. We can do this thing together. Forget Mutual Living."

Had Greg's helmet not been on, Franklin would've seen Greg's eyebrows nearly reach his hairline. At the most, he had expected Franklin to help him out a little bit, but he had never expected Franklin to be so willing to give up that huge monthly paycheck from Mutual Living for something that wasn't even a guarantee. Franklin joked around a lot, but Greg could see it in his eyes that he wasn't joking about this. God couldn't have given him a better best friend.

Surprised that his throat felt clogged with tears, Greg held out his fist in his friend's direction. Franklin nodded his head a few times, then touched fists with Greg.

The light turned green and Greg and Franklin situated themselves on their bikes and drove off. They stopped at the nearest gas station to fuel up, and Greg called his mom to let her know that Franklin and he would be stopping by for a brief visit. Then they headed to Macon.

As they rode, Greg felt free. All of his senses seemed to come alive as he experienced a heightened sense of awareness. He seemed to notice every vehicle on the road, every groove in the pavement, and every bug in the air as they spattered on his face guard and wind-shield.

A couple of hours later, the men found themselves parking their bikes in Greg's parents' driveway. They left their helmets on top of their seats and made their way to the front door of the plantation-style home and rang the bell. Greg was a bit nervous about revealing his new motorcycle to his mother. His gut feeling told him that it wouldn't set well with her.

Mrs. Crinkle greeted them with a wide smile and hugs for both of them. She was so excited to see them that she didn't even pay attention to the vehicles they had arrived on. She ushered them inside, and they made their way into the country kitchen and enjoyed fried chicken, po-tato salad, turnip greens, and corn bread for lunch.

"I figured you'd be hungry," Mrs. Crinkle said as the men stuffed their faces. "So, what brings you here?"

Before Greg could answer, Franklin blurted out, "We just wanted to put some more miles on Halle and see how fast she could go."

"Halle? Don't you mean Shania? And what do you mean by 'miles'?"

Greg tried to hit Franklin's leg under the table, but Franklin was too busy smiling in Mrs. Crinkle's face to pay attention to the incinerating glare Greg was trying his best to send him.

"That's what he named his bike. Halle. And if you ask me, the name fits 'cause that's a pretty bad bike," Franklin said.

Mrs. Crinkle lowered her fork to her plate and her face lost two shades of color. "Please tell me you're talking about a bike with spokes and pedals."

Franklin almost choked on the greens. Finally, he glanced over at Greg, but it was too late. Though Greg still wore the incinerating glare, the damage had already been done. Franklin held up his hands and told him with his eyes that he thought his mother already knew. Greg kicked him under the table and Franklin frowned, then kicked him back.

"You mean to tell me that you had the audacity to ride over here on a *motorcycle?*" Greg's mother asked.

Greg couldn't bring himself to answer her question, but his silence was answer enough.

Mrs. Crinkle's jaw dropped. She gave her son an intense stare, then pushed away from the table and stomped over to the window. She pulled back the heavy drapes and gasped. He might as well have driven a boa constrictor over, rather than a bike.

"Gregory, I *know* you didn't ride that thing over here. Tell me it's not yours."

Greg felt his neck and ears grow hot, and he wanted to reach across the table and slap that goofy grin off of Franklin's face. Franklin was chewing his greens and munching on his corn bread like it was a bag of hot buttery popcorn and he was sitting at the cinema, enjoying the show.

Greg could tell by his mother's tone and expression that there was no diffusing the situation. A part of him felt like a five-year-old. He wanted to say, "I got a bike, but don't forget, Neil got one first." At least that would take some of the heat off of him.

After mulling over the thought of being a tattletale, he decided against it. What would he gain by throwing his only brother under the bus? he reasoned. Instead, he manned up and handled the situation.

Making direct eye contact, Greg explained, "I got the bike on my birthday. It's what I wanted."

Mrs. Crinkle shook her head and retook her seat at the table. "I don't know what's the matter with my two sons. First Neil, and now you?" She sighed in frustration. "I guess I shouldn't be surprised. Ever since you were a child, you've been following Neil's lead."

She knew about Neil's bike? When had that happened?

As if reading his thoughts, she explained, "He sent me a postcard of him and his bike and wrote at the bottom 'Mom, it's my bike. Please don't be mad.'"

Franklin held his side, laughing. "No, that boy didn't. Did he break it to you like that, Mrs. Crinkle?"

"Frank, shut up," Greg said.

"You shut up, Greg. You should've told mom dukes you got a bike. What kind of sorry excuse for a man are you?"

"Say one more word and I'm coming across this table."

"Boys!" Mrs. Crinkle yelled and hit her hand against the tabletop. "You are grown behind men," she said through her teeth, "so act like it."

"He started it," Greg said, then wished he could've retracted the words as soon as they left his mouth. If he felt like a five-year-old before, now he felt like a three-year-old.

"How does Shania feel about this?" Mrs. Crinkle pressed the issue.

Greg didn't want to keep harping on the bike, but he didn't want to be disrespectful, either. "She was understandably mad at first, but now she's okay with it." He plastered a grin on his face. "I didn't come all this way to talk about my bike. Where's Dad?"

"He'll be right back. He had to make a quick run to the store."

Greg mixed his favorite drink of sweet tea and Sprite. He noticed Franklin's disapproving frown and offered to fix him a glass. When Franklin declined, Greg said, "Don't sleep on this drink, man. It's good." He held the glass to his lips and poured it down the hatch.

Mrs. Crinkle said to Franklin, "Greg's been drinking that since he was ten years old."

Franklin smirked and picked up his glass. "I'll stick with a good old-fashioned glass of tea. Thank you very much." He winked.

"So how are you and Shania doing?" his mother asked. "How's she doing with Eat Your Heart Out?"

Greg gave her a quick overview of their relationship, leaving out the part about how they both had been pretty testy with each other over the past few days. Then he told her about Shania's possible catering of the governor's induction ceremony.

"Wow, that's great!" his mother exclaimed. "And what about you, Franklin? Have you stopped bouncing around from woman to woman yet?"

"Yes, ma'am." Franklin nodded. "I've already met my wife. We're just not married yet." And then Franklin went into his long spiel about Kaiya, and how they met, and how much they loved vintage cars, and how they rode through town, side by side on their bikes. He went on and on, too excited to realize that he was talking too much.

Finally Greg cut him off and said, "I think that's enough, Franklin. She gets the point. You're in love."

"Haters," Franklin said and looked at Mrs. Crinkle while shaking his head. "Gotta put my blockers on." He took the pair of shades from atop his head and slid them over his eyes before looking over at Greg.

"I left my Haters Repellant Spray at home, so these blockers'll have to do."

Greg laughed and slapped hands with Franklin. "That was a good one, boy. I like that."

Not long after Greg and Franklin finished off their lunches, they moved into the den and chatted while Mrs. Crinkle cleaned up the kitchen.

When Mr. Crinkle came home, he dropped his shopping bag on the counter and acknowledged Franklin, then gave Greg a manly hug.

"Always good to see you, son." Mr. Crinkle nodded in the direction of the door. "That your bike out there?"

"Yes, sir. The black and chrome one."

"That's a nice bike," he said. "Both of them are pretty good models, actually. When I used to ride, I had a Harley. Black and red Harley. Called her Fire." Stroking his salt-and-pepper beard, Mr. Crinkle told them about his days as a biker.

Greg clung to his father's every word as though he was hearing these stories for the first time. "Tell him about the time you rode cross-country, Dad."

Franklin's eyebrows lifted high. "You rode cross-country, Mr. Crinkle?"

"Rode almost to California once," Mr. Crinkle said, and there was a faraway look in his eyes. "Me and Bruno—you remember Bruno, don't you, Greg?"

"Yes, sir," Greg said, nodding.

Bruno was a good friend of the family, and he kept riding his bike until diabetes took one of his legs. He died of kidney failure just before Greg's thirteenth birthday.

"Me and Bruno made it all the way to Vegas. Then my bike broke down in the desert. Got ahold of some bad oil and it locked my engine. Felt like my whole world had crashed," he said, still stroking his beard. "Know how bad it hurt to make it this close to our destination," he said and pinched the air, "and fail at the very end?" He shook his head back and forth. Even though he was sitting in the den area with his son and Franklin, he might as well have been transported back into time, all those many years ago, and been standing right beside his bike in the dusty desert where it had broken down. "Bruno's bike only had one seat, so we were stuck down there in Vegas for a whole month, until we came up with the money to catch a train back."

"That sucks," Franklin said and sucked his teeth. "Did y'all ever try to make the trip again?"

"We planned to, but . . ." The sparkle in his dad's eyes seemed to dim, and he looked down at his weathered hands and twirled his fingers. "But then I met my wife, and we had Neil. Then we had Aleigha, and I . . . I kept wanting to ride, but like your mama said, it was too dangerous. And I didn't just have myself to worry about. I had to live for my wife and my children. So I left well enough alone."

Mrs. Crinkle peeked her head into the room. "Darling, your plate is ready."

"Thanks, sweetheart. I'm coming."

He slapped his hands against his thighs and pushed up out of the chair. Greg noticed that every time he saw his father, it seemed to be more and more of a struggle for him to move around with much ease.

"You okay, Dad?" Greg asked, stepping forward with his hand outstretched.

Mr. Crinkle waved his son's hand away. "I'm fine, I'm fine." But when he stood to his full height, his back popped and he winced.

Franklin cleared his throat. "Mr. Crinkle, you know, it's never too late to start riding again. Maybe now that your kids are grown and you're retired, you'll start again."

Mr. Crinkle looked at Greg, then at Franklin. "I don't think so. I'll leave that up to the youngsters."

"But, Dad, if that's where your heart is, you owe it to yourself," Greg insisted. "Look at Mr. Bruno. He kept riding 'til he couldn't ride anymore. He didn't give up."

"Who said I gave up?" Mr. Crinkle stood there for a few seconds, and he seemed reflective for a moment. He cleared his throat. "One night, me and your mama got in a bad argument. So I jumped on my bike and took off riding."

Greg tuned into what his dad was saying. He'd heard his dad's motorcycle stories countless times, but he'd never heard this one.

"While I was riding, it started to rain pretty heavily. Something in me told me I should head back, but I was too angry, so I kept on riding. Then I hit a slick spot in the road and had a wipeout." He winced like the thought hurt him, then wiped his hand in the air like he was wiping rain off his memories. "Whole life flashed before my eyes, and in a matter of seconds, I saw my young bride become a widow and saw my kids grow up without a daddy. That scared me. It wasn't worth it." He looked from Greg to Franklin, then back to Greg. "God was giving me a warning, and I took heed to it. I put the bike up, and I ain't never rode again."

Greg couldn't argue with that. Now he understood why his parents had been so against him getting a bike. He wanted to apologize to his father for misjudging him for all those years. Here he was thinking that his father had punked out for a woman, when in all actuality, he was being obedient to God.

Mrs. Crinkle peeked her head in the room again. "I made sweet potato pie. You boys come get you a piece."

Franklin checked his watch. "As much as I'm lovin' this family reunion right about now, we need to head back before it gets dark."

Mrs. Crinkle pouted. "I sure wished you could stay a bit longer, but I understand. I don't want you to be on the road at night. It's already dangerous enough. Let me wrap you up a piece of pie."

She hurried into the kitchen, then returned moments later with two huge hunks of pie wrapped in Saran Wrap. She squeezed Greg and kissed him on the cheek. After releasing him from her embrace, she said to Franklin, "You know you're just like a son to me. So don't be a stranger. You don't only have to come when Greg comes with you."

"Yes, ma'am," Franklin said and stepped into her embrace.

Franklin and Greg took turns using the bathroom, and Mr. Crinkle walked them out. He admired both bikes and told them to be safe. They suited up and took off to the gas station up the street, where they refilled their tanks and made the journey back to Alpharetta.

Back at home, Greg found Shania in the bathroom, mopping, and the strong acidic stench of vomit burned his nose.

"You all right? What happened?" He turned away. Something about seeing throw up made him want to upchuck the contents of his stomach.

"I'm fine," she assured him. "I made some herb baked chicken. I guess it was too greasy for my stomach."

"You sure I don't need to take you to the doctor?" The smell of pine mixed with bleach filled the air.

"I'm sure." She finished mopping and flushed the bucket of water down the toilet before returning the mop and bucket to the supply closet.

"Guess you won't be able to eat any of this, huh?" he asked, holding up the hunk of sweet potato pie.

She glanced at the pie and started smiling. "Somebody must've been to Macon."

"Sure did," he said and disappeared for a moment to set the pie on the kitchen counter.

When he returned to the bathroom, Shania asked, "And how are your parents doing?"

"They're fine. Dad's worrying me a little. Seems like every time I see him, he's slowing down more and more. And Mama just about had a heart attack when she saw my bike."

"I bet so." Shania chuckled, but her smile didn't reach her eyes. It didn't seem like she was feeling too good. He rubbed her lower back in small comforting circles. "You sure you okay? You want to lay down for a bit?"

"Yeah, I'm just . . . so tired. Where's Mother Washington? I thought you were picking her up this morning?"

"No," he said. "The doctors kept her because they wanted to run a few tests on her. I'll have to call over there a little later and see if I can talk to her."

He watched her as she brushed her teeth and gargled. Her face appeared fuller to him, and this wasn't the first time he had seen her look a little wheezy. He tried to remember how long it had been since she'd had her last period. "Is your period on?"

She dabbed her mouth with a face towel and looked at him through the mirror. He could tell that the thought hadn't occurred to her.

Then she whispered, "It never came."

Was she serious?

Twelve

Convinced that her brain would explode if she had one more random thought about having a baby, but annoyed that she couldn't shut her brain off for even five minutes to get some shut-eye, Shania yanked two pillows off the bed and made a fort on the front room sofa. She flipped through the channels, stopping at all the black-and-white movies, hoping their dullness would lull her to sleep, but sleep continued to elude her.

Sometime that night, Greg must've reached for her and realized she was gone, because he came stomping through the house, yelling out her name as though an intruder had broken in and stolen her.

"Greg, I'm right here."

He rushed into the living room, wearing nothing but a pair of silk night pants, and he rubbed one sleep-crusted eye with his fist. "What's wrong? What's going on? You sick again?" He yawned while he talked.

"I couldn't sleep. And I didn't want to wake you with all my shifting. Go back to bed, honey."

"I can't." He yawned again. "I need to hold you."

She smiled. Even in his half-sleep state, he was a total sweetheart. Though she didn't want to, she turned off the TV and held on to his hand as he led her back to bed. He wrapped his arms around her waist, and within seconds, he was snoring softly in her ear. She counted everything from sheep to baby booties, and finally, around six-ish that morning, she drifted off to sleep—only to be awakened an hour and a half later by her alarm clock. Had she not needed to finish the finger foods for the induction ceremony the next day, she would've unplugged the clock and drifted off back to sleep. Instead, she forced herself out of bed and into the bathroom, where she tried to vomit as quietly as possible so Greg wouldn't wake up worried. It didn't work.

Every passing second felt like a minute and each minute felt like an hour waiting for Greg to get back from the drugstore with a pregnancy test. But she didn't need to see the results to confirm what she already knew to be true. With the frustration of finishing everything for the wedding and with Greg's job loss, she had blamed her missed period on stress.

While she waited for him to return, her empty stomach began to feel ravenous. She slipped on her bedroom shoes, went to the kitchen, and fixed herself a hearty breakfast of scrambled eggs, bacon, buttery grits, and raisin toast. At least that was the plan...until she smelled the aroma of the bacon. The smell that once made her mouth water now made her queasy. Back to praying to the porcelain god she went.

Shania hated being sick. She hated the nasty taste that had developed in her mouth even more. Certain that she couldn't handle feeling nauseated and fatigued for the next nine months, a part of her hoped that she had caught some twenty-four-hour bug instead.

She caught a glimpse of herself in the bathroom mirror and shrieked. Little red veins decorated the whites of her eyes, and she had bags underneath. She shook her head as she turned on the faucet and used her hand as a cup while she sipped, rinsed, and spit.

She turned off the faucet and dried her hands and mouth on a hand towel. With her stomach still feeling unsettled, she decided not to eat the breakfast she had prepared. She instead opted for some saltine crackers and orange juice. For some reason, when the citrusy drink hit the back of her throat, she felt less like throwing up.

She stood at the kitchen island, munching on one crunchy, salty cracker after another, thinking about how much her life would change with a baby. She had figured that she and Greg would have children someday, but the thought of that "someday" possibly being now made her heart flutter.

Was it too soon to have a baby? What about the timing? If she was pregnant, Greg *definitely* wouldn't want to go to Jamaica now. He'd want to save every penny for the baby. Furthermore, what kind of example was she setting for her sister? She and Greg hadn't even celebrated their first wedding anniversary, and there was a possibility that she might be with child already?

If Cheyenne found out she had allowed herself to get pregnant so early in her marriage, she'd probably assume that it gave her the right to do the same. And what would Greg's parents think about the situation? Would they think she moved too fast? Oh God, oh God, what had she done?

Then she remembered a conversation she'd had with Mother Washington. The older woman had said, "You're married now. Anytime married folks wanna start havin' babies is fine. Don't let people try to convince you to wait, if that's not what you and your husband wanna do. That's between you and him. Keep folks out your business. What happens in your house needs to stay right there, in your house. Marriage is what you make it. It takes work and commitment, especially after you start havin' babies. Forget about the fairy tale, because when the fairy tale ends, real life begins."

Shania felt like her fairy tale had ended days ago. Yet and still, she pondered the words of wisdom and stuffed another cracker in her mouth. She swallowed hard when she saw Greg come through the door, carrying a plastic bag and wearing anxiety in the creases of his forehead. As he walked toward her, he removed the pregnancy test from the bag and held it in the air.

"Here you go," he said as he placed the test on the counter in front of her.

Shania stared at the test in utter disbelief. She had to ask herself if this was really happening. A few months ago, she was a virgin. In a few short minutes, her entire world could change.

Trying to get rid of some of her nervous energy, she twisted the sleeve of crackers and put the remaining crackers back in the box. She pressed her hands against the edge of the island and sighed.

"Don't be nervous." Greg placed his hand on top of hers and squeezed. "No matter what, we'll be all right."

With that vote of confidence, Shania picked up the test and read the instructions. When she felt comfortable, she went into the bathroom, peed on the stick, and waited.

Unable to take the stress, she left the stick on the back of the toilet and returned to her plate in the kitchen, hoping that she could hold down a few eggs to stop the vicious growling in her stomach. She carried her plate into the bedroom and noticed that Greg had his head bowed and his eyes closed. He must've been in prayer. Was he praying that she was or wasn't pregnant? Probably wasn't. What man would pray that he had a baby on the way when he had just lost his blanket of security?

Once again, she sighed and called herself a fool for not being more careful. She hadn't been taking her pills the way she should've, and she knew it too. She should've made him use condoms, or she should've at least made him pull out. Christ, what was she thinking?

Greg turned his attention to Shania and checked his watch. "You think it's ready?"

Shania stuffed a forkful of eggs in her mouth and nodded, then followed him into the bathroom. She pressed the heels of her palms against her eyes so she wouldn't have to see what she already knew to be true. In her mind, as long as she didn't see it, it wasn't real yet. However, curiosity got the best of her, and she peeked from behind one palm and watched Greg's shaky hand pick up the stick and almost drop it.

"What does it say?" she whispered.

"Look."

She pulled her hands from her eyes and Greg turned the stick around so she could see it. The word *pregnant* filled her vision, and her stomach fluttered. They stood there in silence.

She looked up at Greg and confirmed, "We're pregnant."

She couldn't believe those words had come out of her mouth. Nothing could describe how she felt. A mixture of fear—no, more like terror—and a hint of excitement surged through her body. Next came the long list of questions swirling around in her mind: *Am I really ready? Will I be a good mother? What's Greg thinking? Why is he not smiling? What will my family think? How will this affect my career? What can I eat? Why is he not smiling?*

Shania felt dizzy and took a seat on top of the closed toilet lid.

Greg worked his jaw while he rubbed the back of his neck. "We're having a baby." He sounded surprised and confused, but he still wasn't smiling. "But I . . . I thought you were on the pill?"

With her hands dangling between her thighs, she looked up with teary eyes and said, "I'm sorry. My schedule has been busy and I forgot to take them a couple of times." She felt out of control. It was the same feeling she got whenever she jumped off a diving board, but just before she hit the water. And why, in God's name, was he still not smiling?

He got down on one knee and kissed her left hand. The feel of his soft lips sent a tingle up her spine.

"If you had told me that, I could've used some extra protection." He looked away from her.

She pushed her face against her knees and let the hot tears that she had dammed since yesterday squeeze from beneath her eyelids. "I'm sorry," she whispered repeatedly. "I messed up and I'm sorry."

"Babe, babe," he said, and lifted her head out her lap. He grabbed the hand towel and wiped the tears from her face. "Why're you crying like that? Those aren't happy tears."

"Because you're not happy," she sobbed, and wiped her runny nose with the back of her hand. "You haven't smiled not once."

"I am happy, Shania," he said, and held her chin while he placed kisses against her lips. "I am happy— babe, I swear I am. But this is a bit of a shocker for me, just like it is for you. But don't ever for once believe that I'm not happy about being a father. We might not have planned it, but it is what it is." He turned his lips inward and made a slight popping sound when he turned them back out. "I love you, and I'm happy that you're having my baby."

She tried to muster a smile for him, but her lips refused to cooperate. He leaned closer to her, put his lips against her cheekbone, and sung in a low, deep voice the lyrics to "U & I" by Jodeci.

His horrible singing brought a smile to her lips. "Honey, please, God blessed you with a few talents, but singing is not one of them. Leave that to Jodeci."

He pulled her up and stood with her, wrapping his arms around her. Despite her plea, he continued to sing. He poked his lips out. "You're not going to sing with me?"

Not wanting to ruin the joy in the moment, she sung off-key with him.

Greg grabbed her hairbrush, stood on the toilet, and sang at the top of his lungs.

Shania nearly collapsed on the floor in laughter. He might've been joking, but he was semi-serious, because that large vein was protruding from the side of his neck.

"Are you laughing at my singing?" he asked his wife.

She grabbed her side, trying to hold the giggles in. "How could I not? You sound like a dying cat."

He attacked her with tickling fingers, tickling her under her chin, under her arms, and along her sides. He tickled her until he brought her to her knees and made her plead for mercy. Then, he removed his fingers and placed his cheek against her belly. She held his head in place and stroked his hair.

"I love you, Shania. And even though I can't feel him, I love him already too."

A smile touched her lips. "And how do you know it's a him?"

She felt him smile against her flat belly. "Because I feel it in my spirit. And I promise you and him right now, on this very day, to be the absolute best husband

and father I can be. To take care of you and my son to the absolute best of my ability and to let no harm come to either of you. That's my solemn vow, and I mean it, baby. All jokes aside."

She nodded and whispered, "I believe you." And she did. Wholeheartedly.

After getting a same-day appointment due to a cancellation, the doctor confirmed that Shania was indeed three weeks pregnant. Greg wasn't sure if he could remain standing on his own two feet. He felt happy; there was no doubt about that. Just the same, he was frightened out of his mind.

One could purchase as many pregnancy and parenting books as money could buy, but this baby still wouldn't come with a manual. However, he understood that babies were gifts from God, and even if he felt like the timing wasn't quite right, he knew that if God brought them to this, God would bring them through this—or at least he hoped He would.

Thirteen

Though he wanted to celebrate the pregnancy news with his wife the night before, they couldn't because she had to take care of last-minute details for her obligations the following day. Even now time was of the essence. Not only did she have to meet with the governor and his wife within an hour's time, but she had a wedding to cater today. The one thing he knew would guarantee a smile on Shania's face would be for him to agree to take the trip to Jamaica, so he told her that he wanted to go on the vacation.

She smiled when he told her, and she immediately called her travel agent to tell her to book the trip to Couples Sans Souci in Ocho Rios in four weeks. They tried to quell their excitement about their new baby and the trip, as well as their anxiety about this huge opportunity that Shania would receive if the governor chose her menu.

At the house, Shania made him taste-test each of the five items on her menu, and since he had skipped breakfast, Greg willingly obliged. The food was flawless, and there was no doubt in his mind that when the governor tasted what Shania had created, it was a done deal. A few seconds later, Shania's assistant arrived driving the Eat Your Heart Out catering truck. Together, he and the assistant loaded all the food for the wedding in the back of the truck.

"You go ahead to Highland Hall," Shania told her assistant, "and set up shop. I'll meet you there after I finish meeting with the governor."

"Okay," her assistant said before squealing with delight. "Good luck! I know you got this." She drove off.

Greg helped Shania load her finger foods into the back of the Range Rover, and even though it was only five dishes, he refused to let her pick up a single dish. Then he held open the passenger door for her.

"Greg," she said and caught his face between her hands, "don't take this the wrong way, but this is something I want to do alone, okay? I really want to make a lasting impression on the governor, and with you in the room, it'll make me nervous."

He frowned at her and pushed his lips out. This was one of the greatest opportunities she'd ever been offered, and he wanted to share this special moment with her. But in the same sense, he didn't want to be the cause of her failing to impress the governor simply because he was in the room.

Finally, Greg sighed and nodded. "Okay, babe. I understand." He kissed her forehead. "Even though I won't be there with you physically, I'll be there with you in spirit, rooting you on."

She kissed him long and hard. "Thanks for being so understanding. I love you."

"I love you too." He walked with her around the Range Rover, helped her inside, and then closed the driver door for her. He stood in the driveway, watching her back out. He sent a prayer up to God, asking Him to open the floodgates of heaven and send Shania His strength and His divine favor. Then he returned to the house and started cleaning.

Even though there wasn't much to clean up, Greg figured that since he didn't have a job, and since his wife already had such a busy day today, he could at least take some of the housework off her hands. He washed the few dishes left over from breakfast, mopped the kitchen floor, made up their bed and washed, folded, and put away two loads of laundry. Then he retreated to his office and resumed his job search. He figured that until he knew for certain whether he'd be able to start his own company, he might as well be productive and look for a job.

Once his brain began to hurt from filling out all the online applications, he closed his computer down and called the hospital to check up on Mother Washington. They transferred him to her room, and when she answered the phone, she didn't sound too good.

"Everything's okay? How're you feeling, Mother?" he asked.

"Blessed and highly favored, son," she croaked into the phone.

"You don't sound too good."

"Naw, I don't, do I?" she said, and managed to laugh. "Pastor Ray came up here to see me this morning. He prayed with me and that made me feel a lot better."

Even though she couldn't see him, Greg smiled and nodded his head. "So when are they gonna let you go?"

"Well, suga," she said, then cleared her throat long and hard, "they been pricking me like I'm a pin cushion, running all these tests on me. Said something ain't right with my blood. That's why I be so cold all the time. Today, they talking 'bout giving me a CAT scan. They just like having me over here 'cause I'm good company, and I help these nurses and doctors' day go by faster."

It touched him that even in the midst of her pain and discomfort, she was still able to smile and make light about the situation. However, he noticed that she still hadn't answered his question. "So, when are they going to let you go home?" he asked again. "Shania's already set you up a real nice guest room. You're going to love it, Mother, I guarantee."

"Oh, bless her heart," Mother Washington laughed into the phone. "That Shania's a sweetheart. She tell you she's pregnant yet?"

Her words shocked him so much, he couldn't utter a single word.

"Gregory? You still there?"

"Yes, ma'am," he said, nodding. "But . . . h—how'd you know she was pregnant?"

Mother Washington laughed again. "As soon as I saw her face Sunday morning, I knew she was pregnant. Tell her she having a boy too. And she better name him after you."

A smile tugged at Greg's lips. "How do you know she's having a boy, Mother?"

"I just know some things, suga." She took a deep breath, then sighed into the phone. "Tell her thanks for setting that room up for me, but I don't think I'm gon' be needing it. All is well with my soul."

Greg frowned. "Mother Washington, I can't let you go back to that house, not after what Kristen did to you."

"I spoke to Kristen about what happened, and she apologized for making such a terrible mistake. She swore she didn't mean to do me no harm." She paused. "God's gonna take care of Kristen. And God's gonna take care of me too." She sighed into the phone, then let out another groan. "I love you, Greg, but I's gon' have to get off this phone. Talking so much got my head pounding again. I'm gon' close my eyes and get me some more rest."

"You do that, Mother. I love you, and I'll be up there to see you soon."

"I look forward to it," she said, then ended the call.

About an hour later, Greg's iPhone rang the special tune that only played when his wife called. Holding his breath, he sent a quick prayer to God and answered the phone.

"I got it!" she yelled into his ear.

Greg had to pull the phone away from his ear as she screamed out her victory. "They picked you?" he asked.

"They picked me!" she exclaimed. "There are still two more individuals that they have to look at, but the governor was so impressed with my presentation and the taste of the food, he said he's already made up his mind. We signed the contract right then and there, and he even signed me an advancement check."

"Congratulations, baby! This calls for a celebration. Let's go to Maggiano's."

"Mmm," she moaned into the phone. "I am ravenous, and Italian food sounds like a prescription from the doctor. I should be finished with the wedding around six-ish. Is that good?"

"That's great. Have fun at the wedding, and don't overwork yourself."

"Make sure you call and make those reservations."

Greg got off the phone and called Maggiano's to make reservations. Then he looked through the closet for something nice to wear, not too dressy, but not too casual, either. He settled on a pair of dark khakis and a white button-up, collared shirt.

While waiting for Shania to finish with the wedding, he decided to go by the hospital and check on Mother Washington. She was asleep when he arrived, so instead of waking her, he simply sat by her bedside and watched over her. Then he got on his bike and took a relaxing ride down a long winding back road.

When he returned home, he stripped off his clothes in the bedroom. As he stepped into the shower and cracked the glass door closed, the bathroom door swung open. He pulled back the curtain just a tad and smiled at his wife. "So how'd it go?"

"Perfect," she said and smiled at him while she curled a piece of hair around her finger. "I love weddings. They always bring back the excitement and nostalgia I felt on our wedding day. The bride looked like a princess and the groom looked like her knight in shining armor. The whole wedding was like one big fairytale."

She was glowing with happiness, and Greg loved seeing her like this. He wasn't sure if the glow came from her flawless day or from the baby taking shape in her womb, but whatever the case, he felt himself lengthening from the need to have her.

"Babe," he said softly.

He didn't have to say another word. Somehow she understood what he wanted and needed. Without hesitation, she slipped out of her clothing and joined him. He made love to her against the shower wall, very slow and careful—cautious not to hurt her. The fact that not only was he making love to his wife, but to the future mother of his child, heightened his sexual desire.

After they finished showering, they got dressed and headed over to Maggiano's.

They pulled up at Maggiano's and let the valet park their car. Inside, they ordered a huge plate of smothered vermicelli covered in mozzarella and Parmesan. Together, they ate every bite.

While eating, Greg thought about telling Shania about his plans to start a business. He remembered how upset she had been when he'd made the bike purchase without touching base with her first, and he figured she'd be upset about this decision as well. However, he knew if he told her that he was considering starting his own business, she'd want to invest in him and pay for everything. But he didn't want her money. There was no guarantee that his business would succeed, and he didn't want Shania's nest egg on the line.

"A penny for your thoughts?"

Greg forced a smile for her sake and twirled the vermicelli noodles around the fork tines. This was the perfect opportunity to let her know what all was going on in his head. Instead of mentioning the business loan, he said, "I'm a bit worried about Mother. She didn't sound too good when I talked to her on the phone earlier. I went by the hospital to check on her, but she was sleeping."

Shania lifted her glass to her lips and took a small sip. "Honey, Mother Washington will be fine. She's strong and she's a fighter. I have no doubt that God'll bring her out of this. So don't stress yourself about it." She cleared her throat, then said, "But I've been wondering . . . Why didn't you tell me about that woman at the dealership?"

Greg knew that question was coming eventually. "Babe," he said, "like I told you before, I didn't tell you about her because I didn't think it was important. She was coming on to me, even after I told her I was happily married. When I rejected her, she got all mad. I didn't know she was Mother Washington's daughter."

Shania nodded and chewed thoughtfully before saying, "Listen, honey." She put her fork down. "I trust you, and I believe you, okay? If you said nothing happened between you and that woman, then I believe you. But if our marriage is going to be a success, you need to tell me things, okay? Don't leave me in the dark about situations. I'm more understanding than you give me credit for."

Once again, he heard God whisper, *Here's your chance. Tell her.*

He opened his mouth, closed it, then cleared his throat and stared at their half-eaten plate. He picked up his glass, sipped his drink and said, "So, when are we going to start on the baby's room?"

For the rest of dinner, they refrained from conversing about any touchy subjects. They just talked about their love for each other and the seed that was taking root in Shania's belly. They reminisced on the early stages in their relationship, like whenever Shania would shoot down all Greg's advances while she played hard to get.

They left the restaurant arm in arm, heads held back, and laughing. For once in a very long time, Greg felt a peaceful bond between them, even though a few things still nagged at his conscience.

After Maggiano's, they went to a small club on the far side of town that had a live jazz band that exceeded any other live jazz band he'd ever heard. Greg's favorite two instruments in the band were the low registers from the bass guitar combined with the sultry blows of the alto saxophone.

He glanced over at Shania, who was bouncing in her seat, her head bobbing as she grooved to the relaxing music. They drank lemon water and spoke few words. They let the musicians use their instruments to do the talking for them. The last number that the band played had a very provocative feel to it. Greg glanced over at Shania and the embers of passion burning in her eyes told him that she felt it too.

He leaned over and whispered in her ear, "Let's get out of here."

She understood the implications of that request and quickly jumped out of her seat. However, when they got home, the pasta she had devoured disagreed with her stomach, and she spent the next half hour in the bathroom, retching up the contents of her belly.

Greg thought maybe he could get some after her stomach settled, but by then she wasn't in the mood and told him she just wanted to be held. Greg didn't push the issue. He simply took her to bed and held her in his arms. Was this what he had to look forward to? Months of rejection?

Fourteen

The past two weeks seemed to fly by. Greg had elicited the help of a realtor who attended his church to help him find a location for his shop. The more he thought about it, the more excited he became. He felt like, if push came to shove, he could use his severance money to start his business venture in the event the loan fell through. That'd be enough to get started.

It seemed like he had just fallen asleep when his phone started ringing. Greg popped open one eye and looked at the caller ID. It was Franklin, so he ignored the call. But Franklin kept calling back-to-back. Finally, Greg answered the phone and growled out, "What, man? What do you want?"

"Wake up and get here ASAP."

The sound of his voice caused any remnants of sleep to vanish like steam. Greg jumped up in bed and threw the covers off of him. "What's going on? What's wrong, Frank?"

"Mother Washington is in real bad shape, man."

"What you mean?" Greg exclaimed, already slipping into a pair of jogging pants. "I just went by there earlier today, and she was—"

"Listen, man, me and Kaiya are over here now, and I'm telling you, she's not doing good. The doctors done gave her a three percent chance."

"A three percent chance?" Greg looked at the phone incredulously. He hoped that this was just a sick joke,

Franklin taking his humor overboard. He knew that this wasn't so. Franklin joked around a lot, but he knew his friend wouldn't joke about something like this. He wondered what in the world had gone wrong to cause things to go to such an extreme.

Just as he was about to wake Shania, her phone started ringing. With her eyes still closed, she reached over and grabbed the phone, put it to her ear and said, "Hello?"

Greg only half listened to her conversation while he pulled on a shirt and stuffed his feet into a pair of shoes. But when Shania screamed into the phone, Greg's head whipped around and he hurried to her side, feeling like someone had just sucker punched him in his gut. Her eyes looked like platters, and she was pressing trembling fingers against her lips.

Frightened out of his mind, Greg held his chest and wondered if it was healthy for his heart to palpitate like this so many times in such a short time span.

"What's going on, babe?" he asked, but she held up one finger, quieting him as she continued to listen to whoever was on the other end of the phone.

"But are you okay?" she yelled into the phone. "Okay, okay," she said, throwing back the covers and jumping out of the bed. "I'm on the way now. What hospital are y'all at?" She nodded her head repeatedly. "Okay, I'm on the way."

Greg stared at her, utterly confused. "What . . . what's going on, babe? Was that about Mother Washington?"

"Mother Washington?" She frowned as she hopped in a pair of pants to get them past her thighs. "No, that was Cheyenne. Jonathan's been shot again."

Greg's eyes widened. "Again? How'd he get shot?"

"I don't know," Shania snapped as she pulled off her night slip and searched through her dresser drawer. "I could barely understand Cheyenne, because she was crying so hard. She said something about a drive-by and bullets—I don't know. All I know is that Jonathan got shot." Shania pulled out a blue shirt and pulled it over her head. "*That's* why I told her to leave that boy alone. He is no good for her. All that talk about God and change wasn't nothing but a front, and he almost fooled me too. Almost. He ain't about nothing, don't want to be nothing, and ain't gonna be nothing. I can minister to him until I'm black and blue in the face, but that's not gonna change a thing. I can't change him and Cheyenne can't change him, either. He has to want to change for himself." She rolled her eyes upward. "Cheyenne can do bad all by herself."

Greg didn't have time to listen to his wife rant on and on. He cut her off mid-sentence. "What hospital is he at?"

"South Georgia Medical Center."

He grabbed the keys to his bike, then said, "Okay, well you head that way, and I'm going over to Piedmont. Be careful, and call or text me when you get there."

"Piedmont?" She paused in getting dressed and stared at Greg sideways. "What are you going over there for?"

"Franklin just called me," he said, tussling with his motorcycle jacket. "They're giving Mother Washington a three percent chance to live. I've got to get over there."

As he sped down the road, darting in and out of traffic, Greg asked God what in the world was going on in his life. He'd lost his job, a woman who was like a second mother to him had basically been given a death sentence, and now his brother-in-law had been shot—

again. The more he thought about the negativities in his life, the angrier he became. Then he heard a small voice whisper in his ear, *Whatever is positive, whatever is loving, whatever is of good report, set your mind on these things.*

Greg understood that if he continued to look at all the wrong in his life, he would end up digging himself into an abysmal pit of despair. Not missing a beat, he began to combat his negative thoughts with positive ones. He had a baby on the way. Even without a job, he and his wife were secure and didn't have to worry about a roof over their heads or food in their mouths. His wife had just had an amazing door of opportunity opened for her. His best friend had finally found true love. Most of all, no matter what happened with Mother Washington, she had already assured him that there was peace in her soul. Knowing this, he still prayed that Mother and Jonathan would be all right.

When he arrived at the hospital, he locked his bike and ran along the corridor and made two left turns. At the receptionist desk, he requested Mother Washington's floor and room number. They had moved her over to the intensive care unit. The first person he saw when the elevator door opened was Franklin standing in the middle of the hallway, hugging his riding helmet as though it was a teddy bear.

"Frank."

Franklin looked up and gave Greg the saddest smile he'd ever seen on his friend. They hugged each other and thudded each other's backs. Then Franklin said, "Kaiya's in there with her now."

"How's Mother doing?"

Franklin's skin looked pasty as he spoke. "It's a tumor in her brain."

Greg's heart dropped to his soul.

"And the doctor said it's inoperable."

Greg held his stomach and had to literally fight back vomit. He wished Franklin would shut up, but he kept talking.

"The doctors said that *if* she lives, she'll be in a vegetative state. But that's *if* she lives."

Greg shook his head and stared up at the ceiling, nonverbally asking God why. Kaiya walked out of Mother Washington's room. She had been crying so much that her eyes looked like two watery Roma tomatoes. She rushed into Franklin's outstretched arms, and he held and rocked her from side to side. Greg left them to each other and tapped softly on Mother Washington's door before allowing himself in.

A nurse was in the room, checking Mother's vitals. She looked over her shoulder at Greg and gave him a sympathetic smile. "You must be the son she keeps talking about."

The nurse's words almost sent him to his knees. Only a single thread was holding him up, and he felt that at any second, the thread would snap and he would collapse in despair.

"She's pumped full of morphine," the nurse assured him, "so she's feeling no pain. If you need me, just press the red button." She bowed out of the room.

As soon as Greg laid eyes on Mother Washington, he felt like breaking down. He hated seeing her lying there with tubes sticking out of her. He plastered on a fake smile, hoping she wouldn't pick up on his trepidation. Though he was only a few steps away from the bed, the walk to her bedside seemed like the longest walk he'd ever taken in his life. He took a chair and pulled it to the side of the bed before taking a seat. Mother Washington had a serious expression on her face but attempted to smile when she saw him. He encouraged her not to. He could tell that every move, no matter how minor, made her uncomfortable.

Careful not to disturb the tubes, Greg touched Mother Washington's leg. "You'll be all right," he assured her. It hurt him to speak; it felt like someone had punched him in his throat, and he was trying to talk around the pain.

Her eyes filled with tears as a faint sound escaped her lips. He leaned in closer to hear her stammer, "I don't think so, suga. But all is well with my soul."

He turned his head away and looked at the window so she wouldn't see the tears that were threatening to spill down his face. He knew he needed to be strong, so he blinked repeatedly until the tears dissolved and returned to their ducts.

Looking back at Mother Washington, he noticed that her skin no longer looked brown, but gray. He leaned down and kissed her cold cheek and whispered in her ear, "The God we serve is able to do exceedingly, abundantly, above all we can ask or think."

"Yes, He can." Mother looked at the ceiling and nodded.

Greg didn't like to think about the possibility of Mother Washington dying. He felt the need to open his heart to her and tell her just how much she meant to him. When he opened his mouth, no words came out, just a heart-wrenched sob.

"It's okay to cry, suga," she said, and patted his leg. "Go 'head and cry, chile. Crying won't make you any less of a man."

At her prompting, he dropped his chin against his chest and let the tears flow. He sniffed hard to keep snot from running down his lips while he talked. "All my life," he said, while still looking at his lap, "I always felt like I lived in my brother's shadow. Like I had to work extra hard to prove to my parents that I was just as good a son as he." He wiped his nose with the back of his hand and then dried his hand on his pants. "But when I'm with you, Mother"—he wiped his nose again and looked over at her—"when I'm with you, I don't feel like I have to compete, you know? I can be myself and you don't judge me. You just shower me with love. You've taught me what it means to be a good man, a godly man, and a good husband. I don't know . . . if I can make it . . ." He gasped and tried to catch his breath. "Without you."

Mother looked over at him and gave him that toothless grin that he had fallen in love with. "You can and you will. Sometimes God puts us in situations that we ain't got no control over. When that happens, know that even when you can't trace Him, just trust Him."

Greg nodded his head and his shoulders shook while he sobbed. Then he pulled himself together and said, "Are your feet cold?"

"Chile, yes," she said. "For all the warmth these hospital blankets give me, I might as well be laying here naked."

Greg chuckled, always amazed at how she could make him laugh despite the situation. Carefully, he sat on the edge of the bed and uncovered her feet. They felt like chunks of ice in his hands. As he massaged them, he listened to Mother reminisce on all the good times they'd shared. Before he knew it, Mother Washington had him laughing with her jokes and antics, and for a moment in time he let himself forget about the severity of the situation.

The nurse returned to the room and said, "Ms. Washington, a young lady who says she's your daughter is here to see you. But the doctor told me to only let one visitor in at a time."

Greg lifted his eyebrow at the nurse, then turned to face Mother Washington. "I thought Kaiya has already been in here."

Mother Washington sighed deeply, then shook her head gently from side to side. "It's not Kaiya. It's Kristen."

"No. No!" Greg said, jumping off the bed. He pointed at the nurse, who gave him a frightened look, as though she was about to go call security. "Don't you dare let that woman in here."

"Greg, hush yo' mouth," Mother Washington reprimanded him. "She might be a hateful somebody, but in my heart, she's still my child. And there's something I need to tell her before it's too late. You gon' out there and let her come in here so I can speak to her."

Again, Greg held his chest as his heart palpitated. "What if she tries to hurt you again?"

Mother Washington pointed up at the ceiling. "No weapon formed against me is gonna prosper. That's what my Father told me."

She had a point there. Reluctantly, Greg nodded. "Well, I'll leave out the room for now, but I'm spending the night here with you."

"No, you ain't," she corrected him. "You got a pregnant wife at home to tend to, and you don't need to be sitting here worried about me. Get on outta here and tell that pretty wife of yours I said she better take care of herself and take care of that baby. And, Gregory," she added, almost as an afterthought, "you listening to me?"

Intuition told him to listen closely to what she was about to say.

"No matter the situation, God's always gonna make a way for you to escape."

He expected a few different parting words. For the life of him, he couldn't understand why she was telling him this.

She must've read the confusion on his face because she added, "Even if it don't make no sense now, it will later."

"Okay." Greg nodded and let his lips linger on her cool forehead for a few seconds. "I love you, Mother."

"I love you too, son. And when you get the chance, take a vacation, chile. It'll do you a world of good."

"I plan to," Greg said, smiling. He then told her about his upcoming vacation. He held her hand. "If you don't want us to go, we can cancel the trip."

She coughed out the word "no," cleared her throat, then said, "San-na-oochee?" She frowned. "I ain't never heard of that island."

Greg laughed at her pronunciation. "It's in Jamaica."

"Jamaica," Mother repeated him. "Ahh, I know where that's at. I always wanted to go there."

"Maybe we can take you once you get out of here."

"No, chile," Mother said and patted his hand. "Y'all just go and have a good time for me. Get on out of here now. I got people to see, and places to go."

Greg had to force one foot in front of the other in order to leave her room. He didn't want to leave; he wanted to sit in that chair forever and watch over her like a guardian angel. Deep down inside, he felt that as long as he was in the room with her, God wouldn't let her pass to the other side. He had no idea why he felt that way, because whether he was willing to admit it or not, he knew that when it was time to go, it was time to go.

In the hallway, he was met with the unwelcomed sight of Kristen. Thankfully, she had on some decent clothing, but her shirt was cut dangerously low, showing off her ample bosom. His face grimaced on its own volition.

"Is she dead yet?" Kristen asked matter-of-factly.

Once again, his hand itched to slap her. For that one second in time, he wished he wasn't a Christian, and he wished his parents hadn't instilled such good morals in

him. He was yearning to put his fist through her face
and use physical force to teach her the true meaning of
respect. But instead, he locked his jaw in place and said
through his teeth, "You better not hurt her."

"Or what you gonna do, Daddy?" she asked and slid
her tongue over her bottom teeth. "You can play like
you don't like this if you want to, but that day at the
dealership, somebody got a little happy against my leg.
Or did you forget?"

There she goes again, playing her little games. Greg
didn't think her question warranted a reply. He simply
said, "I'm praying for your soul," while he brushed past
her.

She looked after him, laughing. "'Preciate it!"

He found Franklin and Kaiya in the waiting room,
huddled over the Bible. When Franklin saw him, his
expression asked if Mother Washington was all right.

Greg nodded. "She's happy, she's at peace, and she's
in good spirits. That's all we can ask for, right?"

Both Kaiya and Franklin nodded. Then Greg said,
"Look, man, I gotta run. Same time when all this crazi-
ness happened, my brother-in-law got shot. With the way
things are going, there's no way Shania and I are gonna be
able to go to Ocho Rios in two weeks."

Franklin frowned. "You ain't talking 'bout the same
dude that just got shot not too long ago?"

Greg nodded.

"I thought you said he gave his life to God? Thought
you said he gave up that lifestyle."

"He did," Greg said, shrugging his shoulders. "I don't
know what's all going on, but they got him over there
at South Georgia Medical Center. Shania's en route, so
I'm headed that way now."

"A'ight, man," Franklin said and slapped hands with
his friend. "You be careful."

Greg nodded, then gave Kaiya a hug. He looked back to Franklin. "You take care of her, all right, bro?"

Franklin grinned. "You know I will."

Greg tried not to think about Kristen in Mother Washington's room, yanking the tubes out of her, turning off all the machines, smothering her with a pillow. A thousand negative thoughts filled his mind, but once again, he forced himself to set his mind on positive things. He called Shania to let her know he was on the way, but her phone went straight to voice mail. So he jumped on his bike and flew down the road from one hospital to the next.

When he got to South Georgia Medical Center, he went to the receptionist desk and asked what room Jonathan was in. She told him, and he took the elevator and read the door tags until he came to Jonathan's room. He found Shania and Cheyenne holding each other on the extra bed in the room, both fast asleep beneath a blanket. The blanket had slid off their shoulders, so, careful not to wake them, Greg lifted the blanket and placed a gentle kiss on Shania's head.

Other than having his leg in traction and an IV in his arm, Jonathan didn't look anywhere near as bad as Mother Washington had.

As he approached the bed, Jonathan's eyes fluttered open, and he stared at Greg.

Jonathan cleared his throat. "Hey, Mr. Greg."

"Jonathan." Greg held his bike helmet in his lap and took a seat in a chair that was already next to the bed. "How's Cheyenne?"

He motioned his hand in the direction of Cheyenne and Shania. "As you can see, her and her sister are knocked out sleep." Greg shifted in the chair. "Are you okay?"

Jonathan nodded his head and reached for the pitcher of water beside him. "I mean, it's not like this is the first time I been shot. At least this time the damage ain't as bad." He sipped some water, then cleared his throat again. "Thanks for coming to see me."

Greg chose his words carefully. "To be honest, Jonathan, I'm wondering, why am I here to see you? I mean, I know you got shot, but how did it come to this?"

Jonathan held up a hand to stop Greg. "Before you get started," he said, "let me let you know that your wife done already went ham on me. She called me every name but a child of God and didn't bite her tongue to let me know how she really felt about me. She thinks I'm no better than the trash that the dog dragged in."

Greg was silent as he waited for Jonathan to continue, because he felt in his spirit that there was more Jonathan needed to tell.

"When I was out in the projects, living an illegal lifestyle," he said, "I ain't have nobody to come talk to me and lead me to God. I was hanging with a bunch of dudes who was doing the same things I was doing—smoking, slanging, drinking, sniffing. Ain't nobody talk to me about God. Only time I heard God's name was when somebody got killed and the people on the street would say, 'He's in God's hands now.'" Jonathan cleared his throat and continued. "But I had this one homeboy. He went by the name of J-Dub. He used to always talk about how he wanted to get his life right 'cause he got twin girls to live for. Plus, he'd always talk about how he ain't wanna die and go to hell. So . . ." Jonathan shrugged his shoulder, then winced and gingerly placed a hand against his side.

"You all right?" Greg asked, ready to stand and call a nurse, if need be.

Jonathan waved for him to stay seated and took a few seconds to gather his bearings. Then he continued, "Me and Cheyenne, we came back down to the projects, looking for J-Dub. I was ministering to him about how God had changed me and how He could do the exact same thing for him, since God ain't a respecter of persons, you feel me?"

Greg nodded and didn't fight the smile that was inching across his face. "Yeah, I feel you, Jonathan."

"Well, anyways," he continued, "while we was over there, some people who J-Dub owed drug money to came over, demanding their money. J-Dub told them he ain't have it, so Cheyenne gave them everything she had on her, but it still wasn't enough. The dudes left. Then next thing we knew, *pow pow pow*," he said and turned his fingers into guns to mimic the gunshots. "I kept yelling for Cheyenne to get down, and I jumped on top of her. I was the only one who got hit." Jonathan gestured at his leg. "Bullet tore through my calf muscle." He motioned at his side. "Bullet tore through my side."

"Man," Greg said, amazed at the truth of what really happened, but even more amazed at this young man's courage to put himself in harm's way to bring a lost soul back to Christ. "I bet you're pissed, huh?"

"Pissed?" Jonathan frowned and shook his head. "Naw, man, I ain't pissed." He gestured at his leg again. "The gunshot to my leg wasn't nothing but a flesh wound." He gestured at his side. "Gunshot right here went slam through me. It ain't hit a single vital organ. Doc told me, 'Young man, you are very lucky.' I say, 'Naw, Doc. I ain't lucky. I'm blessed.'"

Greg looked at Jonathan, beaming, and he wished to God he could hug this young man. There was Shania in the bedroom, getting dressed, talking pure trash about this young man, and in all actuality, he could be considered a martyr. He had put his own life on the line to save just a single soul. He didn't know how much more Christlike someone could get than that.

"You know what?" Greg said, standing to his feet. "No matter what Shania says about you, you're all right in my book."

Being careful not to tear the wound in his side, Jonathan touched his fist to Greg's. "I appreciate that, man. But as long as I'm all right in God's book, that's all that matters."

Greg couldn't argue with that. He wondered if Shania would finally admit she was wrong about Jonathan and accept him into the family.

Fifteen

Shania sat in the living room, looking over the paperwork she had received from her doctor. She yawned. There was so much information that she thought her head was going to explode. She read about the first trimester of pregnancy and what to expect, foods to eat, and the importance of prenatal vitamins.

"Great," she said to no one in particular. "Nausea, dizziness, and frequent urination," she read.

Just seeing the word *urination* on the page made her bladder feel full, prompting her to get up and go to the bathroom—again. Shania swore she had to go pee every five minutes, but she didn't mind. All part of the journey toward motherhood, she reasoned.

She hurried up and washed her hands and dried them on a paper towel when she heard her phone ringing. She captured the call before her voice mail picked up. Rayna immediately chimed in, explaining that she was calling to see how Shania was doing.

Shania could hear her doctor's words replaying in her head. The doctor had told her that some people preferred to wait until after the first trimester before telling people about the baby. She understood the logic. The doctor had explained that about 80 percent of miscarriages occur in the first trimester. Even still, she didn't feel right keeping the news from the closest person to her besides Greg.

Convinced she'd pop like a balloon if she held the information in any longer, she blurted out, "'Cuz, you're not going to believe this." She imagined Rayna holding her breath, as she often did when waiting to hear news, whether good or bad. "I'm five weeks pregnant."

"Are you serious?" She didn't sound as surprised as Shania thought she would. "I kind of figured you were, considering how low tolerance you've been lately, combined with your frequent vomiting." Rayna laughed, then said what Shania had previously thought. "Just think...a few months ago you were a virgin. And now, you're about to be a mother. Congrats to you and Greg. Speaking of Greg, how's he feel about it? Is he excited?"

"Yeah, he's pretty excited, considering the circumstances. He went to the doctor with me this past Friday, and he was very supportive. When we went out for dinner yesterday, he talked about starting on the baby's room already." She worried her scalp with her fingers. "No sooner than we mellowed out from our emotional high, life came crashing down around us."

"What do you mean?" Rayna sounded concerned.

"Cheyenne called to tell me that Jonathan had been shot again."

She heard Rayna gasp. "Is he okay?"

"Yes. He had a flesh wound, and the other bullet went right through him. It didn't do any damage."

Exhaling, Rayna said, "Thank goodness."

"As if that wasn't enough, Mother Washington is suffering from a brain tumor."

"Mother Washington?" Rayna gasped again. "Isn't that the elderly lady who Greg checks up on all the time?"

"Yes, girl," Shania said, nodding. "That woman is like a second mother to him. He's actually over there at the hospital now. I wanted to go with him, but he wouldn't let me. He says I need my rest. He's been going through a lot lately, so make sure you keep him lifted up in prayer."

"You know I will."

She yawned again and apologized. "I had a long night."

Rayna said, "I can tell. You sound exhausted. Take care of my godbaby, and get some rest."

Shania loved the way Rayna had presumed she'd be the child's godmother. In Shania's mind, there was no other choice. Besides being family, Rayna was one person she could count on to carry out her wishes.

They ended the call, and Shania's eyelids felt heavy as they drooped over her eyes. She realized that with all the commotion, she hadn't told Cheyenne about the baby. Since she would be her child's aunt, Cheyenne had a right to know.

She reached for the phone but then hesitated with her fingers still outstretched. Guilt gnawed at her. The way she had gone off on Jonathan last night was completely uncalled for. As an active Christian, she knew better than to act like she had and to say the horribly hurtful things she had said. Overwhelming fear and anger had allowed her emotions to get the best of her. She'd felt guilty about how she had gone off on Jonathan, only to find out later that she had jammed her foot in her mouth.

Pride wouldn't let her apologize the night before. Knowing she couldn't put the phone call off any longer, she called her sister and waited for her to answer.

When she finally answered the call, Shania said, "How's he doing?"

"Sister, he's fine," Cheyenne said, and there was a smile in her voice. "The doctor is going to keep him for a few days to make sure his wounds don't get infected, and then he's free to go. I'm so thankful, sister, because this could've been a lot worse. God's hand of protection was all over us."

"Tell me about it!" Shania exclaimed. "Well, I'm glad to hear that he's doing better."

"Mmm-hmm," her sister said, and her tone was a little too chirpy.

A long pause extended between the two and Shania knew that Cheyenne was purposefully waiting for her to break the silence. "Okay," Shania finally breathed into the phone. "Okay," she said again. "I'm sorry."

"For?"

Shania rolled her eyes. "For assuming the worst and showing up at that hospital, acting like an ignorant fool. Sorry for disrespecting you and your husband, and sorry for embarrassing you."

"You didn't embarrass me," Cheyenne said with plenty of feistiness. "You embarrassed yourself."

"Yeah, well . . ." Shania shook her head and toyed with her bottom lip. "It's just . . . he wasn't my prime choice for you, Cheyenne, and you know it. I figured he was just with you for the money. A bad boy who had found a good girl. I thought his conversion was artificial. But considering last night, the only one who seems artificial is me."

Cheyenne sighed. "You're not artificial. You're human. Just like me and just like Jonathan. I mean, think about this. You've always felt the need to be in control, ever since our parents died in that car crash. It's understandable that you would feel that way, because the sudden death of our parents made you feel out of control. You stepped in, and you became like a mother to me, and I will forever appreciate that, sister. But you have to let me go and let me live life for myself and just know that if God never let you down, what makes you think He's going to let me down?"

"Wow," Shania said, nodding her head as she listened to her sister speak. "Powerful words of wisdom. I needed to hear that."

"I'm not mad at you, sister, and I still love you just as much as I always have."

Shania smiled. "Thank you, Cheyenne. I love you too."

Her intuition told her that even though she would still prefer for Cheyenne and Jonathan to wait on making a baby, the decision was ultimately theirs. In her heart, she believed that her sister was mature enough to live life in her own footsteps, despite the choices that Cheyenne made in her life. What better time than now to inform her sister that she and her husband were going to be an aunt and uncle?

"Before you hang up," Shania said quickly, "I have to tell you something."

"And what's that?"

Shania inhaled deeply, then exhaled. "I have a bean in my oven."

It took her sister only a few seconds to catch her meaning. "Awww, sister, I couldn't be happier. I'm going to be an auntie! I guess Jonathan can forgive you for how you flipped out on him in the car and at the hospital. That wasn't you. That was the baby talking." She burst out laughing.

The laughter must've been contagious, because Shania found herself laughing at her sister's silliness. Cheyenne had reacted exactly the way Shania had expected her to. They talked about motherhood and all the things that the baby would need. Cheyenne said she was trusting and believing in God that it would be a girl, because she wanted to go to the store and buy her a ton of pretty little pink dresses. They spent the next thirty minutes talking solely about the baby.

With her head jerking back and eyes straining to stay open, Shania resigned to the fact that she needed to take a nap and told Cheyenne that she'd talk to her later.

Not having enough energy to make it up the stairs and lie in her bed, Shania drifted off right there on the couch.

She wasn't sure how long she had been asleep when she felt Greg shaking her. She fluttered her eyelids and finally opened her eyes long enough to focus on his handsome face. Feeling a little disoriented, she took a moment to gain her composure.

"What?" she muttered, still trying to focus on him. For all her sleepless nights, for him to interrupt such good rest, he'd better have a reason of gold.

"I want you to see something I found," he said and kept shaking her until she finally sat up on the couch and glared at him with her red-veined eyes.

"Greg, I swear this better be good."

Battling with the sleep that continued to call her name, Shania plopped her feet on the floor and forced her body off the couch. She followed Greg to his office, wondering what in the world he was up to. He pulled back the computer chair and motioned for her to have a seat. She sat in the chair, then looked up at him.

"What is it?"

He pointed at the computer screen. "Read it."

Shania swiveled around and stared at the screen, her eyes quickly scanning the information. She clicked her tongue against the roof of her mouth and her eyebrows lifted while she read each line. Ms. Kristen Washington had quite an extensive history. She'd been evicted from her apartment and filed bankruptcy all in the span of one year.

"I paid to run a background check on her." He explained. Greg squatted beside her and read the information along with her.

Shania nibbled on her pointer nail and shook her head. "This is so sad," she whispered. "Do you really think she would go as far as to try to intentionally overdose her own mother?"

"Yes, I do," Greg said, reaching around her to move the mouse. He minimized the screen they were looking at and pulled up a different screen. One read: "Inmate Offender Search" in big bold letters. Greg pointed at Kristen's offender profile. "She served four months in county for an aggravated assault conviction. So no, I wouldn't put it past her."

"Wow, Greg," Shania said, leaning back in the chair. "You really did your homework."

"Babe," he said, taking one of her hands in his, "if Mother makes it through—which I still think she can because God is a healer—then I want her to come live with us forever. As long as Kristen's around, she will never be safe."

His concern for Mother Washington touched her deeply. She kissed his temple and said, "If that's what you feel we need to do, then it's fine with me."

"Thank you, Shania."

Even as he offered her his thanks, her heart went out to him. Deep down inside, she knew that Mother Washington's time here on earth was coming to an end. Mother Washington was like a flickering candle that had burnt down to the wick. She'd lived her life, made her accomplishments, and made her mistakes. Now it was time for her to shed her old building for her mansion in the sky.

Even though Shania had fixed up the guest room and made it warm and inviting, she had done it more so for

Greg than Mother Washington. However, unwilling
to dampen her husband's hope and optimism about
Mother's health, she encouraged him and upheld his
convictions.

Greg stood and said, "Have you talked to Cheyenne?"

Shania turned in the swivel chair to face her husband
and nodded. "Yeah, I talked to her. I told her we are
pregnant."

"Yeah, but did you tell her you were sorry?"

His words hit home, convicting her even more than
the Holy Spirit already had. "Yes, Greg," she said, donning a very sober expression. "I apologized to her."

"Did you apologize to him?"

She cocked an eyebrow, then lowered it slowly. "No,
not yet, but I plan to."

"Good," Greg said and reached around her to close
out of the programs. "It seems like every time something happens in your sister's life, you lose your head."

"No, I don't—"

"Yes, you do, babe," he said, nodding emphatically.
"What about the time when they ran away and eloped?
Cheyenne had kept it a secret until Jonathan got shot
the first time, and you almost killed yourself. Literally.
I had to wake you up with smelling salt."

She leaned back in her chair and stared at him as she
reflected on the day that Cheyenne had told her that
her last name had changed.

Cheyenne had just finished telling Shania about an
argument Jonathan and another guy had outside of the
movie theater. The guy followed Jonathan and Cheyenne back to Jonathan's grandmother's house and shot
Jonathan.

That wasn't all. She then admitted that she and Jonathan had eloped. An invisible vacuum had sucked the air out of the room. Shania had felt as though she couldn't breathe. She had to get out of there. She got up from the couch without saying a word and sprinted to her bedroom faster than South African teenager Caster Semenya during the world championships.

"Shania, come here!" her sister had called out after her.

But Shania ignored her and continued running until she was in her bedroom with the door shut firmly behind her. An anxiety attack threatened to consume her. She felt the same way she'd felt that day when her phone had rung and she'd answered, only to find out that her parents had been wiped out of her life forever.

Without notice, Shania bellowed a gut-wrenching scream, and the sound echoed off the walls, mimicking her, taunting her. Her soul ached, and she felt a migraine coming on. As she held her head, her knees buckled. Next thing she knew, she was sprawled out in the middle of the floor, crying.

The hinges squeaked as the door opened, and she didn't have to look up to know that Cheyenne was standing in the doorway. She figured she must've looked like a two-year-old throwing a temper tantrum, but she didn't care. She felt as if someone had sucker punched her in the gut and stabbed her in the heart.

She felt Cheyenne's hands on her shoulders and she shrugged away her sister's touch. "Sister, please! Calm down. Pull yourself together," Cheyenne had pleaded. "Why are you acting like this?"

"Leave me alone, Cheyenne! How could you do this to me?" she had cried. "Just get out!"

"To you?" For a moment, Cheyenne stood there, looking dazed and confused. "I didn't do anything to you. I did something for me. And you're supposed to be happy for me."

Shania stopped rolling around on the floor and said, "Didn't I tell you to leave me alone? Why are you still here? Get out!"

Cheyenne opened her mouth as if she wanted to say something, but nothing came out. She turned and walked away, leaving Shania to wallow in her misery.

The look of pain on her sister's face made her want to run after her, but she was so disappointed in Cheyenne that she couldn't stand to be around her. There was no telling what she might have said. So instead of chasing her sister down, Shania remained on the floor, crying and weeping until she found strength enough to pull herself to her feet.

She went into the bathroom and splashed cold water on her face. When she looked into the mirror, she didn't recognize the person staring back at her. Her eyes looked like they had been doused with hot sauce. She had an intense headache, and she could see the veins pulsating at her temple. The thought crossed her mind to call Greg and tell him what happened in hopes that he could make sense out of the entire situation, but all she wanted to do was sleep and get rid of her headache. She pat dried her face with a hand towel, then searched her medicine cabinet until she found a bottle of Tylenol PM. Two handfuls of sink water helped ease the pills down her throat.

While waiting for the pills to take effect, Shania crawled into her bed without even bothering to take off her clothes. Pulling the covers over her head, she closed her eyes. Just as quickly as the hot tears escaped, she wiped them away. She continued to do that until she fell asleep.

It seemed like she had only been asleep for a few hours when she felt someone shaking her so hard, it almost gave her whiplash.

"Shania, wake up!" Greg had said as he continued to shake her like a rag doll. "What did you do? What did you do?" he repeated.

"Greg?" she said groggily as she tried to awaken from her deep sleep. At first, she had thought she was dreaming.

He pulled her close to his body, hugging her tightly. "Thank God you're all right. I was so worried about you."

She rubbed the sleep from her eyes and covered her mouth as she yawned. The smell of her breath made her turn her head when she spoke. She didn't want Greg to catch a whiff of it. "What are you doing here? What time is it?"

She looked at the clock, which read 6:30 P.M. Doing a quick mental calculation, she figured that she must've been asleep for two hours. As her brain finally caught up with her body, she remembered the falling-out that she and Cheyenne had, and she felt her blood boil and her head begin to ache all over again.

"What are you trying to do, kill yourself?"

Shocked by his statement, Shania stared up at him, a deep crease lining her forehead. "Greg, are you crazy? What in the world are you talking about?"

"Do you know how long you've been asleep?"

For the life of her, she couldn't figure out why he was so angry, or why he was yelling at her with such intensity. She glanced at the clock again to make sure she had read the time right.

"Yeah, for two hours, roughly. What's the big deal?"

He frowned at her. "What did you take, Shania?"

"Why?"

"Why?" he repeated. His eyes were bulging, and there was a vein popping out right in the middle of his forehead. "You haven't been sleep for two hours. You've slept for an entire day."

Shania's jaw dropped, and she glanced at the clock again, trying to make sense of the situation. How in the world could she have managed to sleep for an entire day? Then she smacked her forehead with the palm of her hand, remembering that a while ago, she had put sleeping pills in her empty Tylenol bottle. If that was the case, she definitely would've been asleep longer than a couple of hours. Somehow the fact that she had fallen asleep in the evening and the fact that it was the evening again threw her for a loop.

"Oh my God." As she realized that she could've overdosed and badly hurt herself, she started to cry. She had been so distraught by Cheyenne's announcement that she hadn't paid attention to what she was doing. "I accidentally took sleeping pills."

"Yeah, well, you could've killed yourself," he reprimanded her, wagging his index finger. "I called you last night, and Cheyenne told me you were sleeping. When you didn't call me back, I got worried. I came over to check on you, but you were still sleeping. We decided to let you get some rest. Your sister told me you were upset, but she didn't tell me why. So, I left and called you first thing this morning, and you were *still* sleeping. But when Cheyenne called me and told me that she tried to wake you up, but you wouldn't budge, babe, I thought you were dead."

The anger in his face dissolved, and she stared into the eyes of a man who had been tortured by his thoughts, expecting to barge into her home only to find the worst.

She reached out and held his cheek. "I'm sorry. I didn't mean to scare you like that."

He turned his face in her hand and nuzzled her palm. "The only thing that stopped your sister from calling an ambulance was the fact that you had a normal pulse. I left work early to come straight over here. God, I'm so glad you're okay."

He held her close and kissed her until her lips were sore.

Once he stopped kissing her, Shania sniffed and wiped her nose. "Where's Cheyenne?"

"She went to the hospital to visit Jonathan. She hasn't been gone that long. I promised to call her to let her know how you're doing. What's going on with you?"

She extended her arms. "Come here. I need a hug."

He sat back down and held her. "Talk to me." He softened his tone.

"I don't even know where to begin."

He tucked a piece of hair behind her ear. "Try the beginning."

Shania inhaled deeply, then exhaled toward the ceiling. "I'm emotionally tired, Greg." She lowered her head to his chest. "I hate to admit this, but a part of me is tired of loving Cheyenne."

"Don't say that. She's your sister, and you love her."

"That's the problem. I love her, but I'm not sure she loves me." Shania raised her head off his chest and looked at him. "You know how disappointed I was when she dropped out of college. And now"—she shook her head—"she ran off and eloped. Our parents are probably flipping in their graves."

"What? She married Jonathan?" He massaged his temple.

"That's why I was so upset. I feel so betrayed by her. She's been making bad decisions for a long time now, and I just . . . I just . . ." Shania scooted back on the bed until she felt her back press against the headboard. She then folded her legs and wrapped her arms around them. "I'm hurt that Cheyenne acts without any regard for anybody else. She's so self-absorbed."

Greg moved on the bed until he was sitting beside her and he laced his fingers through hers. "I understand how you feel, babe. And I agree with you. I think she's too young for marriage." He tightened his hand around hers. "But she's grown, Shania, so you have to let her learn and grow and make her own mistakes. Their union doesn't necessarily have to be a mistake. It doesn't have to be the end of the world. You could look at this from a different perspective."

"How so?" She tilted her head and gave him her full attention.

"You raised her with morals and values." He wrapped his arm around her shoulder. "Through the years, you've been a great role model for her. Maybe seeing you so happy and in love has made her want it for herself. Be thankful that she's not acting like a lot of girls her age. Your sister actually holds the institution of marriage in high esteem. Marriage is honorable in the eyes of God. At least she's not being promiscuous."

Shania rubbed her fingers across her lips, then finally nodded. "You're right, Greg. It's just that I thought she would've finished college, fell in love with someone who had . . . who had *something* going for himself. And then got married, later. Much, much later."

"Yes, Shania. That's what you wanted. That was *your* plan for *her* life. This is her life. Let her live it."

"I don't have a problem with letting her live." She didn't mean to sound defensive, but she was. "My problem with both of them is that they don't have their priorities set. He dropped out of high school and she dropped out of college. That tells me that neither one of them has the commitment to finish what they start. Neither one of them has a job, so how are they going to live? They've got another thing coming if they think they're going to live here with me."

"If they both get jobs, you could help them get an apartment."

"I could do that. But I still think Cheyenne has made things more difficult than they need to be. Her husband has a criminal record and no education. What kind of job is he going to be able to get?"

Greg sighed, released her hand, and stood up. "You know what? It's not for us to worry about. The best thing we can do is pray for them. Pray that he becomes the best husband he can be and that she becomes a wonderful wife. Instead of discouraging them, we need to support them."

"Support them?" Shania couldn't force her mind to comprehend the concept. She turned up her nose.

"Don't turn your nose up at me," he said. "I'm serious. I know you don't want to hear this, but lots of people get married young. Not all of those marriages end in divorce, either."

"Okay." She uncurled her legs and stretched out across the bed. "We can do things your way. But what happens when she pops up pregnant?"

"We'll cross that bridge when we get to it," he sighed.

Shania got out of bed and gave him a hug. "I'm about to freshen up. Would you wait for me downstairs?"

"Sure. You want to order a pizza?"

She smiled. "That sounds good. I'm famished."

"You should be, Sleeping Beauty."

Shania laughed. "Would you order it, please?"

"Yes." He left and closed the door behind him.

That's when Shania had first come to realize that she needed to get a grip. Worrying about Cheyenne had never helped anybody, especially since she never seemed to be worried about herself. Not to mention the fact she was a grown woman. Shania had already raised her. Her job was done. Although it still stung at times, she had to admit that Greg had been right all along. She had to let go of her little sister.

Shania shifted her thoughts back to the present and noticed that Greg had left her sitting alone in his office. She licked her dry lips and got up to pour herself a glass of water, then went in search of her husband. She found him in the media room, on the phone with their pastor. She quietly returned to the living room, picked up her phone, dialed the number, and listened to the phone ring.

She cleared her throat when the operator answered. She then asked for Jonathan's room. Shaking her leg and nibbling on her nails, she waited for the call to connect.

"Hello?"

Shania inhaled. It was now or never. "Jonathan?"

"Yes, ma'am, Ms. Shania?" His voice changed, and she could almost picture him trying to sit a little straighter in bed.

"How're you feeling?"

"Okay, I guess." He let out a nervous chuckle. "Just ready to get out of here and go home."

"I bet so." She exhaled, then took a deep, steadying breath before saying, "Jonathan, I want to apologize for how I acted the other night. I was completely out of line, and there is no excuse for my behavior. I've already apologized to Cheyenne, so now I'm offering an apology to you. Will you please forgive me?"

She held her breath while she waited for him to respond, and, boy, did he take his sweet time in responding.

"Ms. Shania," he finally said, and his voice sounded heavy and serious, "I will forgive you under one condition."

She cocked her eyebrow and frowned. "And what's that?"

"I will forgive you if you allow me to love your sister and give her my whole heart for the rest of my life."

His words filled her throat with tears, and she'd never felt so humbled before in her life. She was so overcome with emotion, she wasn't sure if she could speak. Finally, she nodded her head and choked out, "It's a deal."

After Shania ended the call, she felt a hundred pounds lighter—even though she knew with her appetite as of late, she would be putting on a few pounds soon. She went in search of her husband. Thankfully, he was off the phone. She bribed him with some loving in exchange for him to go on a treasure hunt for a plate of fast food that her stomach could actually hold down. He protested at first, but when she finished pleasing him, he slouched in his chair, let out a content sigh, and said, "Make sure it's not greasy, right?"

She grinned and replied, "That's right."

Alone with her thoughts, she reflected on her conversation with Jonathan. He had sounded so mature. She wished she could get a good read of him. Was he for real? Was he sincere? Did he really love her sister? Only time would tell.

Sixteen

Greg got on his bike and went on the impossible mission of finding food that wasn't greasy or smelly. That alone ruled out most fast-food restaurants. He passed by an establishment that he knew served delicious grilled chicken salads that Shania loved, so he parked his bike and went inside. He ordered a salad for Shania, and the smell of chicken influenced his decision to order hot wings for himself. He drove home quickly, hoping the food would still be piping hot when he got there.

He pulled into his driveway and went inside to find Shania stretching and yawning on the couch. She glanced at him and turned her yawn into a smile when she spotted the bags. He could tell that she must've been pleased by his food choices.

He sat the bags next to her on the sofa while he went into the pantry to get two serving trays for them to place their food on. When he returned, Shania had already removed her large salad from the bag. He extended the legs of the trays and placed one in front of Shania. Removing the clear plastic lid covering the salad, she poured honey mustard dressing on top.

"Glad you remembered to tell them to hold the fried onions," she said as she mixed the chicken strips, lettuce, and dressing.

He bit into a spicy wing, savoring the delicious food while he listened to her chat about apologizing to Jonathan, then about the couple who had called, asking her to cater their wedding.

While Shania was talking, Greg's cell phone rang loud and shrill.

"Go ahead and answer it," she said.

Greg nodded his thanks, licked the tips of his fingers, and wiped them off with a napkin. He retrieved the phone from his pocket, and when he saw that it was his pastor calling, he frowned. They had just gotten off the phone less than an hour ago. Why was he calling back so soon? Frowning, he answered the call.

He tilted his head back and stared at the high ceiling when he heard his pastor say that the tumor in Mother Washington's brain ruptured, and the doctors couldn't stop the bleeding. Mother Washington had died, and he wanted Greg to perform the eulogy.

Something collapsed on the inside of him and the spicy chicken he had placed in his mouth suddenly tasted like a piece of salted cardboard. He spit the chicken into a napkin and wiped the taste off his tongue. On the inside, he felt cold and sterile, only able to mutter the words "I gotta go." Then he hung up the phone.

"What's the matter?" Shania asked.

Unable to speak, Greg got up and went upstairs, where he got on his knees in prayer. While he prayed, his eyes emptied a bucket of tears down his face. With the back of his hand, he hurried and wiped his damp skin. He didn't like to cry, especially not around other people, because he thought it showed weakness.

Knowing that Shania must've been wondering what was going on with him, Greg went back downstairs to give her an explanation.

In the family room, Greg skimmed the familiar art-work, wedding portraits, and oddments, absorbing all that meant home and family. Rubbing his moist hands over his denim-covered thighs, Greg broke the news about Mother Washington to Shania.

Shania stopped eating and stared at him. Her eyes glistened with tears as she spoke. "Greg, I'm so sorry." She reached for him, but he shook his head. Frowning, she retracted her arms. "What happened?" she asked, and her voice cracked.

He lowered his body onto the couch and wrapped his arms around himself. "According to Pastor, the tumor in her brain ruptured."

She touched his shoulder. "Are you okay?"

Biting his lower lip, Greg nodded his head.

"I think we should pray," Shania suggested.

"I already did—"

"I mean together."

She reached out to him, and he stared at her hand as seconds ticked by. Finally, he slipped his hand into hers and took a deep breath, trying to accept that Mother Washington was gone. He then released the air in a slow drag, as if he were blowing out cigarette smoke. He lowered his eyelids and prayed out loud.

Still feeling a bit unsettled after the prayer, Greg told Shania that he wanted to go ride his bike to help clear his mind. The chicken wings had lost their appeal, but apparently Shania hadn't lost her appetite, because she devoured her salad and his wings too.

Outside, Greg looked at the light blue sky with willowy clouds and wondered if Mother Washington's soul had ascended to heaven. He checked his watch, and the time read 6:00 P.M. He figured that he could ride for an hour and still be back before darkness fell.

As he rode along the open road, he thought about the first time he had met Mother Washington. The church had decided to have a program honoring the church mothers. The purpose of the program was to give people their flowers while they were still living, rather than waiting until they were dead and gone to shower them with gifts and love. Pastor Ray had made a point of letting all ten elderly women know how important they were to the church, their families, and the community.

Mother Washington stood out from the bunch in her colorful suit and wisecracking antics. It seemed like every time she opened her mouth, wisdom laced with humor poured out. He'd miss her sense of humor even more than her radiant smile and the way she called him "suga."

Even though rumors about her late husband and estranged daughters had definitely followed Mother, he had never given much ear to them. In the words of Franklin, haters were gonna follow you wherever you went. And for Mother Washington to be such a lovable, giving, selfless woman, it could only be expected that she was going to have people who hated on her. If they hated on Jesus, who did no wrong, how could anyone on earth expect to be exempt from it?

Greg surprised himself at how hard Mother Washington's death had hit him. He knew that he cared about her and that they shared a close bond, but he didn't think losing her would hurt so much.

Tears blurred his vision, and he decided that it was time for him to go back home. He thought about calling Franklin but decided not to. As of late, he and Franklin had been spending less and less time together. But Greg wasn't jealous. He was actually happy that his friend had finally found such positive companionship in a woman. And he knew that Kaiya had to be taking Mother Washington's death just as hard as him, if not more so. There was no doubt in his mind that Franklin was doing his best to comfort Kaiya in her time of need.

With a horde of thoughts bouncing off of each other in his mind, Greg veered off to the nearest exit, intending to turn around. A car honked, catching his attention. He realized that he had clipped the other driver, and he could tell by the obscene gesture that the guy had given him that he wasn't happy about it.

Greg realized that he needed to hurry up and get off the road. Careless mistakes caused accidents and he needed to get his mind right. The realization that he could've been hit made his heart beat a tattoo onto his chest. His faith made him believe that he'd see Mother Washington again someday, but he didn't want that day to be today.

Seventeen

Five days had passed since the death of Mother Washington, and the funeral services were being held this rainy Saturday afternoon. Shania remembered that it had rained the day of her parents' funeral services too. As a little girl she had heard that rain on the day of a funeral meant that the heavens were weeping.

A gloomy cloud hovered over her all morning. She hated attending funerals. After the death of her parents, she stopped going to funerals. The only reason she was attending this one was to support Greg.

Dressed in all black, Shania slicked her hair back into a neat bun. She blotted some pressed powder on her face, applied a thin line of liquid eyeliner on her top lid, and smeared a coat of lip gloss on her full lips. Then she turned sideways in the mirror, trying to determine if the dress she was wearing made her look fat. She decided that it did, so she ditched it in favor of a dress that cinched just below her breasts, making her waist look smaller than it really was.

Her stomach grumbled, reminding her that she hadn't eaten since the night before. Realizing that she couldn't make it through the morning without putting some food in her belly, she decided to fix some breakfast. First, though, she went down the hall to Greg's office to check on him and find out if he wanted anything to eat.

She stood in the doorway, looking at Greg as he read the Bible. With the book resting on his lap, he looked up at Shania.

"How're you feeling this morning?" she asked. "You didn't get a wink of sleep last night."

"I know I didn't." He closed the Bible and scratched the back of his head. "But I'm all right. Just trying to get mentally prepared to speak at the funeral."

Her heart went out to him. "Are you hungry?"

He placed the Bible on his desk and stood up, smoothing the wrinkles from his dark slacks. "I don't have much of an appetite. I'll eat later. You already know there's going to be a dump load of soul food at the reception." He got close enough to hug her and continued. "I know this must be hard for you." He kissed the top of her head. "If you don't want to go, I understand. I wouldn't be mad if you stayed home and got some rest."

She shook her head while he spoke, then leaned on her tiptoes and pressed a kiss against his lips. "I'm going, honey. As much as I hate funerals, there's no way that I'd let you go through this ordeal alone." She tucked her hand in his and gave it a squeeze. "We're a team."

He nodded his head and looked off to the side, as though he had something on his mind. "Yeah," he said, nodding, "we are a team." He kissed her forehead again. "Thanks in advance for making this sacrifice."

The sound of thunder caused Shania to jump, and she tried to laugh away her nervousness. Greg soothed her by rubbing his hands up and down her back. Being with him brought her a sense of comfort that she couldn't explain. She thought about all the times he had been there for her, like when her sister eloped, or both times Jonathan got shot. The least she could do was to be there for him during this difficult time. She knew how much Mother Washington meant to him, and Mother Washington meant a lot to her too. She'd never forgive herself if she didn't go and pay her final respects.

They cut their tender moment short, realizing that they were on limited time. They went into the kitchen, where Shania fixed a light breakfast consisting of mixed fruit and cereal. She was surprised when the food actually stayed down. Each of them appeared to be consumed with their own thoughts, so they didn't talk much while she ate.

At 11:00 A.M., Greg drove them to the church. When they arrived, the parking lot was already full. Had it not been for his reserved space in front of the church, they would've had to park across the street on the grass.

"A lot of people cared about Mother Washington," Greg commented as he parked.

Shania smirked, hoping that this wouldn't be a drama-filled event like so many funerals she had heard about. She wasn't up for any of the nonsense. She'd heard the rumors about Mother Washington's late husband being a pervert, and the thousands of rumors about why Mother Washington had *really* left her previous church. Whether the rumors were true or not, she could care less. She just prayed to God that no one showed up at the funeral acting ignorant and foolish.

Greg helped Shania out of the car before removing his jacket from a hanger in the backseat and putting it on. Luckily, the rain had cooled the temperature a bit and reduced the humidity. However, there was still a slightly sticky feel to the air, and the scent of wet earth was strong.

Shania removed her Jackie O–inspired sunglasses from her purse and secured them on the bridge of her nose. She looked up at the dark gray sky and saw clouds drifting slowly across the celestial sphere. She prayed that the dark clouds would stay over in the far corner of the sky until the burial services were over. Silently praying for strength for her husband and herself, she interlocked her fingers with Greg's and strolled into the building.

Nearly everyone wore black. There were a handful of people dressed in cream or white. The hushed tones in which people spoke sounded almost like bees buzzing around Shania's ears. She looked around into the many faces of the men and women in attendance, and solemn expressions covered their faces like masks.

When the youth from church saw Greg, they called his name and waved, only to be hushed and silenced by their parents. Greg waved back at them, then put a finger to his lips and gave them a wink. Shania smiled inwardly. If he was this great with kids, she had no doubt that being an excellent father would be a breeze.

Leading Shania by the hand, Greg escorted her down the center aisle and to the third pew. A 12 x 18 framed picture of Mother Washington looking quite regal sat propped up on a display stand next to her closed casket, surrounded by red roses and greenery. In the photo, she was proudly displaying the perfect white, pink-gummed dentures that she never, ever wore. It almost seemed as though her eyes were looking directly at Shania's. Shania squinted at the picture and gasped, then rubbed her eyes with both her fists. Either her eyes were playing tricks on her, or Mother Washington had just winked at her.

Greg looked at her, frowning. "You okay?"

Shania wanted to say, "No, I'm not okay. That woman just winked at me in her picture." But she didn't want her husband to think that she'd tripped over the deep end, so she simply smiled and said, "I'm fine. Perfectly fine."

Greg and Shania talked amongst themselves for several minutes, until Greg looked up and spotted Franklin and Kaiya. He waved them over.

Franklin looked dashing in his black three-piece suit with the periwinkle vest and matching tie. For once, he actually looked and acted very mature. He had Kaiya's hand tucked in the crook of his arm, and she looked like pure elegance in her all-black dress with a pair of spiked heels that strapped across her toes and thin ankles.

Franklin hugged Shania first, then gave Greg a hug and a hard thud on the back. "You straight?"

"I'm straight." Greg nodded.

"You sure?"

Greg nodded again. "With God's help, I'm going to make it through this."

"You look stunning, Kaiya," Shania said and watched as the young lady blushed and politely thanked her for her compliment. "And you, Mr. Franklin," Shania said, reaching over to straighten his tie just a bit, "finally look like a real man."

"And you, Ms. Shania," he replied, tapping the space just below her nose but just above her top lip, "finally look like a real man too."

Shania didn't get it at first, but when she realized what he was talking about, she elbowed him in the side, hard enough to make him double over. Her punch forced a groan and a rush of air out of him. They got a few reprimanding stares, and she whispered an apology to the attendees as she glared at Franklin. Self-consciously, she fingered the space above her top lip, then leaned over and whispered in Greg's ear, "Do I really have a moustache?"

Greg chuckled and shook his head. "Franklin's just being the goof that he is."

Shania rolled her eyes at him, then spoke quietly with Kaiya while Franklin and Greg spoke quietly as well. A few minutes later, she glanced at the back of the church and noted the time. She hated to interrupt them, but she shook Greg's arm and said in a low voice, "Honey, we need to take our seats. Service is about to start."

Franklin sat right beside Kaiya, Mother Washington's nieces, nephews, two sisters, and three brothers. Shania and Greg parted ways with them and found empty seats on the second row.

As soon as Shania took a seat, nausea washed over her and the light breakfast that she'd eaten bubbled in her belly. "I think I need to go to the bathroom."

"You need me to go with you?" Greg offered.

"No." She shook her head, and just as she felt her breakfast rising in her throat, she held a hand over her mouth and took off running to the ladies' room. On the way to the restroom, she passed by Kristen, who she immediately remembered from Mother Washington's house, but she didn't have time to worry herself about the woman dressed in a skintight, low-cut dress. With her hand still in place, she rushed through the bathroom doors and missed the toilet by a long shot. Thankfully, she didn't get any chunks on her clothes.

A woman occupied the stall beside her, and when the woman exited the stall, Shania noticed she was holding a belly that had to be about seven or eight months with child.

"First trimester?" the pregnant woman asked.

Shania nodded her head before rinsing out her mouth.

"Is this your first?"

Again, Shania nodded and wiped her mouth with a paper towel. "If I have to deal with this for the whole nine months, you best believe that this'll be the last."

The woman laughed. "It'll get better, I promise. The first trimester is the worst. After you get past the morning sickness, then you'll only have to worry about urinating every two to three seconds." They shared a laugh. Then the woman tiptoed around her vomit and said, "I'll go talk to the ushers—see if they can find someone to clean this up."

"Thank you so much," Shania whispered.

After pulling herself together, she returned to her seat and popped a piece of gum in her mouth before turning to face her husband. With his eyes, he asked her if she was all right. She nodded, and he wrapped his arm around her shoulders.

Pastor Ray stood in front of the sanctuary dressed in his long robe, and he greeted the people. He then said a touching prayer before talking about the cycle of life. Shania could hear sniffles all around her.

After saying some wonderful words about Mother Washington's character, Pastor Ray introduced a soloist who sang "Amazing Grace." Shania felt herself getting choked up. That song always moved her emotionally. It was the same song that they had played at her parents' funeral, during the final viewing of the bodies.

An usher standing in the aisle handed her a couple of tissues, and she dabbed her face and eyes. At the end of the song, the pastor commented about the lovely selection and called on Greg to say the eulogy.

Greg adjusted his dark tie. He didn't exude nervousness, but Shania sensed it, anyway. Even still she felt confident in his abilities. He always did an excellent job whenever he spoke on youth Sundays, so she knew he'd do an excellent job now.

Over the past three days, he had worked hard on
the short biography, and Shania had no doubt in her
mind that his diligence would pay off and make Mother
Washington proud. She gave him a reassuring smile.

Greg took his position behind the podium and spoke
into the microphone. "Mother Washington was one of
a kind. From the first day that she started coming to
this church, she called me son, and had been calling me
that ever since. And when she wasn't calling me son,
she was the only one other than my mama who called
me by my full name." He chuckled, and the congregation laughed with him. He then talked about when and
where Mother Washington was born, where she was
raised, her nursing career, her community service, and
various parts of her life—up until her last days.

"On the days when it gets difficult to accept her ab-
sence in your life . . ." Greg said and stopped a minute
to gather his composure. He blinked rapidly, then
looked out at the congregation, and his chin quivered.
"Remember this. Mother Washington told me that she
was ready to go home. God didn't take her. She left.
Willingly. Furthermore, she told me on repeated occasions that there was no need for me to worry about her,
because she was in good hands, and it was well with
her soul."

Applause followed him to his seat, and an usher
stuffed a handful of tissues in his hand as he stepped
from the pulpit.

Shania thought he did a great job, in spite of the fact
that his voice cracked, and there were times when she
wasn't sure if he'd be able to finish. Regardless, his
cheeks remained dry, though Shania didn't think that
they would.

Greg folded his notes and placed them back in his
jacket pocket, then joined Shania on the pew. She gen-

tly squeezed his hand and glanced at him, as if to say, "Good job." Grinning back at her, he lifted her hand to his lips and placed a soft kiss on the back of her hand.

The services ended, and Shania and Greg followed the procession to the grave site. As they drove to the cemetery, Shania found herself feeling light-headed and faint. Her stomach heaved yet again, and she sat with her arms wrapped around her waist, praying that she didn't throw up in Greg's Mercedes.

At the grave site, she contemplated staying in the car and watching from a distance until she saw the solemn look on Greg's face. The magnitude of the situation must have finally settled over him like arthritis in joints. She knew that she couldn't leave him hanging. Willing her stomach to obey, she patted her belly, massaged her temples, then forced herself out of the car.

Shania and Greg trekked across the grassy field with Shania's two-inch heels leaving small holes in the wet soil. An overcast threatened to pour down on their heads at any moment. Shania gripped Greg's arm as they approached the tent and slowed down, waiting for the immediate family members to take their seats.

As Shania watched the pallbearers carry the shiny coffin from the hearse, she thought about the seasons of life. In particular, she meditated on Ecclesiastes 3:1–2, which states: *To everything there is a season, and a time to every purpose under the heaven: A time to be born, and a time to die; a time to plant, and a time to pluck up that which is planted....*

Shania understood that just as there are seasons, spring, summer, fall, and winter, there are seasons of life. She equated a "time to be born" with the spring of one's life. That's the time when people need proper training so that they can learn who they are and how they fit in.

She figured that "a time to plant" must be the summertime, when people get out of school, find a job, get married, and raise a family. Not necessarily in that order, but still during that season.

"A time to pluck up" has to do with harvesting the resources that have been planted. Harvest times occur in the autumn of one's life.

Ultimately, there's "a time to die." In the winter of one's life cycle, material things no longer matter. Death is the end of the road, the path that leads to eternal life.

Shania sniffled. No matter how much logical sense it made, that still didn't stop the pain of losing a loved one. She thought about her parents every day of her life. Although the pain had lessened over the years and she no longer felt like curling up and dying, there was still a tiny spot in her heart that harbored a sadness that just wouldn't go away.

She had done all of the spiritual things that she knew how to do: pray, read the Bible, meditate, and go to church; yet none of that stopped the hopelessness and depression she felt for so long. Many times the pain had become so unbearable that she thought about committing suicide and ending it all.

Two things stopped her: the fact that her life wasn't hers to take, and her love for Cheyenne and the rest of her family. She understood that she was a child of God. Because she didn't create her life, it wasn't hers to take. If she had killed herself, she believed that she would never see her parents again, anyway. She'd spend all eternity either in purgatory or in hell, but not in heaven, where she believed her parents had gone.

She also knew how devastated her family would've been if she had done such a selfish act. Plus, Cheyenne probably never would've forgiven her, or gotten over that.

Shania thanked God for godly counsel too. She had gone to visit a therapist for one full year to help her through the grieving process. Being able to talk through her struggles helped her to move on and stop being angry with God. Somehow admitting that she had been angry with God almost seemed blasphemous to Shania. Who was she to be angry with Him? she often wondered. Over time she came to realize that her rage was eating her up inside. Once she let go of the anger, she was able to begin the healing process.

A lone raindrop landed on her left shoulder, causing her to look up at the gray sky with scattered white clouds. The dark clouds from earlier had escaped their corner and now hovered directly over the burial tent. She wondered if that was a sign. A sign of what, she had no idea.

Shania observed the people gathering around the open grave site and thought about how sad they looked at that moment. Although they may have been grief-stricken, Shania understood that their lives would go on. In a week or two, the shock would wear off, the pain would cease, and Mother Washington would be on her way to becoming a distant memory to everyone, except her daughters and the people who truly loved her the most.

Shania snapped out of her reflective state when she heard a loud, gut-wrenching bellow. She exchanged confused glances with Greg before focusing her attention on Kristen, who had draped her curvaceous figure across her mother's casket.

"Lord, no!" Kristen cried. "Not my momma." She kicked off her high-heeled shoe and struggled to adjust her body on the slippery surface.

If looks could kill, the expression on Greg's face would've buried her in the same freshly dug hole with her "momma." He hurried to the front of the crowd and motioned for a few of the deacons to get her off the casket. A guy standing at least six feet and five inches tall pulled Kristen off the casket, and her sister tried to console her as Kristen buried her face in her shoulder and sobbed.

Kristen must've set off a chain reaction, because not long afterward, many people broke down, falling on their knees, shouting, even running. Shania had never seen anything like it. She stood there speechless.

Pastor Ray tried to regain some order by sharing a few encouraging words and letting everyone know that Mother Washington had gone on to a better place. He explained that death was a part of life. No one could escape it. He went on to say that life was like parentheses. He compared the first parenthesis to being born. The sentence in the middle was life and the end parenthesis was death. Shania liked that analogy.

People seemed to calm down a bit aside from a few random sniffles. Kristen had stopped showing out and sat down, thank God, and folded her hands on her lap. For the life of her, Shania couldn't understand why someone would want to wear such provocative clothing to church—especially to a funeral.

When Pastor Ray had finished speaking and uttered the words "ashes to ashes, dust to dust," the pallbearers lowered the casket into the ground. As they turned the crank, it started to drizzle. Shania wanted to hurry up and get out of the elements before an outpouring occurred. She nudged Greg and raised her brows, indicating that it was time to go. He nodded and raised his index finger.

Shania's patience grew thin. Her umbrella was in the car, and in her fragile state, she didn't want to get soaked and catch a cold. It wasn't just her health she was putting at risk. However, she clenched her jaw to keep from saying something sarcastic.

Not even a minute later, the rain poured down in sheets, and thunder and lightning rattled Shania's nerves. People took off running to their cars like a stampede. Women were hollering, and some people were slipping and sliding. Shania wanted to laugh so bad that her side hurt.

Just when she thought she couldn't take any more, a huge crack of lightning lit the sky, followed by deafening thunder. A lightning bolt bounced off the metal on the casket and struck Kristen and two other mourners. The explosive sound nearly stopped Shania's heart and hurt her ears.

Kaiya's face twisted when she saw that her sister lay twitching on the ground, and she started screaming.

In shock, Shania stood there staring. For some reason her brain wouldn't register that three people had just been struck by lightning. She had heard about people being struck by lightning, but the odds of it happening were astronomical. And at a funeral? A burnt smell assaulted Shania's nostrils, letting her know that people had indeed been struck.

"Go to the car now!" Greg demanded as he took off his jacket and handed it to Shania.

There was a strong sense of urgency in his voice, so she knew she needed to do exactly as he said. He reached down in his pant pocket and handed her the car keys, then pushed her a tad harder than she would've liked. Considering the circumstances, she let it slide. She held his jacket over her head as she half ran, half speed walked to the car, being careful where she placed her feet so she wouldn't slip.

Within the safe confines of their car, Shania stared out the window and watched Greg and Franklin pick up Kristen and carry her to a limo to get her out of the wetness. She immediately grabbed her cell and dialed 911. A couple of pallbearers picked up the other victims and carried them to limos as well. The minister and a handful of other people followed in a panic. Knowing there was nothing else she could do, other than pray, Shania bowed her head and called on God.

As the rain collided with her windshield, Shania couldn't help but reflect on the day's events. Had Mother Washington truly winked at her in that picture, or was that all her imagination? And if Mother Washington *had* winked at her, was it because she knew about something that they didn't?

Unable to shake the feeling that something just wasn't right, she heard the sound of sirens and realized that an ambulance had arrived. She prayed that the victims would be all right, yet she wondered what all of this meant.

Eighteen

Greg rarely missed church. This Sunday was one of those rare occasions. Since Shania had gotten up feeling sick, he didn't feel comfortable leaving her home alone to fend for herself. He made a few phone calls to the pastor and associate youth minister to let them know he wouldn't be in service. He then fixed Shania some dry toast and orange juice, something he knew she could keep down, and brought it to her in bed. She sat up and ate.

"I still can't believe the fiasco Mother Washington's funeral turned into," Shania said as she bit into the toast. "God rest her soul. I'll bet she was turning over in her casket."

Greg chuckled. "Yeah, I had never seen anything like it. I felt like looking for hidden cameras. I half expected Ashton Kutcher to jump out and say, 'You've been punk'd.'"

"I know, right?" Shania laughed.

"Thank goodness everybody's all right." He leaned back on the fluffy pillow. "Kristen had a minor burn to her shoulder, and the other two were treated for minor injuries. Apparently the lightning didn't directly strike them. Their guardian angels must've been working overtime." He shook his head in amazement. "It took every ounce of my strength not to break out shouting when I saw Kristen shaking from that bolt of electricity. She looked just like this." He jerked one shoulder toward his ear while he made his body twitch all over.

"Gregory Crinkle!" Shania popped his hand, but she was doubled over with laughter. "Minister Crinkle," she said, "now you know that isn't godlike."

He knew it wasn't godlike, but he had been itching to say that ever since he'd heard that pop of lightning and saw her twitching on the ground. "Yeah, I know I'm wrong for laughing at her," he said, "but 'vengeance is mine,' said the Lord, and He sure did serve her a good dose of it."

Shania laughed with him, then finished off her toast. "Sorry that you missed church just to stay home and babysit me."

He kissed her forehead. "Nothing to be sorry for. No other place I'd rather be." He touched her cheek and smiled at her while she drank her juice. "You think your stomach'll be able to hold it down?"

She shrugged. "I hope so. I'll be so glad when the first trimester is over." She pushed the tray to the side and rested her hand on her flat belly. "This baby is kicking my behind."

Although he wouldn't dare say anything, he couldn't have agreed more. He was tired of seeing and smelling throw up, tired of the sour smell that was constantly on his wife's breath, and tired of her pendulum mood swings. He hoped this stage would soon pass. He didn't know if he could survive nine months of this.

While watching her nibble on the toast, he felt himself getting turned on and nuzzled Shania's neck, but she pushed his head away. "Don't feel like it, so don't even try it."

Rolling his eyes, he sighed. *Yeah, this stage better pass and it better pass fast.* "Get yourself some rest," he said and stood there for a few seconds with his briefs hanging low, hoping she'd change her mind. She didn't. So he left her to her juice and dry toast and went to take a shower. A very cold shower.

When Greg got out of the shower, he could hear Shania snoring. He thought about how much their lives were about to change and how much had already changed. A baby on the way . . . was he truly ready?

With his towel tied around his waist, he stood in the doorway and stared at Shania as she shifted, trying to get more comfortable. He wondered if she'd be able to bounce back after having a baby. Would her perky breasts sag? Would she get stretch marks? Suppose her stomach looked like a shriveled-up balloon? Would she be able to lose the baby weight? Then he looked down at the floor. What if he couldn't satisfy her after the baby was born? What if that big ol' seven- or eight-pound baby stretched her to the point where she could no longer enjoy him?

He glanced down at his favorite piece of his anatomy, sighed, then put his right foot on top of the left and leaned against the door frame.

"Stop trippin', man," he whispered to himself. "That's your wife, and she's having your baby."

He exhaled and felt a twinge of guilt for being so shallow. He went back into the bathroom and looked at the man in the mirror. He didn't like what he saw staring back at him. Here his wife was pregnant with his child, trying to create life, and all he could think about was whether or not she'd still have a banging body afterward.

He splashed cold water on his face and allowed it to drip, then mentally told himself to pull it together. He spent the rest of the day pampering his wife, and to his dismay, she became more and more bad-tempered as the day went on. By that night, he was so sick of her attitude and impatient demeanor that he willingly slept in the den on the couch.

Early the next morning, he awoke to the sound of his phone ringing. He didn't recognize the number, so hoping it was one of the many jobs he'd applied for, he cleared his throat and answered the phone using his most professional tone.

"Hello? Gregory Crinkle speaking."

"Gregory Crinkle," a male's voice said, "this is Justin Horne with First-Stop Business Center. I'm calling in reference to a start-up business loan that you applied for."

Greg sat up straight on the couch, instantly fully awakened. "Yes, sir," he said.

"Well, I have great news for you, Mr. Crinkle. Your application has been approved, and the bank has approved you for a loan of up to five hundred thousand dollars."

Greg tucked his bottom lip between his teeth, pointed up at the ceiling, and mentally blessed the name of the Lord.

"Are you still interested in the loan?"

"Yes, sir, definitely. I'm interested." Greg stood to his feet and walked softly into his office so he wouldn't wake Shania. He closed the door, then said, "So what's my next step?"

"We just need you to come into the office, sign the paperwork agreeing to the loan amount and the repayment terms, and then you could have the money directly deposited into your account as early as three to five business days."

"Okay," Greg said, trying his best to conceal his giddiness. "Give me a few minutes to get ready, and then I'm on the way."

As soon as the words left his mouth, his office door swung open and Shania filled the doorway with her face a pale green color and her hair standing all over her head. Obviously, she hadn't slept well through the night.

Greg hurried up and ended the call.

"On the way where?" she asked, lifting a brow.

Greg swallowed, then pretended to be engrossed with a few documents that were setting atop his desk. "To, uh . . . to, uh . . . Franklin's house."

He felt bad about lying to his wife, but how was he supposed to tell her that he was going to the business center to finalize paperwork for a loan that she knew absolutely nothing about?

She crossed her arms and leaned against the door frame. "Isn't Franklin at work?"

Just tell the truth! Greg heard his conscience screaming at him, but by now, he felt stuck between a rock and a hard place. If he told her the truth, she'd be upset because he lied to start with, and then she'd be even more angry that he went and made yet another decision without touching bases with her first. Furthermore, if he told her the truth, she would want to foot the bill herself, and that was something he didn't want or need from her.

Once again, he heard his conscience sing a tongue-twisting proverb he'd learned in his adolescent years: *Oh, what a tangled web we weave when first we practice to deceive.*

He opened his mouth to tell her the truth, but it was almost as though his mouth had a mind of its own. "No, uh. . . . no, he didn't go to work today. He, uh . . . called out."

"Really?"

He couldn't lift his eyes from his desk as he nodded his head and wiped his slick palms on the sides of his pants. He held his breath as he waited for Shania's next words, but instead of speaking, she turned her head and grabbed his bookshelf while she vomited on the floor. Greg squeezed his eyes shut and looked away. The stench was unbearable.

His iPhone rang and he glanced at the screen. It had to have been Franklin calling, because the phone displayed the internal line to Mutual Living. Unsure whether he should answer or not, he stared at the phone until it stopped ringing.

Shania frowned at him but asked no questions. Franklin called again. Greg still made no move to answer the phone. He called yet again.

Shania turned her head sideways as she stared at him. "Are you going to answer that?"

Greg shook his head and Shania stomped over to his desk. For half a second, he thought she was going to answer the phone, but she simply picked it up and looked at the caller ID. When she saw that it was Mutual Living calling, she threw his phone on the desk so hard, it bounced off the desktop, clanged against the floor, and slid beneath his bookshelf. He figured she'd broken it, and if it wasn't broken, then it was probably severely damaged. Shania turned on her heel and stomped out the office.

Greg remaining seated, staring at the phone, wondering, what in God's name had he just done to his wife and to his marriage? He picked up his iPhone and became upset when he saw that Shania had thrown his phone with enough force to shatter the screen. Thank God he had good insurance on the phone. Regardless, that wasn't going to stop him from getting his money. He hurried up and got dressed and went to the lender's office.

***

The next day, Greg fidgeted with his fingers and shifted in the oversized leather chair as he searched the quaint conference room, waiting for the lawyer to arrive. A large mahogany desk resting on top of a Persian rug and a matching bookshelf lined with law books as thick as dictionaries took up most of the space. He had a lot of nervous energy that he didn't know how to expend as he waited for the others to arrive. He still couldn't understand why he had been called at all. The paralegal had been pretty vague when she called and told him that he needed to be present at the reading of Mother Washington's will. He wondered what she could've possibly left him.

He checked his watch and noted the time as 9:25 A.M., but the meeting was supposed to start at nine. He figured the attorney must've been a black man, because if he was white, he would've been there about forty minutes ago.

While he waited, he dialed Franklin's number on his new iPhone. Franklin answered on the first ring. "So what'd she leave you, man? Old folks got dough. That's why they be driving them fancy behind cars all the time, styling and profiling. I bet you Mother Washington was sitting on a bank. How much she leave you, man? Half million? Half a billion? Am I close? How much she leave you?"

"Franklin, shut up."

"Won't you shut me up, G? You bad."

Greg rolled his eyes at his friend and waited for him to finish running his mouth. Then he said, "This meeting was supposed to start twenty-five minutes ago. Why am I still the only one here? Where's Kaiya?"

"Twenty-five minutes ago?" Franklin sounded confused. "Man, you must have your times mixed up. Kaiya told me it starts at nine thirty."

Greg glanced at his watch. "Well, it's about two minutes 'til and I'm still the only one—"

He heard a man's voice outside the door and looked at the open entranceway. A black man dressed in a pin-striped suit entered and introduced himself as Attorney Jeffries. Greg stood and gave him a firm handshake. He felt bad for thinking stereotypically about black people and time.

The attorney placed his briefcase on top of the conference room table and removed some documents.

"This shouldn't take very long at all," the attorney explained as he shuffled through the papers and took a seat at the head of the table. "Are the daughters present as well?"

Greg shrugged his shoulders. "I'm guessing they're on the way."

The attorney glanced at his watch, then nodded. "We'll wait on them. I'll give them a few more minutes."

Nodding, Greg stepped out the room and put the phone to his ear. "You still there, Frank?"

"I'm still here. What's up?"

Greg looked down at his shoes and traced an invisible pattern on the carpet. "Man, I messed up real bad."

"What'd you do?"

He sighed into the phone. "Man, I got approved for the start-up business loan."

"That don't sound bad to me."

"I lied to Shania about it. And she caught me in my lie."

"Greg. G. My man. My dude. Come on, dog!" Franklin smacked his lips in the phone. "It's too early for you to be lying in your marriage, man! You don't start lying until you reach the one-year mark. What's wrong with you, my dude?"

"What kind of advice is that?" Greg listened to his friend, shaking his head. "Where'd you get this one-year mark from? See, that's why I'm married and you're not."

"Hey, the route you headed, me and you both gonna be in the same boat pretty soon. You know Shania don't play that mess."

"I know, I know." Greg groaned into the phone. "What should I do to make it up to her?"

"Maybe tell her the truth."

"The truth? Shania can't handle the truth."

"No, G," Franklin said on a very serious note, "*you* can't handle the truth. You wanna know what the truth is?"

Greg smacked his lips but perked up his ears. "What's the truth, Mr. Know-It-All?"

"The truth is," Franklin continued, "that you're intimidated by your woman's money."

"Intimidated?"

"You want me to spell it for you? I-N-T-I-M—"

"Okay, okay, I get it." Greg cut him off, then lowered his voice when he realized the young paralegal was all up in his conversation. He turned his back to her for more privacy, then said, "Why you say that, Frank?"

"Think about it, G. From day one, you've felt like you have to go over and beyond your call of duty to prove to her that you don't need her money."

"Because I don't need it."

"Fool, you *do* need it!" Franklin smacked his lips and clicked his tongue in the phone and Greg could imagine his friend shaking his head. "Listen to you. You up here willing to go sign up for a loan from the bank, knowing you'd have to pay interest on that loan. It would take you forever and a day to pay that money back, when you could get that loan from your own wife, who you already know is more than willing to invest in you, because she loves you. The only thing she would charge you is your heart."

Franklin's words shut Greg up. Greg couldn't think of a single thing to say in his defense. What Franklin was saying made logical sense, and it was sad that he couldn't have put things into perspective on his own.

He recognized Kristen's voice before he saw her face, and seconds later, Kristen and Kaiya came into view. They both wore dark pantsuits and sunglasses. While Kaiya's pantsuit was very professional and demure, Kristen's pants were too tight, and she wore no shirt under her blazer, so the upper portion of her two mounds were visible to anyone who wanted to look at them.

"Well," Greg said into the phone, "the sisters are here."

Franklin sighed on his end. "I bet Kaiya looks lovely, huh? Looks like she walked right out of a magazine, huh? Tell me what she got on, G. Tell me what she looks like. Put her on the phone. Let me hear her voice."

Greg rolled his eyes and said, "This girl has you sprung, Frank. Not a good look, my man."

"Aww, whatever." Franklin chuckled into the phone.

Greg ended the call, turned his phone off, and returned to the conference room. He had never been to the reading of a will, so he didn't know what to expect. He offered Kaiya the seat he had occupied earlier, and she politely thanked him for it. Kristen sat in the chair beside her sister, and her eyes flashed an invitation to Greg as she crossed her arms beneath her breasts, making her mounds rise even higher within the folds of her blazer. Greg rolled his eyes and looked away. He was not in the mood for her shenanigans.

After the ladies took their seats, Attorney Jeffries cleared his throat and said, "Now that everyone is here, we can get started."

He loosened his tie and put on a pair of reading glasses. He went through the formalities before announcing that Mother Washington had left her house and personal effects to be equally divided between her daughters. This nearly blew Greg away. He would've much preferred to hear that Mother Washington had left Kaiya everything and hadn't even left Kristen the corn off her pinkie toe.

When Attorney Jefferies stipulated that the house could not be sold, Kaiya cleared her throat and Kristen crossed her legs.

"And, ladies," he continued, scanning his eyes down the document in his hands. "That seems like the only thing she left you." He turned his head to address Greg. "But you, sir," he said, lifting his bushy eyebrows, "she left you all the money in her bank account." He looked down at his sheet of paper. "That total came to $54,972.85."

"What?" Kristen screamed. "That's a bald-faced lie."

Leaning forward, Greg rested his elbows on his knees. He furrowed a brow, wondering if he had heard the guy correctly. "Come—come again?"

"And that's not all," Attorney Jeffries continued, still looking at Greg. "She made you the sole beneficiary on her $100,000 life insurance policy."

"What?" Kristen screamed again. She jumped out of her seat and her breasts jiggled in her blazer like two basketballs. "What do you mean she left him"—she pointed at Greg—"all the money? We're her daughters!" Her high-pitched voice went up an octave. "He ain't nothing to her, just her little handyman. You need to clean your glasses off and take another look at that paper 'cause something has got to be wrong!"

Kaiya seemed to shrink within herself as she leaned away from her sister's rage.

Attorney Jeffries's cheeks reddened, and he said indignantly, "Ma'am, I can assure you that I can see just fine. And I'm an attorney. I think I know how to read. I'm telling you what the paper says, nothing more, nothing less."

Kristen's hands gripped the arms of the chair as she retook her seat. "Then there must be some mistake," she said calmly. "Why would our mother do that?" She eyed the attorney, demanding an explanation.

Attorney Jeffries folded his hands on top of his desk and looked at Kaiya. "With Kristen's irresponsibility with money, your mother was afraid that the money would be too much of a temptation for her."

"What do you mean by irresponsibility?" Kristen spat at him. "I'm not irresponsible. I've never done an irresponsible thing in my life."

"Then why'd you get evicted from your apartment?" Greg spoke up, shutting her down completely. "And why'd you have to file Chapter 11?"

She gasped and splayed a hand across her exposed breasts. "How do you . . . how do you know that?"

Greg grinned at her. "Research, baby." The look on her face was worth a million bucks.

The attorney took off his glasses and squeezed the bridge of his nose. "Can we just get through this, please?"

Greg apologized to the attorney, then pretended to zip his lips. He was a bit surprised when Kaiya cleared her throat and spoke up.

"That might be why she didn't leave the money to Kristen, but what about me?" Kaiya wanted to know. "What did she say about me?"

"Mother Washington wanted to be as fair as possible. Your mother didn't want to leave you the money and have you feeling so guilty about it that you end up sharing it with your sister. Because she loved you both equally, she didn't want to put either of you in that situation and add an unnecessary strain to your relationship." He held up a certified cashier's check. "This is for you," he said to Greg. "It's the bank account balance. An insurance representative will be in touch with you soon."

Greg hesitated before accepting the check. He could care less about Kristen because once again, he felt like she was getting her just desserts. But he felt bad for Kaiya. She shouldn't have to suffer because of her sister. He looked into Kaiya's tear-streaked face and offered her a heartfelt apology.

"You can keep that tired apology for yourself," Kristen replied for her sister. She jumped up from her seat, swinging her hair with her eyes flashing. "Get up, Kaiya. Come on, let's go. We should've expected this from Mama from the jump. We always do get the short end of the stick, huh?"

The thought crossed Greg's mind that if the sisters had paid for the funeral out of their pockets, then he should offer to reimburse them, so he mentioned it to Attorney Jefferies.

Before either of the women could answer, the attorney said, "Well, actually, Mother Washington was a planner. She had picked out and paid for her casket, headstone, and burial plot years ago. She wanted to be buried next to her husband."

"Oh," was all Greg could say as he folded the check in half and placed it in his wallet, feeling less and less guilty.

The attorney said in a professional tone, "If there's nothing else, we're done here."

With a disappointed look on her face, Kristen grabbed her things and held up her middle finger at Attorney Jefferies, then pointed a long, sharp fingernail at Greg. "You may think you won. Best believe, it ain't over. What Kristen wants"—she let her eyes drop from the check in his hand to the crotch of his pants—"Kristen gets. Check my track record."

He rolled his eyes. "I already have. I saw your little aggravated assault charge. Is that supposed to intimidate me?"

At the sound of his words, she touched her chest and her eyes widened.

Greg added, "Your threats don't scare me, Kristen. God says, 'Touch not my anointed.' You tried to overdose your own mother and see what happened to you at the funeral? Touch me if you want to."

Kristen pointed a finger at him again. It seemed like she was searching for some smart-aleck reply but came up empty. Finally, she pulled her lips back in a snarl and said, "Go to hell."

"Trust me, you'd beat me there." Greg chuckled in the face of her fury.

Greg gathered his things and shook the attorney's hand. "Thank you, Attorney Jefferies, for everything."

"Here's the number for the insurance company," the attorney said as he handed Greg a piece of paper. "If you don't hear from them over the next few days, be sure to give them a call."

Greg briefly studied the information and explained to the attorney that he and his wife were leaving for Ocho Rios in two days and that he'd deal with the insurance matter when he got back the following week. He thanked him again, then left.

He noticed Kristen yank Kaiya by the arm and all but drag her out of the place.

Once outside, he stared up at the sky and smiled, wondering if Mother Washington was looking down on him from heaven.

Greg felt like new money after leaving the attorney's office. His heart ached that Mother Washington had died, but having a dump load of money sure had a way of helping out with the healing process. He couldn't believe his luck. He immediately thanked God for his blessing and hightailed his motorcycle straight to the nearest Bank of America.

After making a sizable deposit into his bank account, Greg took a detour to his church and met with his pastor. They talked and Greg gave his pastor a check for 10 percent of the money he had just gotten. He believed in tithing and knew that his church could use the money to help the missionaries that had recently gone to Cameroon, Africa. Pastor Ray thanked him for his generous gift, and Greg felt good about what he had done.

Greg still knew that there was one situation that he needed to right. He made one more quick stop and purchased a dozen red roses for Shania.

By the time he reached the house, some of the joy he'd felt since the attorney made his unexpected announcement had ebbed away. A cold ball of regret and dread had replaced it.

"Shania," he called out as soon as he walked through the door, holding the dozen roses in front of his face, as though they were shield.

He waited a moment for her reply so that he could determine where she was.

"What's the matter?" she yelled from the kitchen.

Placing the bouquet behind his back, he hurried into the kitchen and greeted her with a smile. She didn't smile back. She just kept looking down at her chopping board and hacking a carrot into thin slices. For a second, his mind replaced the carrot with his favorite piece of his anatomy, and he visibly cringed.

"What's the matter with you?" She scrunched up her face. Greg forced himself to stop imagining his private part on the chopping board, and whipped the roses from behind his back. She stared at the roses as though he had whipped out the manual to put together a fish tank. Her expression remained the same when she said, "So how'd it go? What'd she leave you? Her Bible?"

Greg forced himself to grin at her dry joke. "Well, she left me a lot more than that." He placed the flowers in a vase, covered the stems three-quarters with water, and carefully slid the vase across the island top while he closed the distance between them.

She picked up a nearby mug of ginger tea and sipped on it while giving him a blank stare.

Greg went on to explain about the money and why Mother Washington had entrusted the money to him instead of her daughters. He also told her about the offering he made to his church.

"So what am I supposed to do? Applaud you?" Shania stood there glaring at him. She picked up her knife, slid the carrot out the way with the blunt edge of the knife, then began chopping celery, using much more force than was required.

The longer Greg stared at the glistening blade, the more nervous he became. Maybe he should wait until she finished cooking and talk to her in a less dangerous part of the house. He didn't watch a lot of crime reality TV, but he'd watched enough to know that a high percentage of homicides, especially domestic homicide, happened in the bathroom or the kitchen.

He took a deep breath to still his trembling nerves and said, "Babe, I lied to you yesterday."

"Really?" She made a sarcastic expression of surprise and slapped one hand against her cheek. "I would've never known!"

"Can you kill the sarcasm?"

"No, Greg, but I'm feeling like killing you!" she exclaimed, wielding the knife in his direction. Based on her volatile temperament lately, he did not put it past her. He held his hands up in surrender and jumped out of her way, but she tossed the knife on the island and it clanged to a stop. "You can't even lie straight, Greg. I looked in your eyes and knew instantly that you were lying."

She put one hand on her hip and glared at him. "How do you expect this marriage to work if you breach our trust? Without trust, a relationship is nothing. Don't you know that?"

"Yes, I do." He nodded and carefully reached across the island for the knife. Once the knife clattered into the sink basin, he felt a lot more at ease. "Baby, listen," he said and went to put his arms around her, but she moved out of the way.

"You can talk to me without touching me."

Her words felt like stakes being driven through his heart; however, he manned up, knowing that he deserved all of this and more. He should've never lied about the situation to start with.

Instead of touching her, he stood as close to her as she would allow and stared at her until she finally focused on his eyes. "I'm sorry, okay? No excuse. I screwed up."

"Yes, you did," she said, nodding her agreement.

"Franklin's right." He leaned on his elbows as he continued to stare at her. "Your money intimidated me, babe. It made me feel like I had to work extra hard to prove to you that I can hold down my own."

She rolled her eyes, then crossed her arms beneath her breasts. "So what'd you lie to me about?"

He inhaled deeply, knowing it was now or never. Finally, he refocused on his wife and said, "I went to sign the papers to finalize a loan yesterday."

Her face pulled into a frown. "A loan? A loan for what?"

He inhaled even deeper. This time, he couldn't look at her when he spoke, so he settled on a spot just above her right shoulder. "A business start-up loan."

She threw her hands in the air and walked out the kitchen. Greg followed after her, trying to get her to understand. He reached for her hands, but she slapped his hands away.

"Greg, just give me a moment."

She tried to press the bedroom door closed, but he jammed his foot between the crack and spoke through the slit in the door. "A moment for what?"

"To think things over," she yelled at him, pressing with all her might to shut the door.

His toes screamed for mercy, but he refused to move his foot. Gritting his teeth against the pain, he said, "Babe, you're scaring me. You make it sound like you're second-guessing your decision to marry me."

"Maybe . . . maybe I am, Greg."

Her words seemed to knock the fight out of both of them. She stopped pushing the door, and he stopped trying to force himself in. If her words had felt like stakes before, they felt like rusted nails now—rusted nails with serrated edges being hammered into his heart.

"You don't mean that, do you?" His words could hardly be considered a whisper. He wasn't sure if she'd heard him until she shrugged her shoulders.

She plopped down on the bed and covered her face with her hands. "What happened to us, Greg?"

His heart ached, seeing her in such pain and knowing full well that he was the cause of it. He stepped into the room and closed the door behind him, then settled on his knees, between her legs.

Her eyes were watery mirrors as she stared at him and repeated her earlier question. "What happened to us? Why did our fairytale end?"

He took her trembling fingers and pressed them against either side of his face and held them in place. "Life isn't a fairytale."

She let out a strained laugh that sounded like a gargle. "God, don't I know it."

"It'll get better for us," he promised her and took her hands from his face and kissed both her palms. "Things will work out for us. I swear it to you."

"Don't swear anything else to me." She cut him off, then shook her head, biting her bottom lip to dam her tears. "Don't make me another vow until you can keep the vows that you promised me before man and God. To love, honor, and respect your wife."

Greg pressed his face into her belly, inhaling her sweet fragrance mixed with the savory scent of the broth she was making. "I do love you, Shania."

Shania struggled out of his touch, and before walking out of the bedroom, she looked over her shoulder at him and said, "Love is an action word."

How was he ever going to prove to her that she was still the love of his life?

Nineteen

Shania and Greg arrived at Montego Bay airport Thursday morning. They waited in the exclusive "Couples Resort" airport lounge and sipped on refreshing drinks of chilled water and pineapple slices until their ride showed up. Greg tried to make small talk, but she ignored him and pretended to be absorbed by a soccer game that was playing on one of the TVs.

Once their van arrived to transport them to their hotel, Shania settled in a seat near the front and took in the scenic view. For some reason, Shania expected the van to arrive, and ten, fifteen minutes later, they arrive at their resort. After an entire hour of having her organs jiggled loose on the bumpy ride, having her elbows and knees aching from the constant knocking against Greg's knees and elbows, and having sweat burn her eyes and puddle at her spine—because even though the air conditioner was on, it obviously wasn't working—she finally said to the driver, whose skin was as black as an onyx gem, "Are we almost there yet?"

Greg glared at her for her impatience, and she glared right back at him. The driver looked in the rearview mirror, winked at her, and said in his Jamaican accent, "About t'irty more minutes, Miss Lady."

She tried to give him a smile, but she was sure it looked more like a grimace. Once again, she settled in her seat to sulk at the bumpy ride and stared out at the dark shades of different natives as they passed by, walking with baskets on their heads, or walking along with two or three shaggy goats following close behind, or bicycling by and waving at their van.

Greg tried to point out different things, but he might as well have been Charlie Brown's teacher saying, "Blah blah blah, blah blah blah."

The only reason why she went along with their plans for this trip was because they had already purchased the tickets and the tickets were nonrefundable. However, she was determined to let Greg know that she was here to have a good time—*by herself*, and he could continue to be the self-absorbed, selfish so-called *husband* that he was.

Thirty minutes seemed to drag by, but Sans Souci emerged majestically from the cliffs of Jamaica's emerald islands. From the distance, the mountains seemed purple with pink tips. Eventually, the bumpy ride came to a stop.

They checked into the resort, and when Shania saw the hibiscus cottage where they were staying, she fell in love with the tropical elegance and breathtaking ambiance. Decorated in ocean blue and white, the cottage exuded peacefulness. Shania immediately noticed the steps to the private Jacuzzi and knew that she'd be spending a lot of time there.

Greg offered the bellman a tip for carrying in their luggage, but the bellman refused. "This is an all-inclusive resort," the bellman explained in a Jamaican accent. "No tips allowed."

"Habit," Greg explained as he stuffed his money back into his wallet and showed the bellman out. "This place is nice," Greg said, and walked up behind Shania before placing a kiss behind her ear. "Is this how we're going to spend our entire vacation? With you mad at me, treating me like an unwanted stepchild?"

It must've been the ambiance of their cottage that caused her to relax in his arms and allow some of the stiffness in her spine to dissolve. She leaned her head against his chest and exhaled deeply, but said no words.

Still holding her, he shuffled them forward until they were standing on the balcony with the thin, billowy yellow and white curtains waving around them as the breezes blew off the ocean. Shania stared outside at the turquoise water that seemed to go on forever until it finally blended in with the sky. She counted the sailboats and canoes drifting across the surface, then looked up at the seagulls soaring above the water, most likely in search for dinner. She then turned her attention to the gigantic banana trees, displaying tight bundles of green bananas, and palm trees whose barks seemed to be splitting and peeling as the trees unraveled. The sound of the ocean lapping at the virginal white shore mixed with the sound of her husband's heartbeat nearly put her to sleep in his arms.

"Tired?" he asked, and she nodded.

Before she could protest, he scooped her up and placed her in the bed. She yawned, and then jet lag and weariness took their toll.

When she awoke, she glanced out the open balcony and realized that the sun had already set in the sky. It wasn't dark out yet but it was quickly heading that way. Greg was sitting at the small, circular table with his Bible and a notepad. When he heard her movement in the bed, he looked her way and smiled. "So you finally decided to join the land of the living?"

"Sorry about that," Shania apologized, covering her yawn with her hand. She stretched, listening to her joints crack and pop; then she pushed off the bed to her feet. "How long was I asleep?"

Greg twisted his lip and glanced at his wristwatch. "About two hours."

She nodded. "Not too bad." She stood in front of the balcony, stared out at the water and stretched again. The catnap had helped bring clarity to her situation. There was no point in coming to such an exotic island and stubbornly remaining in such an ugly mood. So she turned to face her husband and said in a tone much more polite than the one she had previously been using, "What do you want to do first?"

He closed his Bible and hooked his pen to his notepad. "What do you want to do first?"

Yawning, Shania said, "There's so much to see. I think we should take a tour of the resort."

"Sounds like a plan to me."

They finished unpacking, changed clothes, and went straight to the beach. The sun smiled down on them as their feet left footprints in the gritty grains of sand.

"This is heaven," Shania said as her sarong blew gently with the breeze.

Greg reached for her hand and clasped his hand in hers. Everything in her screamed to yank her hand back. Just because she was playing nice didn't mean she had to be all lovey-dovey with him. He was still in the doghouse for telling her that bald-faced lie and then having the nerve to start his own business without even including her in his plans. But, she forced a smile on her face and let him continue to hold her hand as they made their way across the shore.

A woman wearing an orange bikini, who had to have been a Jamaican native, walked by with her curvaceous figure and her flat belly. Even though she smiled in acknowledgement to both of them, Shania felt self-conscious. No, she wasn't showing yet, but she felt bloated. And she certainly didn't think she looked good enough to wear a two-piece. She eyed the shapely woman and noticed that Greg was eyeing her too. She released his hand and stopped walking.

"I know you weren't just looking at that woman." She felt her cheeks getting hot and an overwhelming urge to punch Greg in the chest.

He started to stutter. "What are you talking about?" He threw his hands in the air.

Shania put her hand on her hip. "Don't try to play me, Gregory. I saw you looking at that woman." Tears welled in her eyes.

Greg sighed. "For crying out loud, Shania, you're being ridiculous. All I did was glance at the woman. It's not that serious." He took a couple of steps and stopped when he noticed that Shania hadn't moved. "What?" He sounded irritated.

Shania threw her hands in the air. "I'm going back to the room."

"Seriously, babe."

She trekked through the sand.

"This is what I have to look forward to for the rest of the week?" he called after her.

She could hear Greg calling her name, but she didn't stop or turn around. The thought of Greg ogling another woman made the tears flow. She felt fat and undesirable.

When she came to a walking path, she dusted off her feet and put on the sandals she had been holding in her hand. By then, she had calmed down some and almost felt like returning to the shore to find Greg and apologize for being so sensitive.

"Shania?" she heard a male voice call out to her. She immediately turned around, wondering who it could possibly be. Nobody on this island knew her except for Greg, yet someone had just called her name, and it didn't sound like her husband. Through blurry eyes, she tried to make out who it was, but saw nothing more than the leaves in the bushes and the hibiscus flowers fluttering in the breeze.

Figuring it had to be her imagination, she whipped her head around to continue walking, but no sooner had she turned than she heard the leaves beside her rustle, and then something hard clanged against the side of her head and her world went black.

Twenty

When Shania awoke, she heard God himself whisper for her not to move and not to open her eyes. So she did exactly what He said. She kept still and she didn't open her eyes. Yet and still, the back of her head throbbed something awful, and if she didn't know any better, she'd have thought someone took out her heart and sewed it into her skull. Three thoughts ran simultaneously through her mind: What had happened? Where was she? And where was Greg?

As far as the first question went, all she could remember was heading toward her hotel and then hearing some man call her name. She knew she had been hit with something, but what, she had no idea. As far as where she was, she thought about peeking her eyes open to see what she could see, but reasoned against doing so. If God had told her to keep her eyes closed, then by golly, she would keep her eyes closed.

First, she focused on what she could feel. There was something hard and coarse digging into her wrists, which were tied in front of her. That same coarse feeling was around her ankles. That alone made her aware that she was someone's prisoner, and the thought sent her heart into overdrive. Tendrils of fear slid in and out of her pores, and she had to grit her teeth to keep from trembling.

Then she focused on what she could hear. There were footsteps close by, back and forth. There must have been a wooden floor. A door was somewhere, opening and closing. The sound of waves lapping at the sea. So she knew she was somewhere close to the ocean.

Next she focused on what she could smell. Careful not to allow her nostrils to flare too much, she sniffed the air. There was incense, the faint tinge of cigarette smoke and sandalwood.

And then a voice. A male voice. Not the male voice that had called her name earlier, but a different male voice. It sounded younger, softer. Not quite a boy's voice, but not quite a full-grown man's, either.

"Ya awake?"

His voice was close to her ear, but not so close as to make her uncomfortable. She could smell cigarette smoke and a trace of alcohol on his breath. She wondered why she was his prisoner and what was he going to do to her—or what had he already done?

"Ya awake?" he asked again in his thick Jamaican accent. Then she felt his hand on her ankle, shaking her lightly. She almost recoiled from his touch, but because she was still supposed to be "asleep," she remained as still as possible and willed herself not to tense up.

The sound of hinges squeaking and then heavy footsteps stomped across the floor. Along with the new individual in the room came a horrible stench that nearly turned her stomach. It smelled like a pot of roasted onions that were left out in the sun for a few days and had spoiled and started to rot. Finally, there was a voice to go along with the horrible smell and heavy footsteps.

"She still not awake?" His voice was much thicker and heavily accented than the younger man's. And furthermore, whenever he talked, it sounded like he had a huge loogie stuck somewhere in his throat and he needed to hawk it out.

As soon as he opened his mouth, Shania immediately recognized the voice and knew that this was the man who had hit her even before the younger guy said, "I t'ink ya hit her too hard, mon. Now what we gon' do? Crazy Lady said not ta kill her."

Crazy Lady? Shania almost frowned, then remembered that she was supposed to be asleep, so she forced her face to remain relaxed.

But when she felt two greasy fingers press against the side of her neck and smelled that up close and personal whiff of this man's funk, her stomach threatened an upheaval, and it took nothing less than the strength and mercy of God to keep her from upchucking on this man.

"No, she not dead yet," he said, "but dat a mean bump on da back of her head."

The younger guy said, "Is Crazy Lady finished wit da man yet?"

"No," he said, and she heard his footsteps carry him and his odor further away from the bed. She sent a silent thanks up to God. "No, she not finish yet. He still alive."

Shania listened attentively to their words, figuring that "he" must be Greg. Instantly, she regretted treating him as harsh as she had and wished that she could rewind time back to that moment at the seashore when she had left him standing there. In this moment, she realized that all the arguments they'd had up to now seemed so trivial in the face of grave danger. All the silent treatment and cold shoulders she'd given her husband were lost moments, lost time that she could never make up.

It truly pained her to even think that her husband's last memory of her could be watching her storm down the shore, and her last memory of him could be his utter exasperation with her sour attitude.

Shania hadn't realized she'd been holding her breath until the man had spoken those last words. She cracked her lips and inhaled as deep as she could without being conspicuous, and willed the tears of pure relief to remain in her eyes. As long as her husband was still alive, there was hope.

"But da Crazy Lady needs ta hurry up 'cause me got t'ings to do," the stinky man said and let out a grunt.

"She gon' pay us da rest tonight, yes?"

The stinky man grunted and Shania assumed that meant yes. The two men were quiet and Shania found herself wondering, where was she, where was Greg, and who in God's name was the Crazy Lady? If she could figure out some answers to these questions, she was sure that she could start piecing a way out of this mess.

The stench of the stinky man had her stomach doing flip-flops, and she could count on her fingers how long she'd be able to hold it in before she emptied the contents of her stomach on the floor.

The stinky man said, "I will go check wit' Crazy Lady again. Keep an eye on her."

His footsteps moved across the room. She heard the hinges creak as the door opened. As soon as she heard the door slam closed, Shania leaned over the side of the bed and retched until the only thing left in her stomach to throw up was bile and hydrochloric acid. So she threw that up too.

There was no way that she could throw up and still pretend like she was asleep, so the young man ran to her bedside. She opened her eyes and stared at him. He was not a bad-looking individual. He had to be about Jonathan's age and actually favored him a bit. The only difference was that he was as black as a midnight sky and had teeth as white as the sand on the Jamaican shore. Plus, he was much, much taller than Jonathan.

There was a softness to his brown eyes that fanned Shania's flame of hope.

"Ya okay?" he asked and seemed genuinely concerned.

Shania shook her head and asked for a sip of water. When he left to get the water, she took this moment to take in her surroundings. She still had no idea where she was at, but it seemed like she was in some little hut with a wooden floor and a thatched roof. This must've been someone's house, but whose house, she had no idea.

When the young boy returned, she was glad to see him palming a bottled water instead of a cup of water. The last thing she wanted to do was risk her or her child's health by drinking a foreign country's unclean water.

She gladly accepted the bottled water and tried to wash the disgusting taste out of her mouth by downing the entire bottle. While she drank, she noticed that the young guy was watching her with a look of awe. She finished the bottle, and he gladly took it from her and trashed it. Then he sat at the end of the makeshift bed and stared at her.

"Ya beautiful asleep, but ya even more beautiful awake. Ya from da States, no?"

There was something melodic about his voice. She nodded, then scrunched her nose. "There's a really bad smell in here." She wasn't just talking about her vomit.

The young guy laughed. "Me friend. He 'tink really bad, mon. He don' take no good baths, and he don' wash under his arms much. T'en he wonder why he no find a woman."

Despite her circumstances, Shania found herself laughing with the young guy.

Then he gestured at her head. "Tat's a pretty bad knot on ya head."

She wanted to touch the spot, but she couldn't. Her arms were securely tied. It seemed like she was building a good rapport with the young man, and she didn't want to do anything to ruin her chances at survival. Instinct told her that if she sat around chatting aimlessly with him until Big Stinky came around, she was as good as dead. So carefully choosing her words, she said, "How old are you?"

"Twenty-one, miss."

"You don't go to school?"

He glanced down at the floor for a few seconds, then looked back up at her. "Not 'cause me no want to. Me family no can afford school for me. I a Rasta. Ya don' know what a Rasta is because you and your husband have money. Ya don' have ta deal wit' ma reality."

So that's what this was about. Money. She should've known. "What's your name?"

He looked at her as though she was crazy and shook his head. "Now how I look, pretty lady, tellin' you ma name? I no wanna go ta jail. And t'is type of stuff is da stuff ya go to jail for long time."

Shania sent a prayer up to God, silently asking Him to place the words she needed to say to influence this young man directly in her mouth. He had goals and he had a heart. She knew if she dug deep enough, there was a chance that she could reach him. The same way God had allowed her to reach Jonathan, she prayed that He allowed her to reach this young man too. Then she took in a deep breath and said, "You are better than this. Do you know that?"

Again, he looked at her as though she was crazy.

"When life gives you an opportunity, what do you do?"

The young boy walked across the room and pulled back the heavy curtain as he glanced out the window.

Then he returned his attention to her. "Life gives me no opportunity," he said, and there was a bitterness to his tone and expression.

Realizing that at any moment Big Stinky could barge in the room, Shania mustered up all her courage and said, "Life does give opportunities, even to people like you. Think about it this way." She cleared her throat. "You saw me and my husband, and you figured we had money. So you kidnapped us, thinking that you could ransom us and make some fast money. Wasn't that an opportunity that you decided to take?"

Even though he kept his eyes riveted to the floor, she could tell that he was listening to her.

She shifted in her bed, unable to get comfortable in her restraints. "Don't you know that God will use your enemies as your footstool? You don't know me, anymore than I know you, but I know a man around your age who put his life on the line to go back to the hood and save one of his friends. He got shot twice because of it. Do you think he regretted getting caught in the line of fire just to save his friend?" She shook her head. "No. It was something he was willing to do. He took a chance because he saw that chance as his opportunity. So let me ask you something. If the only reason why I'm tied down to this bed is because of money, then untie me and allow me to bless you. Allow me to invest in you so you can go back to your hood and tell other people in your same situation that positive opportunities still exist and miracles still happen."

She held her breath, waiting for his response, knowing full well that this might be her only opportunity to save herself, her child, and her husband. The young man walked to the window and looked out the curtain again.

Finally, he took a deep breath, then held up his shirt, giving her a small glimpse of his washboard abs. He pulled out a rustic knife from his waistband. At the sight of the knife, every molecule of air escaped her lungs, and she struggled to breath. Her eyes seemed glued to the knife as she stared at its bamboo handle and the rustic blade that seemed as though it was hand-molded from sheet metal.

With the knife clutched in his hand at his side, he walked over to the bed she was tied to and slowly raised the knife above his head. "I didn't wan' ta do dis," he said and worked his jaw while he worked the knife in his hands, "but I gotta."

Her heart sounded like an African drum as she stared into his big brown eyes and waited for the blow that would end her life. Just as the blade swung down from above his head, she squeezed her eyes closed and prayed that he would hit her heart and death would follow swiftly.

In the darkness, Greg lay shackled to the bed, wondering how in the world was he going to get out of this mess. Since he had no concept of time, he had no idea how long the woman had been gone, and even less of an idea of when she would return. He knew that at any given moment, the door could fly open and that crazy woman could come in and end his life.

As he continued to repeat the Twenty-third Psalm, a calming peace came over him, and he recalled the Bible verse that Jesus had told his disciples before he went to take up the cross. *My peace I give unto you.* It sounded ludicrous to be shackled and tied to a bed in the pitch-black darkness, unsure of whether he'd live or die, unsure of whether his wife and child were alive

or not, and to still have a peace that surpassed all understanding.

As though Mother Washington herself had descended
into the room, he felt her presence surrounding him.
The words that she had spoken to him in her hospital
bed came to him loud, clear, and crisp: *"No matter the
situation, God's always gonna make a way for you to
escape."*

Somehow, despite it all, he believed it.

With eyes of faith, he looked past the desolateness
that his current situation offered and leaned on his
unshakable faith that if God brought him to this, the
Lord would bring him through this. He also knew that
faith without action was dead. If he sat here and waited
for faith to save him without lifting a single finger to
bring about that salvation, he was just as good as dead.
He racked his brain, trying to figure out something he
could do to show God that he hadn't given up on the
situation.

Once again, he tried to wiggle his feet out of their
shackles, but that plan wasn't working. He wanted to
try to wiggle his wrists free, but the last time he had
tried to get his hands free, he had pulled and tugged
until his wrists were raw and blood had oozed down
his inner forearms. At that thought . . . he suddenly had
an idea. Gritting his teeth against the pain, he began
twisting his wrists in the shackles, scratching off even
more flesh from his wrists. The old wounds reopened
and the blood started flowing again. Greg strained to
twist his arms in such a direction that the blood would
flow toward his palms rather than toward his elbows.

Because of the awkward position he was reclined in,
his back muscles spasmed, and his neck ached something awful, but he knew he couldn't quit. His life, and
possibly Shania's and their unborn child's life, relied

on whether he made it out of this or not. Perspiration dripped from his forehead and rolled into his mouth, stung his eyes and stung the fresh wounds that he'd created, but it didn't deter him.

Slowly but surely, gravity began to push the blood flowing down his arms in the other direction painstakingly slowly. Once the blood reached the bottom portion of his palms, he folded his long fingers forward until his fingertips felt the cool wetness of his blood. He tried to twist the blood all around the shackles, using it as lubrication; then he folded his hand in half lengthwise and tried to slip his hand out of the cuffs. It took a few attempts, and the muscles in his upper back and neck felt like they were on fire, but he continued to strain and twist until one hand finally popped free from the shackles. Even though it felt like he had broken his thumb and pinkie finger, he'd never felt so good before in his life. One limb down, three to go.

With one free hand, it was easier to slip his other hand free. Once both hands were free, he removed his blindfold before flexing his aching hands, wondering if he'd have to suffer from arthritis and carpal tunnel for the rest of his life. But yet and still, he thanked God that he was making progress.

Unsure of how much longer he had until the crazy woman returned, he forced his sore hands to cooperate, and then began trying to undo the knotted rope around his knees. He had no idea who had tied this rope, but whoever had tied it knew exactly what he or she was doing. Greg dug and clawed at the rope, but without any fingernails, he couldn't make any progress.

He twisted his body and leaned over the side of the bed, feeling on the floor for any object that might help him saw through the rope. His fingers felt nothing on the floor but the vomit he had chucked earlier.

"My Father who art in heaven," Greg said into the darkness, and was surprised to notice that the swelling in his tongue had gone down tremendously, "I know that you didn't bring me this far to leave me now. I've done all I can do. Now I need you to step in and show yourself strong."

Greg heard the locks at the door being undone, and his heart went into overdrive. A cold chill rolled over his entire body and his teeth chattered. The fight-or-flight survival response kicked in, making all of his senses acute. The locks clicking open sounded as loud as gunshots.

His vision suddenly sharpened, and even though the room was black, he could make out the shape of a dresser, a TV, and a lamp stand. The blood that had poured from his wrists smelled overwhelmingly strong and coppery.

When the last lock slid open and the doorknob turned, Greg almost peed on himself. He laid back on the bed and put his arms out to either side of him. As long as she kept the lights off, she couldn't really tell that he had slipped out of the handcuffs.

As soon as he thought that thought, the light flipped on and Greg squeezed his eyes shut because the sudden brightness of the light was painful to his eyes.

"Greg."

When he heard Shania whisper his name, he knew that God was playing a cruel trick on him. Her voice sounded so real, so close. He could even smell the scent of her skin—the citrusy shampoo she'd used to wash her hair before they left the house.

"Greg."

This time he popped his eyes open and stared, and indeed, it was his wife. Relief at seeing her alive and well nearly suffocated him. He wanted to grab her and kiss her and hold her. He wanted to lose himself in her arms and be transported out of this nightmare. But when he saw that ugly bump protruding out the back of her head, rage seeped through his veins.

"You're hurt," he said. "Who did this to you?"

"We don't have time," she said, rushing to the bed and using some weird-looking knife to cut the rope loose from around his knees. "I'll explain it all later, but for now, we just have to get out of here before she comes back." He watched her grit her teeth as she sawed through the rope and hoped she didn't accidentally cut his legs.

"Before who comes back?" he asked as the rope gave way and he was finally able to pull his knees apart.

"The key, Ahdale," she whispered, her hands tugging at his shackles. She turned her head and looked back at the open door. "Ahdale, I need the key!"

"Ahdale? Who is Ahdale? Who are you talking to?"

Before she could answer him, a dark-skinned man stuck his head in the door and whispered in a thick Jamaican accent, "Here she come! Hide! Help will come. I promise you!" Then the man pulled the door closed and Greg nearly cried when he heard the locks clicking in place yet again.

Shania sprinted across the room, hit the lights, returning them back to darkness. Next the closet door squeaked open and closed. Seconds after Shania hid in the closet, Greg listened to the locks on the door clicking open yet again. His mind couldn't quite grasp everything that was happening. Somehow, he felt like he had just been tossed into a tsunami, the tsunami blew him into a hurricane, and then the hurricane sucked him into a tornado. He just wanted this madness to end.

The light flickered on again. Greg squeezed his eyes against the pain that the bright light caused.

"Well, well, well. Someone's been mighty busy since I've been gone," the woman said, and Greg's heart rattled in his chest as he tilted his head up and looked at his captor. His eyes almost crossed up when he saw those big brown eyes and that jet-black hair and what should've been a demure, soft smile.

"Kaiya?"

"Who were you expecting?" she asked. "Kristen?"

"I—I . . ." Greg stared at her, completely at a loss of words. He felt like he'd been hit by a train, then flattened with a steamroller. "But you're a sweet girl. . . ."

"Yeah, yeah, yeah," she said, and walked into the room, slamming and locking all three dead bolts. She removed a gun from the back of her waistband and scratched her head with the barrel. He figured this must be the same gun that she'd jammed into his mouth earlier.

"All my life, I've been sweet little Kaiya," she said. "So quiet, so submissive, take whatever punches life hands me and then I'm supposed to just go with the flow. But you know what?" She grinned at him. "I'm tired of it, Greg. I'm tired of taking the punches. I'm ready to throw a few myself." She giggled, then sat on the edge of the bed and let her eyes stare at his crotch. "Kristen told me to just let it go, but I didn't want to. I'm tired of letting stuff go." She paused. "You're much bigger than your friend in the size department." She rolled her eyes and shrugged. "I mean, it's not like I got to sample it or anything. He was just too darn holy for me. 'Let's wait until we get married,'" she mocked Franklin. "'I want to spend the rest of my life with you. You're my gift straight from heaven.' And yadda yadda yadda, blah blah blah."

Even in his current predicament, his heart went out to Franklin. Franklin had sincerely cared about this girl, was seriously considering marrying her—but thank God her true side had been exposed before his friend made the biggest mistake of his life.

Greg wanted to glance at the closet to make sure Shania was okay, but he feared that looking in that direction might give away her hiding place. So he forced himself to keep his eyes solely on Kaiya.

"I didn't want to take it to this extent," she told him and leaned against the bedpost. "You're probably wondering how I knew where you were. Well, you mentioned at the hospital and again at the lawyer's office that you were going to Ocho Rios. I just mentioned to Franklin that I might want us to take a trip there and asked him where you were staying. Simple as that." She smirked. "All I wanted was my cut of the money, Greg, and you took it from me. You took it from us. We deserved that money. Do you realize what we've been through?"

Greg didn't want to have a conversation with her, but the longer he kept her talking, the longer he kept himself alive. The young boy had said help was on the way. He had to believe it; that was his only hope.

"No, I don't know what all you've been through. Tell me so I can understand, Kaiya."

"You heard rumors. Don't tell me you didn't hear the rumors."

Greg nodded repeatedly. "I've heard quite a few rumors. But you can't believe everything you hear."

"Well, believe this," Kaiya snapped and stared at the gun, passing it from one hand to the next. "Mama wasn't the precious little saint that she tried to make herself out to be. Did she ever tell you why me and Kristen never came over to visit her?"

Greg shook his head.

"I'm sure she wouldn't tell you—or anybody for that matter," Kaiya said, and her words dripped venom. "Because she was ashamed of what she allowed to happen to us." Kaiya walked across the room and leaned against the dresser, which was situated adjacent to the closet. "Her husband, our uncle, Henry—he raped Kristen, Greg. Repeatedly. From the time she took us in. He started with Kristen, and when he tried to move on to me, Kristen protected me. She wouldn't let him touch me, so he raped her from the time she was a little girl until she became a teenager and finally went away to college. I lived in constant fear. That's why I became so shy. There were also other little girls at the church who claimed he would offer them money if they'd let him touch them."

Greg wasn't sure if she was telling the truth or not. He realized that the more she talked, the more she moved around the room and the more distracted she became. If she could get close enough to him, there was a possibility that he could snatch the gun out of her hand and become in control of the situation.

So, to keep her talking, he said, "Did y'all ever tell Mother Washington about the rape?"

"Did we?" She guffawed and made her eyes huge. "Kristen told her numerous times about what her *husband* was doing to her, but she just thought Kristen was hot in the pants. Plus, Mama was old school. She didn't believe in divorce." Anger and hate danced in her eyes. "See, Uncle Henry was a deacon at the church, and Mama didn't want to believe that her husband, a deacon, our very own uncle, would be sick enough to molest his own niece, or offer money to those fast-tailed girls at the church."

Lost in thought, Kaiya sat the gun on the dresser and turned her back to Greg. He wished to God there was a way he could tell Shania to come out the closet and grab the gun before Kaiya could turn around.

"When Uncle Henry was dying, the church didn't want to help Mama, because they knew Uncle Henry had been messing with a lot of little girls in that church. The pastor and church staff just covered it up. The members there felt like he was getting just what he deserved, to die such a slow and painful death. It was only then that Mama finally believed that what Kristen had been telling her for all those many years might have actually been true." She turned and looked at Greg, tears shining at the forefront of her flashing eyes. "You think she ever apologized to us?"

Greg swallowed. If this girl was lying, she sure was a good actor. But, hey, she had acted like Little Miss Innocent for this long. Why couldn't she be acting like Little Miss Victim now? Greg cleared his throat. "Mother Washington never apologized to y'all?"

"Yeah, she did," Kaiya said and laughed a humorless laugh. "On her deathbed. She waited until she knew she was dying to finally apologize. We were gonna accept her apology too. Until she pulled that little trick with her will. To make us suffer for that many years and then not even have the decency to leave us her money? Do you think that's fair to us?"

Greg shook his head, and he figured Kaiya probably thought that he was agreeing with her, but actually, he was shaking his head at how pathetic she sounded. Going to this extent, refusing to forgive someone, just because she didn't get enough money?

"So you agree with me?"

It took all Greg's willpower to nod his head. "If I would've known this information at the reading of the will," he said, "I would've signed over everything to you two girls. You deserve it."

Kaiya looked surprised at his willingness to cooperate. "So . . . you don't have a problem with signing your money over into my bank account?"

Greg held his breath when he saw the closet door crack open in his peripheral. Kaiya had her back to the closet, but yet and still, Greg didn't want Shania to risk putting her life on the line in order to save him. He wished there was a way to tell her to get back in the closet and shut the door, but any signal that he threw Shania would be read by Kaiya. And once Kaiya caught wind of what was going on, it would all be over. They'd all die.

Greg held up his right hand as though he was swearing to tell the truth. "Just tell me what I need to do, and it's yours. I don't need Mother Washington's money. I didn't even want it to start with. You can have it all."

Kaiya looked at him as though she wasn't sure if she should believe him or not. "Well . . . you know," she said carefully, "after you sign everything over to me, I'll still have to kill you, because you can identify me to the police. Your wife doesn't know what's going on, though. She's with the two Jamaicans, and she has no idea that I'm involved in this. So I'll kill you, but I'll let her live. Is that okay? That's pretty fair, don't you think?" She sounded as though her rationale made logical sense. She raised a brow, waiting for his response.

Greg held his breath as he peripherally watched Shania inch her way over to the dresser. If Kaiya turned around, Shania was as good as dead. And with his feet shackled to the bed, what could he do to save her? Absolutely nothing. He sent a prayer up to God to keep his wife shielded and covered with His angels, and then he refocused on Kaiya. As long as he kept Kaiya looking at him, she couldn't turn around and see his wife moving toward her gun.

Again, Greg nodded his head. "That's fine with me. I'm willing to lay down my life for my wife. If I have to die for her to live, then so be it."

Still looking a bit unsure about the situation, Kaiya finally nodded, then reached into her pocket and re-trieved a cell phone. She dialed a number and tossed the phone over to him, along with a notepad with ac-count numbers scribbled on it. "Talk to them," she said, "and tell them you want to transfer your funds from your personal account into that new account."

Greg put the phone to his ear, then pretended as though the call had dropped. He watched Shania hold her breath as her fingers closed the few spaces between her hand and the butt of the gun. He wondered if Kaiya could see his heart slapping unnaturally hard against his chest cavity.

"Just press redial," Kaiya snapped, putting a hand on her hip.

Greg pretended to press redial a few times. "It's not working," he lied.

"Oh my goodness," she yelled at him. "How hard can it be to use this little piece of technology?" She walked over to him and held out her hand. "Let me see the phone."

Just as she said her last word, a sudden thunder-ing against the door made him and her both gasp. She whipped her head around, and just as her eyes landed on Shania, Shania's hand wrapped around the gun.

"Open the door!" a male voice demanded. "It's the police. Open the door!"

Greg saw Kaiya running toward the dresser, and he knew that once she got ahold of that gun, she would take it from Shania and kill them both. Shania had too much heart and too much love for God to actually pull the trigger. Greg sent a silent prayer up to God and yelled at the top of his lungs, "She's gonna kill me! Shoot the locks! Please, shoot the locks!"

As the police shot the three dead-bolt locks, Greg realized that if they broke into the room while Shania was still holding the gun, they'd probably assume that she was the guilty culprit and blow holes all through her. The thought nearly killed him, and he stared at her hard and yelled, "Shania, baby, throw the gun!"

She stared at him with wide eyes; then her eyes shifted to Kaiya, who was quickly closing in on her.

"Throw the gun, babe!" he yelled again.

But she waited too late and Kaiya slammed into her body, nearly knocking her off her feet. However, she stood her ground while Kaiya elbowed her in the face as she attempted to twist the gun out of her hand. Just as the police kicked the door in and filled the room with their guns aimed at both Kaiya and Shania, demanding that everyone drop their weapons, Shania let go of the gun and shoved Kaiya with all her might. Kaiya stumbled backward until she bumped her head hard on the corner of the dresser.

Everyone in the room seemed to freeze and time stood still. Kaiya let out a gasp, and all eyes turned and looked at her. She hit the floor with a thud and blood seeped from the back of her head. Was she dead?

Twenty-one

Shania and Greg were safe in the confines of their home when Greg asked Franklin to come over so that he could tell him about the trip and the baby. The two stood outside talking, preparing to take a motorcycle ride.

"Frank, I wanted you to be one of the first to know," Greg said. "Shania's pregnant."

He smiled. "I see somebody been puttin' in the work," he joked.

They both laughed.

"For real, though," Franklin said, "that's great. I think you and Shania gonna make wonderful parents." He paused. "I know I'm the godfather, right?"

"Of course," Greg assured him. He cleared his throat. Patting the seat on Halle, he changed the subject to the trip. "How did you know Kaiya was up to something?"

"So what happened was this," Franklin said. "I kept calling Kaiya's phone and she never answered, so I got worried. It wasn't like her not to answer her phone. So I called her sister's number, and Kristen just flat out told me everything, all of Kaiya's plans—I mean everything. At first I didn't believe it, but when I kept calling you and Shania and y'all never answered the phone or returned my calls, I knew something wasn't right. And when I called the hotel y'all was staying at and they said they hadn't seen y'all since earlier that day when y'all first checked in, I knew Kristen must've been telling the truth. I immediately called the Jamaican authorities to tell them what was going on."

"Thanks, man," Greg said, giving his friend a dap. "I'm a little confused, though." He scratched his scalp. "As evil as Kristen is, why did she confide in you and throw her sister under the bus?"

"She said she tried to talk her sister out of doing anything stupid, but when she couldn't, she became worried that her sister might get hurt in the process. She told me that although she didn't have anything to do with what Kaiya had planned, she knew that deep down this was really about Kaiya trying to square things with her for all the years she served as her protector." Franklin sighed deeply. "I lost someone who I thought was very dear to me."

"But you know what I've come to learn, Franklin?"

His friend lifted his eyebrows to show that he was listening.

"The Lord gives, and the Lord takes away. If you believe in God, and you believe in your faith, then you have to believe that nothing that happens in your life is a coincidence, or accidental. There's a reason why God brought Kaiya in your life, and there's a reason why he took her out of it. Do you believe that?"

Franklin nodded. "Yeah, I believe it. But you know what I've come to learn?"

This time Greg lifted his eyebrows.

"When something seems too good to be true"—Franklin donned his helmet—"it probably is."

Greg pointed two fingers at his friend and laughed. "Now, I'm gonna give it you. You right about that one." Greg donned his helmet and put down his face guard. "You know Shania told me that after she has the baby, she's going to let me take her for a ride on my bike."

Franklin's smile filled his face. "Yo', you think she's serious?"

Greg nodded his head. "I think she really is. After such a near death experience, she's finally realized the importance of living life with no limitations and no regrets."

"And what have you learned?" Franklin asked, leaning back on his bike.

Greg stared up at the pillowy clouds in the sky and shielded his eyes against the sun. "That tomorrow isn't promised to anyone, so live each day as if it's your last. And that my wife is my teammate, not my competition."

Franklin nodded his head while he listened to his friend speak. "I think that's amazing how your wife invested all that money to start a scholarship program for the kids in the Jamaican ghetto."

"Yeah." Greg nodded and pulled at his chin hair. "I think that's amazing too. I'm praying to God that that young boy, Ahdale, doesn't stop until he makes it all the way to the top. Since he hadn't been in any previous trouble, and he cooperated with the police, he got off with a slap on the wrist." He exhaled. "His partner in crime wasn't so lucky. He's got to serve some time." Then Greg added, "Come on, man, let's check out the new building that I plan to purchase. Can't wait to get in there and start fixing up these vintage cars. Maybe I'll hire Jonathan when he finishes school. You think that's a good idea?"

"Man, the best idea you had was to start your own business. 'Bout time that you started making some decisions that actually make sense. You a thirty-five-year-old, grown behind, rusty behind man, and you just now growing up."

"Better late than never, right?"

"Yeah, yeah, whatever," Franklin teased.

The two friends revved up their bikes. Then Franklin said, "Quick question, my man, then I'll leave you alone."

"What's up?"

Franklin gnawed at his bottom lip. "You think it'd be wrong if I, uh . . . if I helped Kristen make it through her . . . her time of grief?"

"And how would you help her through it, Frank?"

Franklin worked his bottom lip and sucked at his teeth. "By laying hands on her, G. I wanna lay hands on her. She needs these hands laid on her."

Greg shook his head at his friend. Then before driving off, he said, "At least one of us grew up."

Discussion Questions

1. Do you think Greg was wrong for not telling Shania about what took place between him and Kristen at the car dealership? Should spouses tell each other about every encounter they have whenever an individual tries to come on to them?

2. When Greg barges into Mother Washington's home and finds her on the bathroom floor, Kristen tells him that it was an honest accident. Do you think she was telling the truth, or did you side with Greg's convictions? Why or why not?

3. Men are often intimidated by a woman who has a higher income and a higher level of education. Considering the fact that tradition has placed men in the role of being the main breadwinner, how do you feel about Greg's response to his job loss and his unwillingness to allow his wife to treat him like a "charity case"? Do you think he was wrong for wanting to start up his own business without his wife's financial funding? Or do you think there was a better way to handle the situation? If so, how?

4. Kaiya tells Greg something deeply personal about her and Kristen. Did you believe Kaiya was really telling the truth about the situation? If so,

did this make you look at Mother Washington differently?

5. Do you think Mother Washington was wrong in how she left her estate? Do you think Greg was wrong for willingly accepting everything she'd left him?

6. Did you figure out who Crazy Lady was?

7. When Shania found out that Jonathan had been shot yet again, she immediately assumed the worst. Can you fault her for believing that Jonathan had returned to his old ways? Do you think she could've handled the situation in a better manner?

8. While reading, did you note some ironies in this story, like the fact that for Franklin to be such a jokester and to not truly understand the heaviness of responsibility, he was still able to give his friend good, sound advice and shed wisdom on quite a few situations? What other ironies did you note?

9. How do you think watching his father put his passion on the back burner for his wife and kids affected Greg and his decisions in life?

10. Even though Greg had quite a few flaws within himself concerning marriage, Shania was not a perfect wife, either. What are some examples of ways she handled situations within her marriage that you think she could've responded in a more effective way?

Urban Christian His Glory Book Club!

Established in January 2007, *UC His Glory Book Club* is another way to introduce **Urban Christian** and its authors. We are an online book club supporting Urban Christian authors by purchasing, reading, and providing written reviews of the authors' books. *UC His Glory Book Club* welcomes both men and women of the literary world who have a passion for reading Christian-based fiction.

UC His Glory Book Club is the brainchild of Joylynn Jossel, author and Executive Editor of Urban Christian, and Kendra Norman-Bellamy, author and copy editor for Urban Christian. The book club will provide support, positive feedback, encouragement, and a forum whereby members can openly discuss and review the literary works of Urban Christian authors. In the future, we anticipate broadening our spectrum of services to include online author chats, author spotlights, interviews with your favorite Urban Christian author(s), special online groups for *UC His Glory Book Club* members, the ability to post reviews on the website and amazon.com, membership ID cards, a *UC His Glory* Yahoo! Group and much more.

Even though there will be no membership fees attached to becoming a member of *UC His Glory Book Club,* we do expect our members to be active, committed, and to follow the guidelines of the book club.

UC His Glory Book Club members pledge to:

- Follow the guidelines of *UC His Glory Book Club*.
- Provide input, opinions, and reviews that build up, rather than tear down.
- Commit to purchasing, reading, and discussing featured book(s) of the month.
- Respect the Christian beliefs of *UC His Glory Book Club*.
- Believe that Jesus is the Christ, Son of the Living God.

We look forward to the online fellowship.

Many Blessings to You!
Shelia E. Lipsey
President
UC His Glory Book Club
**Visit the official Urban Christian His Glory Book Club website at:
www.uchisglorybookclub.net

Notes

Notes

Notes

2.9

Notes

9

ORDER FORM
URBAN BOOKS, LLC
78 E. Industry Ct
Deer Park, NY 11729

Name: (please print):_____

Address: _____

City/State: _____

Zip: _____

QTY	TITLES	PRICE
	A Man's Worth	$14.95
	Abundant Rain	$14.95
	Battle Of Jericho	$14.95
	By The Grace Of God	$14.95
	Dance Into Destiny	$14.95
	Divorcing The Devil	$14.95
	Forsaken	$14.95
	Grace And Mercy	$14.95
	Guilty Of Love	$14.95
	His Woman, His Wife, His Widow	$14.95
	Illusions	$14.95
	The LoveChild	$14.95

Shipping and handling-add $3.50 for 1st book, then $1.75 for each additional book.
Please send a check payable to:
Urban Books, LLC
Please allow 4-6 weeks for delivery

ORDER FORM
URBAN BOOKS, LLC
78 E. Industry Ct
Deer Park, NY 11729

Name: (please print):_____

Address: _____

City/State: _____

Zip: _____

QTY	TITLES	PRICE

Shipping and handling-add $3.50 for 1st book, then $1.75 for each additional book.
Please send a check payable to:
Urban Books, LLC
Please allow 4-6 weeks for delivery

ORDER FORM
URBAN BOOKS, LLC
78 E. Industry Ct
Deer Park, NY 11729

Name:(please print):_____

Address: _____

City/State: _____

Zip: _____

QTY	TITLES	PRICE

Shipping and handling-add $3.50 for 1st book, then $1.75 for each additional book.

Please send a check payable to:
   Urban Books, LLC
Please allow 4-6 weeks for delivery

ORDER FORM
URBAN BOOKS, LLC
78 E. Industry Ct
Deer Park, NY 11729

Name:(please print):_____

Address: _____

City/State: _____

Zip: _____

QTY	TITLES	PRICE

Shipping and handling-add $3.50 for 1st book, then $1.75 for each additional book.

Please send a check payable to:

Urban Books, LLC

Please allow 4-6 weeks for delivery